BRIDE
OF THE
SHADOW KING

BRIDE OF THE SHADOW KING

GENEVIEVE JACK

USA TODAY BESTSELLING AUTHOR

ABOUT THIS BOOK

It takes a monster to save a lost kingdom.
Speak the vow
Face your demons.
Prepare to pay the price.

Now that I've reconnected with my power, Damien and I must fulfill the sacred promise we made—to his father, to the goddess, and to ourselves. We will take back Stygarde.

But building an army from a population broken by war and starvation feels impossible. Every potential ally demands a price, and still our forces remain pitifully insufficient to face an enemy that holds our greatest weakness: Stygarde's children, innocent lives used as human shields to paralyze our every move.

The dark elves know we won't sacrifice the defenseless for victory. They have no such scruples.

Then we find him—an ally powerful enough to tip the scales in our favor. But his price cuts deeper than gold or land. He wants something Damien can never give, something that would shatter the trust we've built between us. We swore to save this kingdom together, but that oath may be the very thing that dooms us. To keep my promise to the goddess, I may have to break the one I made to the man I love.

I

THUNDER ON THE MOUNTAIN

ELOISE

When I was a child, I used to fear the dark. I remember begging my father for a night-light to chase away the shadows under my bed, shadows I thought were monsters. Little did I know then how I would change. Darkness means safety. Darkness means time to rest, to heal, to plan.

Darkness is the beginning of everything.

The clash of Stygian blades echoes through the pitch-black cavern where Damien trains the men and women of the mountain dweller clan. It's the sound of war, the sound of battle. A sound Damien is no stranger to. As the prince of Stygarde, he once faced the elves of Willowgulch as he led his elite team of warriors, called the umbrae, against their invading army. Despite my best efforts to keep my thoughts optimistic, my mind pictures him there, his boots landing on blood-soaked soil, his sword connecting with the elves' deadly sunlight magic.

I fear that war is again close at hand.

It's been a month since we arrived and convinced Seamus, Lord of Mount Damocles and chieftain of the mountain dwellers who live here, to ally with us to take back the kingdom of Stygarde. Four weeks that we've relied on their protection and hospitality. We've had to. We have nowhere else to go.

But both Damien and I know we are on borrowed time. When New Stygarde found us living among the witches of Dimhollow on the forever-winter landscape of Mount Perilon, we escaped via an enchanted tunnel carved into the center of the mountain, one whose existence was made known to us by the wise witch Catarina. Her assistance saved our lives. Afterward, Damien led us across the wilds of Tenebris to Mount Damocles, where the moat of lava, the sweltering heat, and the oppressive living conditions repel all but the clan of mountain dwellers who call this place home.

The temperature *is* almost unbearable here. It takes a lot to make a shadow sweat, but Damien's dark back glistens with perspiration as he swings Dawnbreaker, the blade forged in this very mountain by the shade he spars with, the chieftain himself, Seamus. I confess, my own skin heats another degree at the sight of my mate, his muscles rippling with the force of each blow, the wings and tail of his battle form flexing with his movements. His hair has grown longer with our time here, and a stray curl sweeps around his horns and daringly across his furrowed brow. I sigh at the remembrance of how that hair felt between my thighs last night, and something low within me flutters.

Seamus's much shorter sword meets Damien's strike

for strike, the stocky shade expertly manipulating the long beard that is the mark of his gender among his people. I don't know how he avoids tripping over it, even in battle form, but he has proven himself a worthy warrior and leader over our time here. Damien says he's the closest to a true umbrae among these men. It's a huge compliment. These people have traditionally been weapons makers, not soldiers, but Damien has done his best to teach them what he knows.

Each and every fighter in this room understands that they are at a physical disadvantage to the army of New Stygarde. Each and every fighter in this room is willing to die to return Damien to the throne.

My spine tingles and my eyes mist with tears at the inevitability of what is to come. This isn't just about Damien anymore. Before we descended to the Darklands to face Thanesia, Catarina married us in a secret ceremony. Damien might be the rightful heir to the kingdom of Stygarde, but I am his queen, which means the fate of these men is as much on my conscience as on his. I would never ask them to do what I'm unwilling to do myself.

I am willing to die to put Damien back on that throne.

I am willing to die to save the children of Stygarde from the evil I experienced firsthand when I was a captive of the dark elves of Willowgulch.

Which is why I'm honest with myself this morning. New Stygarde *will* find us here. The dark, belly of this mountain might be the last place they'll look, the place they'll avoid until the very end, but they will come here, and Damien and I will have to run. We'll have to find more men, more troops, before we have a chance in hell of facing New Stygarde's army, and we'll have to build our forces while dodging their attempts to stop us.

Together, we must succeed—for the sake of the people, for the sake of the children.

"I hate to distract you from such a pretty sight," Amala says at my side, startling me into a smile. She's Seamus's wife, Lady of Mount Damocles, and has become a much-appreciated friend and confidante during my time here.

"Do you want to watch with me?" I ask playfully, nudging the rotund woman whose mostly bald head bobs with her easy laughter. "I think you might enjoy the view just as well." I tip my head in the direction of Seamus.

Her crooked smile is nothing short of wicked. "Ah, I suppose it couldn't hurt to give the boys an audience. Although, that's not why I'm here. The girls in the kitchen are making your Rosinenzopf recipe and can't remember the proportion of dried berries."

"Ah, it was two cups, but tell them to soak them in the honey mixture or they won't be sweet enough." Grapes do not exist on Tenebris, so there are no raisins for the braided sweet bread recipe my grams used to make. But they do have something called crinkle berries, which have the texture of raisins but are less sweet. Soaking them fixes that problem.

"Ah, I'll remind them."

"Do you think they need my help? I don't mind kneading the dough."

She thumps me on the back. "We always love having your help, El, but I think today, you have your own work to do." She raises an eyebrow. "And your mate made me swear I wouldn't give you an excuse to quit your exercises early."

She's referring to me practicing my ability to shift.

I huff. "It's not you distracting me that's the problem."

"Still blocked?"

I nod. I haven't been able to shift completely into shadow since the first time I did it to save Damien's life. Only a few weeks ago, I was able to shadoweave, completely transforming into darkness in order to kill the thirteen elves trying to assassinate him. But the extreme emotional circumstances seemed to help me achieve what I did that night. Since then, I haven't been able to fully transform, no matter how hard I try. And normal shade abilities like coaxing the shadows to perform even the smallest tasks for me remain frustratingly out of reach. As does transforming into the horned and winged form shades use in battle. I may technically be a shade, but I have a lot to learn about the new body gifted to me by the goddess.

"I managed to pour myself a drink today, although very little water ended up in the glass, and I broke the vessel when my shadows dropped it," I confess.

She squeezes my shoulder supportively. "It's something. I can't imagine it's easy, having so many physical changes at once. Have you been practicing the meditations I gave you?" Amala is a healer, and her methods extend into the spiritual. While I appreciate her help, her meditation, which involves a full hour of throat chanting, isn't my cup of tea. I gave it a try, but when it only resulted in my throat going hoarse, with no improvement to my shifting ability, I quit.

"I'll keep practicing," I say vaguely.

"And I'll keep asking the goddess to bless you both." Amala pats my shoulder in lieu of goodbye, and with one last ogle of her husband, she shifts into shadow and funnels in the direction of the kitchen.

Seeing her shift so easily, I try again, willing my cells to come apart and join with the shadows in the corner of the ledge I'm on, but aside from grunting from the effort like I'm severely constipated, nothing happens. I hang my head in frustration.

I'm delighted when Damien barks a command in the pit below, and the trainees still and sheathe their swords. A break. Finally. My mate often seems invincible, but I can tell he needs food and water—and probably blood. Plus, it's a good excuse for me to rest. It's not like I'm making any progress anyway.

Although the small platform I'm on is carved into the wall of the cavern and heavily cloaked in shadow, Damien whirls to face me as soon as the men disperse, as if I'm a beacon in the darkness. Our eyes lock, and in the time it takes for him to twist into a column of darkness and surf the shadows to me, he is by my side in his corse or polite form—no wings, horns, or tail.

"You're supposed to be practicing, little bird," he says through a smirk.

"I am! I'm taking a break. You warned me not to force it."

He runs his callused fingers over the skin of my cheek and then combs them through the red curls behind my ear. "How's it going?"

"Some success today using shadows to pick up a pitcher of water."

His teeth flash white in the darkness. "It's a start."

"As for sprouting wings and horns, as far as I can tell, the goddess Thanesia left that off my gift list." I shrug.

Damien's smile tilts. "You have no need for battle form, my little bird. Your talents are better used off the battlefield."

The tattoo on my back tingles. By talents, he means my magic, and just the thought raises the bond between me and Phantom, my familiar. Once a fox and now a dragon, they are the embodiment of my ancestors and the anchor to my spirit magic. I sense them waiting for me in the darkness, invisible but close.

"I can think of several occasions over the last year when a battle form would have come in handy."

His face falls, and I wonder if he's thinking about my abduction by the dark elf king. The days I spent as his captive were the most terrifying of my existence. I still have nightmares. But I refuse to ruin the moment and my day wasting my thoughts on King Adril Entrydal. I move closer to Damien, caressing his back to the base of his spine, and lick my bottom lip. "Besides, I would love to know what it's like to have a tail. Yours is so much fun."

"Mmmm." He places a firm kiss on my waiting mouth. "Naughty little bird. I'll show it to you now if you like. How fast can you make it back to our chambers?"

I pound his shoulder with my fist because he knows damn well I'd have to get there the old-fashioned way. He grabs my hand and tugs me hard against his chest, laughing in a way that makes my heart swell with love for him.

We're interrupted when a young mountain dweller in a brown uniform bursts into the hall, waving his arms.

"Seamus! High alert! There's someone at the gate!"

Seamus sets down his goblet and turns to the boy. "Did you get a good look at him?"

The boy grabs his head. "It's the master of the guard, Banias, and six other uniformed soldiers from New Stygarde. They are armed, my lord."

Seamus exchanges a knowing glance with Damien and me. We've prepared for this. With a nod of my head, I feel my tattoo tingle, and my bond with Phantom grows taut. I whisper an incantation, and a shield of invisibility comes over us. Beside me, Damien completely disappears.

Below us, Seamus thumps the boy on the shoulder and points his chin toward the front gate. "All right, then," he says in his hearty timbre. "Let's go welcome our guests."

I find Damien's hand with my own, and he pops into existence again. "As long as we're touching, we can see each other," I whisper. "Just don't let any of the bad guys touch you, or the effect will be the same."

"Noted," he says. "Come on. We need to hear this." Damien leads me down the narrow stony outcroppings that serve as stairs and hurries after Seamus. He leads the way from the training hall toward the front, formal entrance to the mountain fortress. Two enormous doors decorated with Stygian steel scrollwork wait for us.

When Seamus brought us here, he used a secret passageway and train system that previously was only available to mountain dwellers. Built under the mountain, the passageway avoids the moat of lava and the intense, upward climb to these doors. Invited in, as we were, our obstacles were few. I get some satisfaction knowing that Banias had to reach this place the hard way.

With the turn of a crank that requires two men to operate, the three-story-high doors slowly swing open. Seven men dressed in white uniforms that sparkle silver in the moonlight stand at the threshold, swords displayed prominently on their hips.

Damien's arms circle my waist, and he pulls me against his chest, then tucks us both into an alcove in the wall. Although we're silent and unseen, Seamus knows we're here. He knows we're listening.

"Sir Banias." Seamus bows. "What an unexpected surprise."

Banias stumbles in. I do not miss the way his legs wobble or sweat trails in rivulets over his temples. The corners of Seamus's lips twitch in a barely suppressed smile.

"My men need water, Seamus. Now! By order of New Stygarde," Banias barks.

"Of course," Seamus says, pointing a finger at one of his men and nodding for them to retrieve said water. The shade returns quickly with goblets and a pitcher and begins to pour.

Banias takes a sip and makes a face like he might vomit.

"You understand there is no way to cool the water here, I assume, and that the volcanic activity infuses it with the taste of sulfur?" Seamus strokes his beard and watches as Banias forces himself to swallow another gulp. His men follow his example, choking down the hot, stinking water.

While it is true that there is no refrigeration in Mount Damocles, I've had plenty of delicious water here. The mountain dwellers are extremely talented craftsmen who long ago mastered filtration. I can only imagine the flavor of the swill they've served to Banias and company and have to keep myself from laughing.

"Am I wrong to think you haven't come all this way for a drink?" Seamus asks.

Until recently, Brahm used to brag that Banias rarely left his side. That changed after we broke free of the king and queen's control. They've sent their best to retrieve us because they fear us. They should.

Banias reaches inside his armor and removes a sweat-soaked roll of parchment. "I'm here by royal decree." He straightens and announces in a loud, clear voice, "Damien Hymir and his mate Eloise Harcourt are traitors to the crown and enemies of New Stygarde. Anyone caught harboring these fugitives will be put to death." He turns back to Seamus, his dark eyes finding the shorter man's and holding his gaze. "As clan chieftain of the mountain dwellers, you speak on behalf of all within these walls. Do you know the whereabouts of former prince Damien or his mate?"

Seamus snorts and pokes a sausage-shaped finger at the still-open doors. "No one comes through that gate without my knowledge, Banias, and I swear on my mother's and my grandmother's graves that neither Damien nor his mate passed through those doors."

I tense as Banias studies the man for what seems like an abnormal stretch of time, then nods once. "You're telling the truth," he says, shoulder relaxing as he leans back on his heels. "Although, where they've gone is beyond me. We've turned over every territory in Tenebris."

"Even Dimhollow?" Seamus asks.

Banias snorts. "Even Dimhollow. Those cursed witches allowed us into their weird, uncanny village." He shivers. "They're not there."

"Perhaps they left Tenebris?"

I have to hand it to Seamus. The way he plants that possibility is as gentle as the first drops of rain on freshly tilled soil.

"Doubtful," Banias says. "We interrogated the captain of every fleet in Aendor, and no one admits to ferrying them to other lands. No. If they escaped Tenebris, they did it on their own against unbelievable odds. I, for one, don't think they're capable."

Seamus strokes his beard again. "So…given that they aren't here, will you be returning to New Stygarde, then?" He gestures his stubby fingers toward the door. "I'm afraid leaving them open like this is against our security protocols."

Banias snorts. "Close them if you like. It will take my men some time to search this mountain."

"You plan to search the entire mountain?" Seamus laughs as if Banias must be joking, but the master of the guard does not break a smile.

"That's exactly what I plan to do. My men must have access to all areas, both public and private, and we will expect meals and lodging." Banias removes his leather gloves and drops them into Seamus's hands. "I look forward to your hospitality."

Amala eases into the room as gracefully as the wind.

"Wife, would you tell your lady's maids to prepare our finest rooms for these gentlemen?" Seamus asks.

She bows. "I'd be honored." She flutters her lashes at Banias. "Of course, we will have to clear those rooms first, as they are currently occupied by our elders. If you'll please wait here, my servants will be with you in just a moment."

Banias agrees, his face a mask of exhaustion as he attempts to acclimate to the heat. Amala slips from the room, and we follow her, not uttering a word until she leads us to the trapdoor and the tunnel under the mountain. We descend the staircase and drop our invisibility once the door is sealed above us.

"Your rabble beasts have been packed with everything from your rooms as well as ample provisions from our stores." She wipes under her eyes. "Those filthy bastards. I hate that you must leave like this."

We both embrace her. "We knew this day would come, my lady, and we can't put you at further risk," Damien says.

"I'm going to miss you so much," I add, hugging her as tightly as I can.

"We'll send word, when it's time." Damien squeezes her shoulder.

Amala releases me and sniffs, lifting her chin. "You will make a fine king one day, Damien Hymir, and justice will be served." Her eyes drift toward the ceiling. "Now, I must go."

We say our goodbyes and watch her ascend into the mountain palace.

"She's prepared rooms for them at the back of the mountain," Damien says with a chuckle.

I grin. "By this time tomorrow, their skin should be as crispy as a roast duck's."

As he leads me toward the underground car where our rabble beasts wait, any lightness I feel over Banias's circumstances fades with my growing apprehension. Once again, we've escaped New Stygarde.

But no place is safe for us now.
Not until we win this war.

2

IT'S THE JOURNEY

DAMIEN

"So what's the plan?" Eloise asks. We lead the rabble beasts from the camouflaged underground tunnels of Mount Damocles toward the network of caves near the base of the mountain. Although we knew this day would come, we've never broached specifics. How could we? There were too many variables. No matter how well you prepare for an exodus like ours, you are never truly ready.

"I wish I had an answer to that question," I grumble. "I have a goal, not a plan. My goal is to raise an army powerful enough to take back my kingdom from Brahm and Nevina. But with Banias and his men hunting us, I'm afraid any plans we might have will have to adjust to our day-to-day realities."

"Fair." She mounts Romulus, who is now completely healed from his former injuries. The rabble beast prances in place, elated to be out from under the mountain. A cool breeze filters to us from the north, rustling Eloise's red curls. "By the goddess, do you feel that? I think I just breathed my first full breath in a month." She smiles at the moon.

Similarly, Borus chuffs and stomps with obvious excitement as I mount him. Both beasts have spent far too long in a stable of stone. They're restless to run. "Although I'm thankful to the mountain dwellers for their hospitality, I have to agree. One never acclimates to that heat."

"Of course, I'm excited for Banias to give it a try. Have fun searching the mountain, bootlicker." She flips a middle finger in Banias's direction.

I snort. "So…"

"So…" Our eyes meet, and the trust I see in hers spurs my courage and sparks the decision I've hesitated to make. There's no right answer. Any choice could lead us in a direction that gets us killed. But together with this woman at my side, I'm ready to face what comes.

"Aendor," I say confidently. "Tempest has been organizing a rebellion in the region for years. It's the most logical place for us."

"I know that was always the end goal, but do you think it's safe? Brahm has to suspect Tempest after what happened at the Harvest Festival. We haven't received a raven from her in weeks. For all we know, Aendor is no safer than Mount Damocles."

"Banias said he interrogated the captains of the shipping fleet in Aendor. No doubt he searched the territory at the same time. They might still have soldiers stationed in the region, but we know they aren't their best men, because those men are here. By the time we reach Aendor, they'll have exhausted their search, know for sure we're not there, and will assume we wouldn't dare risk reaching out to Tempest again. With your magic disguising us, we'll infiltrate the palace and find the lord and lady of Aendor. They'll know how to hide us."

I kick Borus into a walk, steering him toward the trail that leads into the dark forest on the edge of the Borderlands. Eloise sidles up next to me, leaning back in Romulus's saddle.

"Aendor is completely on the opposite side of Tenebris, though. Do you think it's safe to stay on the road that long? Even disguised?"

Turning my face toward the moon, I suppress a dry chuckle. It's a fair question, but she already knows the answer, even if she hasn't admitted it to herself yet. "As safe as anywhere else."

"Right." She rubs the back of her neck. "Unless..." She sits up straighter.

"Unless?"

"You know, we could leave the planet, Damien. I am the key. We could return to Earth temporarily."

I consider the possibility. The way is open to her now, and we presumably have the blessing of the goddess to pass through the Darklands. But if there's one thing I've learned, it's that all magic has consequences. "No."

"No?"

"You're capable, and I'm relieved the option is available should we have no other choice, but ultimately, Stygarde is my destiny." I press a hand into my chest and turn to her. "*Our* destiny. Our people don't have the privilege of hiding on another planet. Our time with the mountain dwellers has made one thing abundantly clear to me. To win this war, we need allies, and that means getting to know the people of Stygarde again. The common people.

People I never had the chance to truly know when I was their prince. I must earn their trust if I am to win their fealty, and we can't do that from Earth."

"True."

"Besides, last time we traveled through the underworld, it drained both of us. We need our strength and your magic to face what is to come."

She narrows her eyes. "Blah, blah, blah. I think you just enjoy riding long distances."

I grin at the way she teases me to lighten the mood. "We've done it before, when we left Dimhollow."

"Yes, and we almost got ourselves killed."

"This time, we have your magic." I cast a wink in her direction. "Besides, I am completely serious about using our travels strategically to understand the state of our kingdom and try to recruit others to our cause. Learn where Brahm has stationed troops. Start to form a battle plan for when the time comes."

"Our kingdom," she says through a grin. "I like the sound of that."

"Me too," I say.

"Then let's go. I'll disguise us using magic, but we should probably come up with a story for who we are before we run into someone with questions for two weary travelers."

I scratch the side of my jaw, considering. "We could pose as Rivertoads. They're wanderers and often travel these back roads."

"Why do I sense hesitation in your voice?"

I raise a brow. "The fact that they often travel the path we're on means we are most likely to come across one of them, and, presumably, they know their own."

"Okay, well, who wouldn't they know?"

"A brother and sister from one of the west villages? People starved out of their homes and seeking a better life."

"I thought Ariadne said they weren't allowed to leave?"

"The citizens of Bolvet Village can't legally leave. But the Zephrine region is bigger than Bolvet. The region is sprawling, and certain rural families would not be beholden to the law."

"One disguise, coming right up." She raises a hand and circles it above her head. Her curly red hair straightens and takes on a pitch-black hue, while her clothing transforms into a mess of rags. Her eyes, usually green, twinkle copper in the moonlight. "Does this work?"

"Less wretched. We may have to buy goods. We don't want to appear completely destitute."

Another wave of her hand and she's in humble riding attire, something similar to what the mountain dwellers wear. "Perfect," I say.

She trails her fingers in my direction, and my hands transform to slender versions of my own. I look down at my narrower self. Eloise couldn't always perform magic this easily, but when she resurrected Phantom, she gained access to all the powers of all her ancestors. No longer does she need to carry a grimoire—she has direct access to the experience of the authors of every spell in her parents' book. Phantom changed everything.

"What do I look like?"

"Blond. Blue eyes. Thin and lanky," Eloise says. "Very handsome. What should we call each other?"

"Velis and Marquis?" I suggest.

"Okay. Which one of us is Velis?"

I laugh. "Velis is quite obviously a woman's name."

"Is it, though?" She quirks a brow.

With a snort, I clarify, "It is on this planet."

"Fine. Velis, it is. But my rabble beast's name is Scout."

"Scout? Why Scout?"

"I always wanted a horse named Scout, since I was nine and read *To Kill a Mockingbird*. Sadly, my parents never delivered a pony for Christmas."

"*To Kill a Mockingbird*? Were you a violent child?"

"It's not about actually killing birds," she explains. "It's just something one of the characters in the story says. It's a sin to kill a mockingbird because they are one of nature's gentlest creatures."

"Scout, it is," I mumble.

"What should we call Borus?" she asks me, giggling to herself. "How do you feel about Atticus?"

The word falls between us as we turn the corner and moonlight sweeps across an odd, branchless tree that appears to be sprouting...arms. Eloise gasps when we draw closer, her hand cupping her mouth.

"Is that? Oh my God, Damien, it's a man, strung up by his feet!" She hops off Borus and runs to the body, placing her fingers on his neck. I already know he's dead.

"This is an execution," I tell her, dismounting and drawing closer to the blood-covered face. "I've seen this before. Sadly, this is what passes for justice among dark elves. They use light to keep their victims from shifting, then hang them from a tree by their feet before slitting their throats. It's a painful and slow way for a shade to die."

"Help me cut him down."

I draw Dawnbreaker and sever the thick rope

stringing up the dead man, then grunt as the body hits the ground. Although he can't feel it, it's hard to watch.

"What's this?" A small object tumbled from the man's pocket when he hit the ground, and she holds it up to the light. It's a small wooden carving of a stag. "A toy? Do you think he had children?"

I stare at the tiny stag, then look back at the man.

"What is it? You look like you've seen a ghost." Eloise places a hand on my shoulder, a hand I don't recognize as we are both still disguised.

I swallow hard before answering. "The stag is familiar. Not this stag, particularly, but the type of carving." I shake my head. "I think I know this man." I kneel beside the body, but the face is so swollen and caked in blood that I can't be sure.

"Eloise, could you?" I gesture toward the man.

A snap of her fingers and the blood is gone, the face slightly less swollen. That's when I know for sure. I grunt in miserable recognition.

"Who is it?"

"The owner of the general store in Bolvet."

"No," Eloise says with a low, melancholy release of breath. "Wasn't he the only one successfully smuggling food and other goods into the village?"

I nod. "And he has children. Children I believe he was raising alone." I stand and turn back toward the tree, running my hands over the bark.

"What if the children are waiting? What if they're alone?" she says more to herself than to me.

I find a lump under the bark and dig my fingers in.

"What are you doing?"

"When the elves execute someone, they usually list the

charges and post them on the tree. Ah, here it is." My fingers catch on the corner of a folded piece of parchment, and I slowly work it out from behind the bark. The thick paper unrolls in my hands, and my stomach turns when I see the decorative crest at the top. "This was issued by New Stygarde, not Willowgulch."

Scowling, Eloise comes to my side for a better look.

"It says he was convicted of hunting the queen's stags without permission and therefore was sentenced to death. The order is signed by King Brahm."

"So, they starve their own people and then execute them when they try to hunt food for their children?" Eloise is spitting mad. Streaks of red cut through the illusion of her dark hair.

"Careful, little bird," I whisper, "Your anger is showing in more ways than one." Taking a strand between my fingers, I hold it up for her to see. She glances down at the red curl, and her eyes widen. I drop the strand of hair, and it turns dark and straight again before it hits her shoulder.

"We need to take his body home, Damien, check on his children. Maybe Ariadne will know someone in the village who can take them in."

"I agree." I bend down to lift the man into my arms and then drape his lifeless body across Borus's back. "I'll walk. You ride Romulus."

Thankfully, she doesn't argue with me about riding, but then she knows the world we live in by now. Knows we can't draw unwanted attention.

"Do you know his name?" Eloise asks softly.

"No."

We fall into silence, the weight of loss heavy between us. We did not know this man well, but he was ours, a citizen of Stygarde, murdered by his own king. I can see in her eyes that she feels it too, the pain of having failed him somehow. We are already on borrowed time. Tolerating Brahm and Nevina on the throne has cost us the lives of just citizens.

At last, the forest opens, and I gaze upon the city of Bolvet, a place I haven't seen in months, since we came here to buy Eloise her wardrobe. I have to stop to make sure what I'm seeing is real.

"Goddess, help us," she murmurs.

The village is flattened and scorched. Not a single building remains standing in its entirety. Partial roofless rooms, littered with fallen beams, are all that's left of a once quaint and welcoming skyline. I shake my head in devastated disbelief.

"What the hell happened here?" Eloise whispers.

"I don't know. But it's our duty to find out."

3

THE REMNANT

ELOISE

As Damien leads our rabble beasts toward the ruins, my heart pounds in my throat and my stomach sinks. Bolvet looks like a wasteland. Even from a distance, the moon reveals a place I would never recognize as the village where the most masterful dressmaker on the planet once fitted me for a wardrobe. Only a few months ago, I danced the night away among laughing towns-people at a thatch-roofed tavern at the heart of Bolvet. Now, I can't even make out the rubble that once was that circular building.

No one is dancing now. This place is war-torn. This place is a graveyard.

We reach the main street and pass by what remains of Ariadne's dress shop. It's mostly ash, although her door remains, painted with a large red X. "What do you think that means?" I ask Damien.

"It's a decree. The red X means she was marked as a traitor. She was executed."

I gasp, and my eyes instantly fill with tears. "Should we —" I gesture toward what used to be her building, but if her body is in there, it has long since burned and is buried under a ton of rubble and ash.

"Nothing can be done except to grieve." He glances back at me, and I see tears in his eyes. All the blue has drained from the illusion I've disguised him in under the swell of his emotions, leaving his pupils pale and diamond-hard. I feel it along our bond—a deep, heart-wrenching loss. Ariadne was a friend. I'd met her once, but he'd known her for a lifetime.

He places a hand on the shoulder of the dead man we came here for. It's hard to believe any of his family lived through this, especially his children, but we trudge on, toward where the general store once was.

"I can still smell the smoke," I say.

He sniffs. "This happened recently. Days ago."

I stop Romulus and dismount, needing to be by his side if I am to face this. Damien waits for me to catch up and takes my hand in his. We walk together toward the remains of the general store and then past the ruins of the tavern at the town's center. "Does Bolvet have a cemetery?" I finally ask. We still need to bury the man slung across Borus, and the stench of his body tells me we shouldn't wait.

Damien nods once, understanding immediately, and starts for the back of the village. Unlike the cemetery behind Stygarde Castle, which is meticulously landscaped, this one is simple, mostly prairie with a few trees. But as we move closer, I see similar sculptures nestled in the overgrown grasses, sculptures that depict the person buried beneath them. In Bolvet's case, the sculptures aren't life-sized. The effigies stand about eighteen inches tall and look like they were handmade by loved ones rather than professional artists. Although I can feel the sacredness of this space, these are modest graves.

Silently, we navigate to the back of the cemetery, passing a few mounds of freshly turned earth. New graves. No sculptures to mark them. I wonder who dug them? I wonder how long ago they were made. I wonder who was brave enough to stay behind to bury the dead.

We reach an unused area peppered with tiny purple flowers at the very back. I'm about to offer to use magic to dig the grave when we both spot a shovel abandoned against a nearby tree, as if left by the last gravedigger who worked here. Without a word, Damien picks it up and begins to dig.

The magical disguise I've wrapped around Damien makes him look soft, but under it all, he is anything but. He has a suitable hole dug in no time. Together, we pull the unknown man off Borus's back and carefully lower him into the grave. We fall into an uneasy vigil in our grief. The only sounds that break the heavy silence are the skittering animals in the forest beyond and the occasional rustle of leaves on the wind.

"Should we say something?" I finally ask.

Damien frowns. "The time for words is past, little bird. Now is the time for action." He digs the shovel into the dirt and tosses it on the grave. "I will avenge you, unknown friend."

"Who are you, and where did you find his body?" a raspy voice asks from behind us.

We both whirl to find the owner and barman of Bolvet's tavern, Warbill, watching us from the shelter of the neighboring trees. He looks even older than the day I met him, all bones and torn garments. His face sags, and his eyes are red-rimmed.

"Warbill," Damien says softly. "Is that you, old friend?"

"Thank the goddess," I add.

He looks confused. Warbill's rheumy gaze shifts from me to Damien and back again. "Do I know you?"

Of course, we're still in disguise. I reach for my bond with Phantom and follow my ancestors' advice to drop the illusion. Flipping my hand over, I whisper, *"Revelverte."* Damien's blond hair turns dark again, and his body bulks into its natural form. I hold up my hand and see my fingers are my own.

Warbill drops to one knee, head bowed. "My king."

"Please, stand," Damien says. "Be at ease."

Warbill stands but a slight tremble blights his hands, and his skin hangs off his bones. Shades are hard to kill and don't age like humans. Warbill's appearance is symptomatic of long-term starvation.

"Is there a safe place we can talk?" I ask in a whisper.

Warbill nods. "Safer than here. Although, I'm afraid no place on Tenebris is truly safe for any of us anymore, most especially you, my lady."

Damien clears his throat. "Not your lady, your queen," he corrects. Warbill does a double take, and my cheeks grow hot under his scrutiny. "A witch priestess in Dimhollow wed us before New Stygarde descended on the village."

"My fealty is yours, my queen." Placing a hand over his

heart, Warbill starts to kneel again, and I am quick to stop him with a hand on his shoulder.

"Please. You said there was a place to talk."

He nods and gestures for us to follow him into the woods.

Without a trail to guide us, we have to stay close as the tightly spaced trees drown out the moon, and the thick undergrowth makes me wish I could easily shift into shadow form to navigate them. But then, even if I could, Borus and Romulus, who follow single file behind Damien and me, could not. Warbill appears to be too weak to shift anyway. Which leaves us picking our way through the forest in familiar, human fashion.

The minutes tick by in silence until we reach a break in the trees and a small log cabin comes into view. A curl of smoke rises from the chimney, cutting a path through the glow of the moon. Inside, firelight penetrates the darkness. Hearth and home. A cozy cabin to starve in.

Warbill opens the door. "You'll never guess who I found lurking in the cemetery," he says to someone inside. A graying head pokes out the door.

"Ariadne!" I gasp. The dressmaker rushes out to me, and we embrace, before Damien pulls her into his arms, his eyes full of tears. "We thought you were dead! Your shop—"

"After years of oppression at the hands of New Stygarde, building a secret passageway out of Ariadne's seemed worth the investment. Warbill and I tried to help the others, but most were too weak to shift. The two of us barely made it here."

Damien recovers from the shock of finding her alive

and turns to me, his expression grave. "A protective ward?"

I nod. "And a stag," I suggest back to him at the sight of Ariadne, whose bones I can count through her pale skin.

"You'll find no stags near here," Warbill says. "New Stygarde drove off the herd in their efforts to starve us. Nothing but vespers—and only if you're lucky enough to find one of the few that remain."

I shake my head at Brahm and Nevina's cruelty and then call Phantom. I don't have to open my mouth, just reach for the bond, and they arrive. The colossal white dragon forms in the clearing and lowers their head to look at me. A noise comes from deep within Ariadne's throat, and she lurches back into the cabin, eyes ever wider. From inside, Warbill looks just as shaken.

"It's all right," I say, trying my best to comfort them. "This is Phantom. They're my familiar. They won't hurt you."

Eyes bulging, Warbill clears his throat before asking, "They?"

"Um, the body of this dragon contains more than one soul, both male and female."

Warbill mumbles, "Oh." But his expression remains confused.

I rest my hands on either side of Phantom's snout. "We need a stag. The largest one you can find. These people are hungry."

The dragon smiles a mouthful of razor-sharp teeth, each as long as I am tall. "You can count on us," the beast says in my grandmother's voice. "Grandpa Henry was one hell of a huntsman, if he does say so himself. We won't let you down."

I kiss the scales of their snout. "Thank you. Careful no one sees you."

"Of course, my dear." They spread their wings and shoot into the sky, disappearing the moment they break the tree line.

"Goddess bless us all," Ariadne says breathlessly. "You've tamed the dragon! I always thought she was a myth."

"They," I correct. "They are an extension of my spirit magic."

Damien adds, "My queen *is* the dragon." The love and admiration in his eyes are almost too much to bear.

"Well, come in," Warbill says. "It sounds like you have a story to tell, and I'm afraid we do too, one I wish we didn't have to."

With a nod, Damien moves toward the door, his hand settling on my cheek as the others pad deeper into the cabin. "Do you need to wait until Phantom returns to lay the wards?"

I blink up at him and offer the type of self-assured smile I know drives him crazy with desire. "Nope." I pop the *p* at the end. "I've been practicing. This should be child's play."

He lowers his chin, bringing his face close to mine, and cocks a brow. Through a crooked smile, he says, "Then I'll let you play." His gaze turns heated. "I love to watch you play. Especially when we're alone."

I chuckle. "Judging by the size of that cabin, I don't believe we'll be alone anytime soon."

A deep sigh rumbles from his chest as he turns and slips inside the door, closing it behind him.

I draw a deep breath into my lungs and reach for a

strand of my power, weaving it with another I pluck from the ether. I cast my protective net over the small cabin in silence, to the sound of night creatures and the rustle of leaves in the breeze. My smile falters as my thoughts return, time and again, to the man we buried and to our starving friends inside.

My anger swells like the magma in Mount Damocles, thick and hot and yearning for destruction. Nevina and Brahm don't know what kind of wasps' nest they've stirred up by messing with our friends. I will not stop until they've paid for what they did to Bolvet Village. Until they've paid for every life they've taken from us.

$$4$$

STRANGER NO MORE

DAMIEN

"His name was Victus," Warbill says. "The man you buried. The owner of the general store. He escaped with his children just before the silver coats lit the fires."

"Silver coats?" Eloise asks.

"That's what Banias has renamed the umbrae. They've all adopted the preferred white and silver colors of their queen. Elven colors."

I wince, remembering what Banias was wearing when he visited Mount Damocles. Umbrae warriors always dressed in black to blend into the night. Elven warriors often wore dark green and brown to blend into the forest. The only reason for the New Stygarde troops to wear silver is because they want to stand out, to intimidate, to show superiority when they are bullying their way through the kingdom. It's a brazen color.

"You were saying about Victus?" I ask Warbill.

"Lady Eudora and Lord Prandle received word the silver coats were heading to Bolvet and evacuated the village. Anyone who was strong enough to shadoweave left with them for Aendor. We have no idea how many made it out. Ariadne and I stayed behind to help those who had to ride. We managed to get a few on the road. Victus volunteered to lead the group out because his children were too young to shift."

"Victus was no fool," Ariadne adds. "Since his wife died and he started trading with the Rivertoads, he'd learned to sleep with one eye open. No one was as travel-savvy as he. The shade understood how to avoid the silver coats. He was meticulously careful and had friends in low places, friends he thought would protect him. We assumed they'd survived, until now."

I scratch my cheek, remembering the man and the waif of a girl I'd seen standing behind him in the store the day I visited. "You say he had his children with him when he fled? I found his body strung up on the road to the Borderlands with a New Stygarde execution decree."

Ariadne clutches her chest. "Then the silver coats have the children."

I stare into the fire. "Most likely. How many children were with him?"

"Only two. His children. Anyone else with young ones had fled Bolvet long ago. There's a girl, Zarissa, and a boy who is a year older, Zander," Warbill says.

"I'll get them back. I swear it." A muscle in my jaw cramps as my teeth grind on the promise.

"Of course you will," Ariadne says, leaning forward in her chair. The light from the fire reflects in her rheumy eyes. "You have the dragon! By the goddess, all of us believed it had died."

"It did."

They both look at each other and then back at me.

"Eloise practices spirit magic. The dragon was dead and now is animated by her ancestors. They are the source of her magic." Although Eloise tried to explain this before, it bears repeating, considering the rarity of her abilities.

"Goddess, so she's a witch?" Warbill shakes his head in abject wonder.

Ariadne's hand flutters against her chest. "She told me she was a vampire. I tasted—" She cuts herself off, not wanting to admit directly to me that she once tasted Eloise's blood. She clears her throat. "I am sure she was not a witch when I fitted her for her wardrobe."

I lean forward, resting my elbows on my knees. "Eloise lost her powers temporarily when she came to this world, but she does practice magic, spirit magic. Yes, she is a type of witch, but she is much more. The goddess Thanesia has made her a shade."

"Made a shade? How is such a thing possible?" Ariadne curls her lip.

"Through blood and death and quite dangerous magic," I explain.

Warbill tucks a strand of his greasy hair behind his ear. "And when did you make her your queen?"

Ariadne stands, her excitement sending a flush into her pale cheeks.

"During our time in Dimhollow. Catarina, a high priestess of the coven, married us. It is binding and the manifestation of my greatest wish."

Ariadne turns to the fire and angrily folds her arms.

"You don't approve?" I ask. Strange. I always thought Ariadne liked Eloise.

"The dress, Damien!" She turns to me, hands spread. "I wanted to be the one to design her wedding gown. What was she wearing when these vows took place?"

I think back to that day. I see her eyes clearly, the look of joy on her face. I feel her hands in mine. "I don't remember." I shrug.

Ariadne grabs the sides of her head. "It's a travesty! It's a great miscarriage of justice."

I give a deep, rumbling laugh. "I promise you she is my stars and moon, my beginning and end, blood of my blood, and my shade from the burning light. She is my destiny, my fate's reward, my true and only mate, and your queen. What she wore is insignificant."

"Insignificant? Oh, my heart!" Ariadne clutches her chest.

Warbill's laugh fills the space. "Just save yourself some time, Damien, and promise her that once you take back Stygarde, you'll host a proper wedding and coronation at the castle."

I smile and look up at my old friend and her tear-filled eyes. "I promise you, Ariadne. We will have a proper wedding."

"And you will allow *me* to design her dress."

"Eloise would desire no one else, and there is no one better."

Her shoulders finally relax, and she sinks back into her chair. "Good. As long as there's a plan."

"What is the plan?" Warbill asks more seriously. "How do you propose to take back the kingdom?"

I let out a long-suffering groan, frustrated with my lack of control. "We need more men. I have the allegiance of the mountain dwellers, but they number only a thousand, without an umbrae among them. Tempest has more. A network of rebels, but I'm unsure how many."

"The mountain dweller's weapons will come in handy," Warbill says. "You know my sword is yours. I will get strong again once I'm able to feed, and I remember how to fight. There is power yet in these old bones."

I nod. "Having a former umbrae at my side means everything, Warbill. I welcome your allegiance."

"How many men can New Stygarde claim?" Ariadne asks.

"I don't know," I admit. "We've been cut off from the shadow network to avoid detection. Tempest sent word by raven occasionally, but we had to be careful."

Warbill frowns. "Last I heard, Victus projected fifteen thousand."

"Fifteen thousand?" Ariadne's eyes widen. "How? That is more than even King Malek boasted."

"That's what Victus had heard from the Rivertoads, whose travels made them privy to more than we are in the west, but he never explained the number.

I suppose there are those like Banias, who simply saw an opportunity for profit and power among the new regime and stayed. And don't forget that New Stygarde has the allegiance of Willowgulch as well. The dark elf king will spare no expense to support his daughter's reign, and he will no doubt employ his own troops, including elven hunters, to defend and expand her rule."

"I don't suppose Tempest is hiding another fourteen thousand men," I grumble.

Warbill scoffs. "Her efforts are not without merit. Last I heard, she and Lord Thane had five thousand on board, a number that grows every day as people flee their ravaged villages. Many of them are former umbrae."

"An experienced umbrae is worth three inexperienced soldiers, but it's not enough. Not with what we're facing." Although I hate the idea of hurting Stygarde's children, there may be no other way to stop Brahm and Nevina than to go through them. Highly skilled warriors are capable of keeping collateral damage to a minimum. Umbrae are trained to neutralize rather than kill innocents. But such discretion is only possible if we have enough men. An overpowered army will be too busy surviving to protect anything in their path.

"What about the witches?" Warbill asks.

"Sworn to remain neutral."

"Fucking cowards," Ariadne spits.

I shake my head and hold up one hand. "I'll have none of that. The witches saved our lives. They are not indifferent to our suffering, but their numbers are few and they're not soldiers. Their magic and training are primarily defensive by nature. We can't judge them for being honest about what they are and where their strengths lie."

Warbill rubs the back of his neck. "You may find others like me who haven't made it to Aendor, but who could be convinced to join the cause. I'm afraid at this point, though, they will be few and far between. Drawing them out will mean revealing yourselves, which will be risky. There is one place to find more men, though. Strong ones, practiced in killing."

"Where?"

"The Rivertoads."

"Mercenaries," I hiss. "Sure, they can fight, but they'll turn on you the moment they're tempted by more coin."

Warbill settles into his chair. "You've been gone a long time."

"What's that supposed to mean?"

"Just that old prejudices run deep."

I cringe. "I harbor no prejudices. My feelings about the Rivertoads are based on facts and experience. It is known."

"I'm not sure about that, Damien. It's not always about money with them. Victus said they helped him defy New Stygarde to keep the general store stocked, even when it was not profitable for them to do so. Brahm betrayed them. Before your father died, Brahm ran up an enormous debt with them he's never repaid. And New Stygarde has begun restricting their movements. They're travelers. Have been since before I was born."

I stare into the fire, watching it crackle and sputter. We'll need more wood for the night. The logs are mostly ash. Then again, the chill I'm suddenly feeling has nothing to do with the fire. I don't like Rivertoads. My father found them untrustworthy, unclean, uncivilized. Only a month ago, a group of them, hired by King Entrydal, attempted to assassinate me. I will never trust a Rivertoad to do the right thing.

"How many men do the Rivertoads have for hire?"

"According to Victus, thousands," Warbill says.

I swivel my head to look at him, convinced he must be joking. "Impossible."

"No." Warbill's eyebrows lift. "When Brahm rose to power, many individuals left the villages and joined up with the travelers. You have to understand that the River-toads made it possible to hide. They aren't governed the way Bolvet was, the way any of the regions are. More often than not, they slip under the radar. That appeals to anyone trying to make a new start, even if it comes with constant movement and an expectation that one might have to perform the occasional act of service."

"Hmmm." By act of service, he means killing or stealing in exchange for goods or money. Exactly what Rivertoads are known for.

As I look upon the two starving shades before me, I know why some would resort to joining the Rivertoads. And I know that if there are loyal umbrae warriors left alive, and they could not make it to Aendor, joining up with the travelers would have promised safety and freedom.

"Then it sounds like my next stop is to pay the River-toads a visit. Do you know the name of their current leader?"

"King of the Rivertoads? No. They're secretive about their leadership, but Victus did tell me one thing after a bit of drinking in my tavern. He said, if I ever needed help, to find the caravan and wait until it stopped for the night to approach. A few of the wagons open in the evening to serve food and drink to anyone with quills. All the Rivertoads gather there. It's their social hub, the center of their community life. Victus said to ask for what you want, and if someone can get it for you and you're willing to pay, they do."

I shove down the sour feeling that churns in my belly at the thought of asking filthy Rivertoads for help with anything. But if there's a chance some of my former umbrae are there, I have no choice. "Then it looks like our next stop is to pay a visit to the caravan."

We're interrupted when the door flies open, and Eloise smiles at us from the doorway. "Who's hungry? I'm afraid you'll have to come outside to eat. There's no way this thing is going to fit through the door."

She steps aside to reveal the largest stag I have seen since my return to Tenebris.

5

ABOUT THE CHILDREN

ELOISE

Cozy as the fire beside me might be, nothing warms my heart more than witnessing the effect the stag's blood and meat have on Ariadne and Warbill. Almost instantly, their glazed and foggy eyes clear, and color returns to their cheeks and hair. Although both are still far too thin, I notice Ariadne's exposed bones become less pronounced. It will take time for the two of them to recover completely, but the rejuvenative powers shades enjoy are incredible, and I know they will heal far faster than any human could. It means everything to me to know I've helped.

Far from what I'd assumed, Damien, Warbill, and Ariadne had no problem moving the beast indoors. The three shades drained its blood into a barrel like the finest wine and, in mere minutes, had butchered the creature. Obviously starving, Ariadne and Warbill gulped down goblets of blood and feasted on the most tender pieces of meat, while Damien showed me how to preserve the rest by hanging it in strips to dry. One leg he placed on a spit to roast over the fire.

Now, I sip from the warm goblet in my hands as the scent of roasting meat permeates the cabin and Damien fills me in on the conversation they had while I was laying the wards.

"So, we need to find the Rivertoad king and ask him to join our cause?" I clarify.

Damien snorts. "More like offer to buy his men. No Rivertoad has ever done the right thing for the sake of doing the right thing."

I frown at the look Warbill casts in my mate's direction. There's something there. I sense Warbill doesn't agree with my mate's assessment of the Rivertoads. I make a mental note to ask Damien about it later.

"And what about the children of the man we found? Victus?" I ask. "Do we know where they are?"

Ariadne scowls. "Taken by New Stygarde, we assume. Or Willowgulch, although I hate to think about those two young ones in King Entrydal's clutches."

This has me on my feet. "Do you have anything of the children's? Or a photograph of them?"

"Photograph?" Warbill asks.

"A painting? Illustration?"

They shake their heads.

"I saved the carving," Damien says, handing the small stag to me, the one that fell out of Victus's pocket.

I stare down at the item, not sure if it will work, and then head for the door.

"Where are you going, little bird?" Damien asks.

"To do a spell to find those children."

Damien opens his mouth to say something more, but Ariadne cuts him off. "I can show you what they look like."

I stop, praying she can do what she says she can do. Phantom has a spell, but it will work better if I can recognize them.

She spreads her hands, and shadows gather from the corners of the room. I'm in awe of the control she wields. I haven't mastered pouring water from a pitcher, and she's painting a lifelike, full-body portrait of a boy and a girl right in front of me. I study the image, committing it to memory.

"What are their names?"

"Zander and Zarissa. Their mother was Ulcuta. They will trust you if you mention their mother. So few remember her name."

I nod.

"Little dragon, it would be foolish to draw attention to our location right now. As much as I would like those children back, we can't do anything...rash."

I open the door and look my mate right in the eye. "All I'm going to do is use magic to determine their location."

His eyes become suspicious slits. "And then what?"

"And then, I'm going to weigh my chances of successfully stealing them back." I leave the cabin, closing the door behind me.

He's outside and in the clearing before I can even call Phantom. He doesn't have to open the door, just funnels under it and is standing next to me. "This isn't a good idea."

"No," I admit. "But I won't allow King Entrydal to

touch those children. Not after what he did to me. Not while I'm breathing."

Our gazes connect for one beat and then two. His lip curls in displeasure with my plan, but he releases a breath of resolve. "How can I help?"

I reach out for Phantom, and my grandmother shows me how to do the spell. "Do you have a map of Tenebris?"

"I can create one for you from shadow," he offers.

"Good. Then I just need the lace from your boot."

Without hesitation, he unfastens one lace and passes the string to me.

"You're being incredibly understanding about this for a man who wants to tackle me to the ground to protect me."

"You can feel that?"

"The bond doesn't lie."

He snorts. "No, it doesn't. But I've learned when you set your mind to something, little dragon, it's in my best interest as your mate not to get in your way."

"Wise man."

He smirks. "Wise is not what I'm feeling at the moment."

"Nevertheless, the map. Please." I point at the moon-washed clearing. In Tenebris, day and night are separated by the rise and fall of the moon, not the sun. It's late in the day, which means we're running out of light. Without light, there can be no shadows, and although Damien can still control the darkness, I won't be able to see the map he creates clearly. "Hurry, we don't have much time before nightfall."

He spreads his hands as Ariadne did, and Stygarde Castle forms to the south, Blackspire Palace to the north in Willowgulch, Aendor and Dimhollow to the east, Mount Damocles and Zephrine to the west, the Borderlands and dark forest slicing across the middle. I place myself outside of Bolvet inside the Zephrine region, our actual location, and dangle the carved stag. Around and around it goes, the circle it carves growing wider and then oblong until it stops at an angle, the animal pointing southeast, toward a section of the Borderlands. I move until it's dangling straight down. "Where is this?"

"Looks like right outside of Carver Village on the edge of the Borderlands."

"Then they haven't reached New Stygarde yet. They're in Lady Odette's territory?"

"If the magic is accurate, yes."

"The pendulum isn't swinging. Maybe they've stopped for the night. We have a shot." I call Phantom, reaching down my bond to ask them a question. Damien startles when the dragon appears.

"We are hours from that location, hours we'd have to travel through dangerous and well-guarded terrain on rabble beasts. The children will not be able to shadoweave, and neither can you."

I stare into Phantom's beautiful blue eye and run my hand along their flank. "I don't need the rabble beasts."

Damien looks between Phantom and me. "You can't be serious, Eloise. You've never tried riding Phantom. You have no idea what will happen."

"How much different can they be from Romulus?"

Damien pinches the bridge of his nose like I've given him an intense headache. But when he speaks to me, he uses his hands. Damien might be from Tenebris, but at the moment, he could pass for full-blooded Italian. "Phantom is a dead dragon animated by your magic. Carrying your weight will be a drain on your magic. Even if you're able to reach the children, you might not have enough power left to save them or carry them back. And if Phantom falls, you fall with them."

"I—" I really want to tell him where to shove it, but damn if he doesn't have a point. "Honestly, I hadn't thought of that."

"We can do it," Phantom says in Grams's voice. "We're stronger now. We've eaten and rested. Let us help the children." They lie down before me and offer their leg as a ramp to climb onto their back.

I glance back at Damien, and our eyes lock. We are partners, equals. I don't need to ask his permission, and I know if I go, he'll forgive me. But the trust we share is sacred. I trust his opinion. I trust his advice. He knows this world far better than I do, and he knows my power and limitations almost as well as I do. I hold his gaze and allow the unasked question to swirl between us, the unspoken conversation to play out in the tightness in his jaw and the roll of my shoulder, the lift of my chin.

"We go now," he says.

"We?"

"Yes, little bird. I'm going with you."

"We can't both—" I gesture at Phantom.

"I won't ride. I'll shadoweave. Believe me, I can keep up." He starts for the tree line, the shadows making up the map drawing in like spiderwebs caught in sticky fingers, following their master and blending into the edges of his form. He casts a wicked grin over his shoulder at me. "Can you?"

A laugh barks up my throat. "Game on, lover." I run up

Phantom's leg, a feat that would have been impossible for my former human self, and straddle the dragon's back, just in front of their wings. Their scales are slippery, and I have to grab one of the bony projections that rise from their neck to keep myself from falling off.

"This isn't going to work," I say to them. "It's too slippery."

"A little magic should do the trick. Your great-great-uncle Alfred has just the thing. Do us a solid and remove yourself for one moment."

With a simple shift of my weight, I slip off the beast and land on my feet.

"Now, picture a saddle and speak very clearly '*Vehi Fugere*' then snap your fingers thrice."

"Vehi Fugere!" I say quickly, adding in the three snaps as required. A saddle appears on my dragon. With a glance in the direction Damien went, I leap on, rest my feet in the stirrups, and hook my fingers through one of three straps that runs across the saddle. I'm relieved to see there's space for the children, the straps made to go over their legs and hold them in place. As always, Phantom has thought of everything. I have no need of reins. My bond with Phantom means all I need to do is think something, and they'll do it.

"Perfect. Let's go, before Damien beats us there."

"As you wish, darling." Phantom launches themselves into the air, my hand gripping the band until my knuckles turn white as my legs squeeze to maintain my seat. It's like being shot from a cannon. My red curls tug back from my face, and my eyes tear from the shearing wind. I swallow down a yelp.

"I've cloaked us in invisibility so that we don't draw unwanted attention," Phantom says into the wind.

I send them a mental note that I approve. I'm reluctant to open my mouth to say the words, worried that at the speed I'm traveling, I won't be able to close it again. I lower my chest closer to their back and hang on for dear life.

After a few minutes in the air, they level out, their wings barely flapping as they soar through the darkness, the moon's light melting beyond the horizon as Tenebris day turns into Tenebris night. Although this new shade body can see in the dark, it takes my eyes time to adjust to the inky blackness.

Once I do, the night becomes a glorious thing. I draw air into my lungs, the wind howling in my ears, the woods beneath us like a dark green carpet. Up here, it's peaceful and calm. Nothing else on this world flies so high. We're alone. We're safe.

"It's nice to feel you happy," Phantom says. "We all think so. You've been anxious for days."

"That will happen when an entire kingdom wants you dead."

Phantom laughs a deep, charcoal-lined laugh. "Darling, is that all? You've been dead three times before. We're all dead in here. Dead isn't anything to fear. Fear for the living. Fear for the ones suffering under those tyrants' rule."

I think about that long and hard. "You're right. The most important thing is helping free this kingdom from Brahm and Nevina and returning Damien to the throne. The only thing to fear is failure to do that. Failure to help our people." I blow out a deep breath. "I'm glad I have you all with me to put things in perspective."

"We're glad to have you too, darling. Hold on tight. I think I see the camp we're looking for, and I hear children crying."

Oh no. "Get us on the ground. Let's see what we're dealing with."

Phantom drops, and my stomach lurches. My fingers grip the strap as my bottom lifts off the saddle, and I stifle another scream. By the time Phantom's feet meet the forest underbrush, my heart is hammering in my chest and I'm wide awake. I dismount and give the beast a thank-you pat, then watch them disappear from view. Approaching the forest's edge, I move toward the sound of children sobbing, and then something grabs me from behind. Damien. He brings a finger to his lips.

"Beat you," I whisper.

He slants me a playful grin. "I've been here a quarter hour."

I scoff, then turn serious and nod toward the clearing. The children are there, all right. Phantom didn't steer us wrong. But extracting them won't be easy. Zander and Zarissa are locked inside a crate enchanted with elven magic. It's the same sort of box the hunters caged me in, and I feel bile rise in my throat, remembering the pain I suffered anytime I was jostled into the bars. The children are hugging each other and sobbing, their eyes and cheeks red from their tears.

"Those bars are charged with sunlight. We can't touch them," I whisper.

"Dawnbreaker will take care of the bars." He taps the hilt of his sword.

I survey the rest of the campsite. Rabble beasts are corralled inside a small pen, and the glow of a lantern comes from inside a tent. A doused fire smolders between the cart and the tent.

"Do you find this just a tad too convenient?" I ask Damien.

He frowns. "Children left alone to sob at the edge of the woods like bait? Yes. They're expecting us."

"So, how do we slip the worm off the hook without alerting the fisherman?"

He rubs his chin. "I'm afraid that hook will have to be dealt with, one way or another. If we touch the box to open it, the magic will make us mortal. If this is a trap, that's exactly what they want. I can cut the box open with Dawnbreaker, but the sound will set off the same alarm bells. One of us will have to cover the other one until we can get the children out."

I place a hand on his arm. "What if we were able to slip the entire hook off the line?"

"How's that?"

"They don't know Phantom exists. I'll have the dragon move the entire box to another clearing, cart and all."

"I doubt Phantom can touch that thing either."

"Not directly." I point to the rabble beasts and then the leather straps of their halters and reins that hang on a branch of a nearby tree.

"Clever little dragon," he whispers.

"You'll have to do it. I can't control the shadows well enough to build the rigging."

"Watch and learn." He slips me a crooked smile, and then the shadows gather. The moon has set, but with my night vision, I easily make out what he's doing from the light cast by the smoldering embers and the lamp in the tent. The shadows heed his command, maneuvering the leather to form a net around the box without a single shadow directly touching any part of the spelled wood. The dexterity and coordination he demonstrates are better than anything I could ever have accomplished. I'm positively awed. He buckles straps and secures knots, all so silently that even the rabble beasts don't look up from their grazing.

"Your turn," he whispers.

I call Phantom, projecting what I want them to do. The only clue to my invisible dragon's arrival is a strong gust of wind from the flap of their wings that blows across the embers. Phantom grasps the loop of the harness in their claws. The box and cart lift from the ground and are engulfed by the dragon's invisibility. We have them!

"Phantom sees a clearing to the west. They're taking the kids there. Follow me." I turn to run in the direction Phantom is beaming into my head, but I stop short when a familiar face emerges from the glowing tent.

Nevina lifts her eyes to the invisible Phantom. Although she can't see the dragon or the children, somehow she knows exactly where they are.

A bow appears in her hand, and she nocks a sunlight arrow, drawing the string back to her shoulder.

I grab Damien's arm, but he's already locked on her. "There must be tracker magic on the cr—"

The arrow flies. I fall.

6

SYMPATHETIC MAGIC

DAMIEN

I catch Eloise in my arms as her body seizes, and she crumples to the ground, blood blooming across her thigh. Carefully, I test the wound, but I find no direct cause of the injury or for the way her eyes roll back in her head and her spine arches in a rigid, bone-bending fit when I probe it. Nevina's arrow struck Phantom, and Eloise bled. *Damn it*! We should have foreseen this. Their bond goes both ways. Eloise is suffering the effects of Phantom's injury. Which means I must get Eloise to Phantom and remove that arrow from the dragon's leg or she won't heal. And I need to do it before Nevina finds us, or the dragon, and finishes the job.

Calling on the darkness, I surf the night, becoming one with the cool air as I rush west, searching for the clearing Eloise mentioned. Nevina's passionate curses reach me as she finds her rabble beast's tack missing and her soldiers scramble to produce a replacement. Shades are generally faster than elves, and we can see better in the dark when the moon has set, but that's assuming we can fully shift and surf the darkness. I can't do that with Eloise in my arms. That said, while elven hunters are trained to move silently and quickly in full dark, Nevina is no hunter. She'll have to use her magic to track the box and her lamp to guide her way.

My head start means I'll get there first. The question is, can I fix what's happened before Nevina catches up? I move as fast as I can with Eloise's rigid body clutched to my chest. Truly, she weighs next to nothing, and I wonder if she's been eating enough. How much stag did she have tonight? How much blood? As always, she was more concerned with Ariadne's and Warbill's health than her own. What she still doesn't understand is that her health, her existence, is more important than anyone's on this planet. She is the dragon, our best hope for freedom.

World be damned, she is the force that keeps my heart beating. I swear to the goddess that if we make it out of this alive, I will force her to take better care of herself. No more unnecessary risks.

The forest opens sooner than expected, and I find the dragon in a mass of downed trees, the box and cart smashed a few yards to the east. The beast never made it to the clearing and must have crashed into the edge of the wood. I rush to Phantom's side, set Eloise gently beside the dragon, and grip the sunlight arrow protruding from their thigh with both hands. It burns, and I feel my body changing, becoming mortal, but I don't hesitate. Bracing my foot on the creature's white scales, I use all my remaining might to pull the arrow free, and then I toss the evil thing as far as I can throw it. My palms have blistered, but as soon as I'm free of it, they begin to heal. I hope to the goddess that the same will happen with Phantom and, by connection, Eloise.

Immediately, her body relaxes. The rigidity in her arms and legs gives way. Her breath evens out. She doesn't wake, but she appears to be sleeping now instead of tortured with internal pain.

"Did Dad send you to save us?"

I turn to find a set of wide blue eyes staring up at me. The boy, Zander, looks just like his father, with a head of tousled brown hair and the intense stare of a shade who has seen too much, too young. His sister, Zarissa, clings to his side and is covered in tiny cuts and burns. Although both their shirts are bloody, they're alive and they appear to be healing.

"Are you injured?"

"No, sir. The box broke when we fell, and my sister was burned, but we're okay now," Zander says.

Zarissa holds out her arm where a bar-thick stripe of blisters mars her skin. "Zander dragged me away from the elf magic."

"Good. You did the right thing. But you both must follow my orders now, exactly, or the elf queen will have you again. Understand?"

Both children nod.

"First, I must know. Did you eat or drink anything since your capture?" Nevina once placed a magical tracker inside Eloise by convincing her to eat a single gumdrop. Nevina definitely knew exactly where the crate was, but was the tracker in the crate itself or inside the children? Before I take these children with us, I must be sure they aren't magically tagged.

"No," the boy says. "Dad told us never to eat or drink anything from an elf or silver coat. They gave us that." He points at a broken bowl beside the crate. A puddle of blue sludge remains in it. "But we didn't touch it."

"Nothing from the shade soldiers either? No candy? No food?"

"No," they both say in unison. "They offered it to us, but we know better," Zander adds.

I hear the dry rasp in his voice now and notice the severe thinness of Zarissa's arms, the fatigue that seems to weigh both of them. They're telling the truth. Thank the goddess. That severely limits the chances they're tagged. "Excellent. You've done very well. I know you're tired and you can't shift, but I'm going to need you to follow me, as fast as you can run. Got it?"

Zarissa swallows hard, but they both nod.

I lift Eloise's unconscious body into my arms again, noticing that she's no longer bleeding. As the dragon has healed, so has she. But no signs of life come from Phantom, and Eloise remains asleep. I leave the dragon, and I run, pacing myself so the children can keep up. To their credit, they give it their all. Victus taught them well. But I hear the thundering of rabble beast feet in the distance, the sound of voices cursing when they find the cart and, I assume, the dragon. And then a lone rider closer behind us. Closing in.

I glance over my shoulder to see a shade in a silver uniform no more than five hundred yards back. A New Stygarde soldier—one I don't recognize. He sees us, and he locks on. I try to move faster, but I can't with Eloise in my arms. Can't risk losing the children.

Like the thunder of a nearing storm, he closes in. There's only one thing to do.

I stop, set Eloise down, and draw Dawnbreaker. My blade feels exceptionally heavy in my hands as I turn to face the soldier. I might best this one, but there will be more. There will be elf magic. Sunlight. I'll have to hold them off until Eloise wakes.

"Get behind me," I tell the children. They obey, the boy searching the ground and picking up a heavy stick. Already brave, this one. My throat tightens at the desperation I see in his eyes.

I sink deeper. Raise my sword higher. I meet the silver coat's eyes...and frown. This is no soldier. He's barely a man, with the build of a teenager and the glazed eyes of one drugged to serve Nevina. Only a dozen yards away now, I know this is someone's child...their stolen child. As innocent as the two little ones behind me. I sheathe my sword. I can't kill the boy. I'll have to knock him out with my bare hands.

I prepare myself for a fight. He closes in.

And then, he's *gone.*

Fire consumes him. I raise my arms to protect my face from the radiating heat. The blast of dragon fire drives down from above, a swirling inferno contained within a perfect column of incinerating intensity. Although I can't see Phantom, I know they are behind this, the only creature capable of this destruction. It swallows the shade and the beast he rides on, singes the trees, the underbrush, the ground. Never have I seen anything like this. It burns as hot as a star. I take several steps back until my legs bump into Eloise.

She's sitting up, and her normally green eyes are glowing as blue as the dragon's.

When I turn my face back toward the soldier, the fire stops. I lower my arm and can't believe my eyes. The man is no longer. Now, there is only ash in the shape of what once was soldier and steed. The wind picks up, and the cremated flesh breaks apart and snows down between the blackened trees.

Phantom lands in front of me and chuffs. I follow their gaze to Eloise, who is now rubbing her head and blinking up at me.

"Little dragon?"

Eyelashes fluttering, she says, "Ow. Why does my leg hurt?" She rubs her thigh where the blood stains her clothes. I don't have time to answer her before she sees the children and immediately forgets her aching leg. "You must be Zander and Zarissa."

"Yes, ma'am," Zarissa says.

"Thank the goddess!"

"Eloise..." Under the guise of helping her to her feet, I pull her into my arms and hold her there. She hugs me back.

"Are you all right?" she asks me, as if she didn't just give me the fright of my life.

I nod. "Let's get back to the cabin. Quickly. It's not safe here."

"Wait! The children...they might have a tracker—"

"No. They ingested nothing."

She nods. "I'll check them on the way back, just to be sure. Help me get them on Phantom." She leads us toward the dragon and mounts quickly. I help Zander and Zarissa strap into the ingeniously designed saddle.

"As fast as you can fly," I say to her, meeting her eyes.

"What happened while I was out?" she asks.

My jaw ticks as I grind my teeth. "As. Fast. As. You. Can. Fly," I repeat.

She returns a nod and grips the strap in front of her. "Hang on!" she tells the children. Phantom shoots into the night sky and disappears.

Thank the goddess. I offer a prayer for her to make it back to the cottage safely and break into shadow, blending into the night. I'm about to take off toward the cabin when the sound of pounding feet heralds a pair of rabble beasts ridden by Nevina and another soldier. I stop and wait, nothing but a shadow. A shadow with ears.

"Where is Xerxes?" she snaps at the soldier beside her. "I ordered him to search this part of the forest. If he somehow disobeyed my orders, he will pay with his life."

The elf soldier at her side dismounts, squats down and scoops a handful of ash from the charred forest floor, sniffing it ruefully. He allows the ash to sift through his fingers. "It appears he already has, my queen."

At first, Nevina looks angry, then she releases a dark chuckle. "No loss. Plenty more shade children where he came from. If the rebels wish to execute their own, I won't stop them."

A chill runs through me. This is how New Stygarde has bolstered their army. All those children Brahm and Nevina stole from the villagers, all those children demanded as a blood tithe to the kingdom—they aren't just using them as servants and labor; they're training them as soldiers, sacrificial pawns to play against the rebellion. My teeth clench with my desire to kill her.

She looks around her, seeming to notice the scorched

earth fully for the first time, devastation that could only be caused by intense heat. "Only a dragon could do this," she says softly. "I knew it wasn't just magic levitating that crate. They have the beast."

"It appears so."

"Where did she find the dragon?" Nevina seethes. "I was told it was dead!"

"I do not know, my queen. No one has seen the creature in centuries."

She shakes her head. "We must double our efforts. Send word to the hunters and the Rivertoads. Double the bounty on their heads." She yanks the reins, bruising her rabble beast's mouth as she signals for it to turn. "Come. We must inform the king."

To my relief, they ride off toward the campsite, never knowing they were mere feet from me. I move in the opposite direction, my heart sinking and my stomach turning to lead. We had one advantage. Up until today, New Stygarde didn't know about Phantom. The dragon was our secret weapon, along with Eloise's newfound magic.

That advantage is gone.

Not a single being on Tenebris hasn't heard of the dragon. It's what started the old war to begin with. King Entrydal wanted the dragon for its magic. My father, King Malek, believed the beast should remain free. Neither Nevina nor her father knows about Aurora's prophecy, that the son of King Malek will protect Dimhollow and bring peace to Tenebris with a dragon at his side. Peace to Tenebris. Not just Stygarde. All of Tenebris.

Eloise is the dragon.

And I fear what's in store when my brother and his elf queen realize what that means.

7

THE PROPHECY

Ariadne helps me find blankets for the children, and we set them up on a pallet in front of the fire. On the way here, with Phantom's help, I scanned them for tracking spells. I found nothing. They're safe, as safe as two orphans can be in this world.

They weather the news of their father's death with the sort of reaction I'd expect from battle-worn warriors rather than children. Zarissa's eyes fill with tears, but none actually fall. Zander doesn't even flinch. He simply nods and then reminds me that his sister hasn't eaten in days. His sister. He only asks for her, those haunting, oversized eyes of his fixed on me. With a lump in my throat, I prepare two heaping bowls of stag meat and goblets of blood, and I watch as they both dive in, choking a little when they try to swallow too much, too fast.

The small cabin has one bed, which Ariadne and Warbill have platonically shared since fleeing Bolvet.

Ariadne offers to give it up for the children, but Zander is quick to point out that he and his sister prefer to be close to the fire. True or not, the discussion ends there. At this point, we've done everything we can do for them.

Warbill leaves to chop more firewood, but I don't think it's ash in his eyes making them water as he moves past me for the door. I can't stop thinking about Victus, how he gave his life to save these children from New Stygarde. How these two are all that is left, the only free progeny of Bolvet Village.

"Was Damien not with you?" Ariadne asks. We stand at the back of the cabin watching the children eat and avoiding any discussion of the future. "Where is he?"

"I don't know," I say honestly. "He left when I did. Maybe he ran into some trouble. I should go look for—" The door opens, and a dark man with an even darker scowl walks in. Damien's boots thunk on the wood floor. His cloak is trimmed in shadows that writhe and coil off it like curls of smoke, then disappear as he steps into the light. The moment he sees me, he seems to see only me and draws me into a needful embrace.

Ariadne excuses herself to help Warbill with the firewood, leaving us alone, aside from the children, who are distracted with their food on the other side of the cabin.

"You made it," I whisper. "I was beginning to worry."

He draws back, his eyes drifting to the children. "Worry is not uncalled-for in this situation," he says quietly.

"What happened?

"I saw Nevina." I draw in a sharp breath, and he quickly adds, "She didn't see me. The soldier who died in the fire, his name was Xerxes. He was one of the sacrifices, a child drugged to do her dirty work."

"What?" Guilt gnaws at my heart.

"It's not your fault, Eloise. Neither you nor Phantom could have known. I only suspected when I got a closeup view of him, and I wasn't certain until I heard Nevina confirm it."

"So she's not just training the children as soldiers. She's enchanting them to force their compliance." My stomach turns with the news. Before we left the castle, we suspected Nevina would use the child sacrifices as her human shield against the rebellion. But forcing them to fight as pawns sacrificed to defend her is beyond the pale.

"Much harder to rise up when it could mean the death of your child. Harder still when your child is enchanted to fight you to the death."

Tears well in my eyes, and I cover my face with my hands.

"There's one more thing," he says sadly.

"What could be more than this?"

"She knows about the dragon, Eloise."

I shake my head. "Phantom was invisible. She can't know for sure."

"She knows. She saw the scorch marks Phantom left when he incinerated Xerxes. Only a few creatures could carry a cart into the sky like that, and of those creatures, only one breathes fire. I don't think she saw Phantom's fallen body. She seemed surprised when she discovered what remained of Xerxes. But she knows."

"Phantom fell?" I try to remember, but all I can draw up is a memory of having a sore leg.

"Nevina had no business being in those woods tonight.

If this had been about a crime or simply transporting the children, her silver coats could have done that. But the queen was there, and she'd placed a tracker in the crate." He shakes his head. "Possibly it was in the children's food. Zander and Zarissa said the soldiers tried to get them to eat, but they refused. The bowl of porridge was still in the crate."

"But why would she do that? Why would she be there herself, unless…" I feel sick.

"I believe she was using the children as bait. We were meant to find Victus, and we were meant to try to rescue the children. She was counting on it."

"But she didn't count on Phantom."

He shakes his head. "She didn't count on Phantom. I don't think she knew what she was shooting at when she released that arrow, but she knows now." His expression turns grave. "She has doubled the bounty on our heads."

"Fuck."

He nods slowly, his lips pressed into a flat line. "I don't know how far Catarina's prophecy spread, but shades and elves have been fighting over that dragon for centuries. The magical properties of dragon scales and…dragon flesh…are well-known. If you controlling the dragon isn't enough to send the king and queen into a frenzy, the moment Nevina or Brahm learns that the witches foresaw a son of Malek bringing peace to Tenebris with a dragon by his side, they will come at us with everything they have."

"How could they have heard Aurora's prophecy? It's not like the witches have an open relationship with New Stygarde."

"You have to remember that, until our return, Caterina

believed me to be dead and that Brahm was the son and Nevina was the dragon referred to in the prophecy. I have no idea to whom she relayed that interpretation, if anyone, but we can't rule out the possibility that someone else knows. Word travels quickly in Tenebris."

I look over my shoulder at the children. "I'm not sorry we risked everything to rescue them. In fact, I'm thankful for it. It's a good reminder why we're doing this."

He growls. "It was a trap, Eloise. It won't be the last one."

"I know." Our eyes meet and hold. "I'm not sorry."

He curls his lip and releases a beleaguered sigh. "We did learn one thing tonight that we didn't know before."

"What's that?"

"Phantom is a major asset, but they are also your greatest vulnerability. I don't think Nevina saw anything to suspect that, when she shot Phantom, it hurt you. But keeping that connection a secret is imperative. And keeping Phantom safe is as well."

I swallow hard. Phantom and I are linked. If something happens to them, it happens to me. It makes sense, but it also raises questions. Phantom is embodied by the souls of my ancestors. They can't be killed, only sent back to the Darklands. But if someone were able to do that, would the abrupt loss of the bond temporarily suspend my powers until I found another host? Cause me to pass out? Kill me? I don't know. If it's true, it increases the risk of using Phantom on the front lines of this war, regardless of the power they have as a fire-breathing dragon.

"Understood," I say solemnly.

He pulls me closer and kisses the top of my head.

"So, we stay here tonight and continue to Aendor in the morning?"

Damien draws back and rubs his chin. "Warbill is right. There is only one place we're going to find enough skilled fighters to attack New Stygarde."

"The Rivertoads."

He nods. "As much as I hate the idea, I think we need to catch up to the caravan, disguised as before, and find out their numbers and their price." He scowls down at me, his diamond eyes turning hard.

"You don't like this plan. You don't trust them at all, do you?"

He reaches up to brush his fingers through my hair. "When Brahm was at his worst, only the Rivertoads would serve him. He'd spend days drunk, following their caravan and blowing the kingdom's money."

"I thought your kind couldn't get drunk?"

"Not on human alcohol. But here, we have certain plants, certain mushrooms, that have an intoxicating effect when smoked or brewed. The Rivertoads never turned Brahm away until he ran out of coin. Rivertoads almost killed us on the way to Mount Damocles. They would have killed me, if not for you. No one should trust a Rivertoad, Eloise. Their only loyalty is to the highest bidder. They have no conscience and no limits. They'll work for elves or shades or witches, sometimes fighting on both sides of a skirmish. I don't relish having to use them, but we may not have a choice. I owe it to you and this kingdom to pursue every option when it comes to fighting this war, and that includes the Rivertoads."

"What use are soldiers we can't trust?"

"Good question. Warbill seems to believe that Victus

forged a relationship with the travelers. According to what he heard, the Rivertoads are as frustrated with this regime as the other regions of the kingdom. For the first time, their routes of travel are being disrupted by new laws and taxes. It's possible we have aligning priorities."

"The enemy of my enemy is my friend?"

He slants me a sad smile. "That's one way of putting it."

"So, we talk to their leader and convince him that joining us is for their own good. Promise them freedom once you're back on the throne."

"Sounds easier than it is. For one, no one knows who the leader of the Rivertoads actually is."

"What? How is that possible?"

"Rivertoads are extremely secretive about their political structure. I've heard they're ruled by a king, but the person holding that title seems to change frequently. In the past, by the time my father figured out who it was, they'd been replaced. Their rulers are not named by bloodline, although I can't say how it is done. My family never understood their culture."

I ponder that as I watch the children hunker down in the nest of blankets in front of the fire. They look so tiny. So vulnerable. "We should get some rest," I say. "I need my strength tomorrow if we are going to trick the Rivertoads into believing we're someone else and trusting us with vital information. I need to be at my strongest."

He moves toward the bed, but I stop him with a hand at the center of his chest. "Ariadne and Warbill claimed the bed. I'm afraid we have the floor. Lucky for us, Ariadne brought some material with her when she fled her shop. We have something that will serve as a blanket."

I dig in the wardrobe and find some heavyweight

fabric that looks and feels like wool. Damien helps me spread it out in front of the small wood-burning stove in the kitchen area. He lies down first and offers me his shoulder. I cuddle into his side, resting my head on his broad chest, the thump of his heart beneath my cheek a steady, soothing sound. He tosses his cloak over both of us, and we fall into an uneasy sleep, waking only for a moment when Warbill and Ariadne return.

8

JOURNEY

DAMIEN

My bride deserves the softest bed, the sweetest waking, and a breakfast fit for the queen she is. Unfortunately, when we open our eyes again, we are on the same hard floor on which we fell asleep. The material beneath us is no match for the rough, splintered wood under it. I have no coffee to offer her, just more blood and drying meat. Now that she's a shade, it will keep her strong, but I suspect she doesn't enjoy it. I can see the fatigue setting in. We haven't even mounted our steeds, and already, she looks tired.

"Damien, whatever is causing that scowl on your face and the absolute brooding coming across the bond, you're wrong." She takes my face in her hands. "Everything is going to work out. You know it will. The prophecy says so. The one with the dragon wins, remember? Trust the goddess. Have a little faith."

"Did you know when you married me you'd become

the queen of a broken kingdom, of battle-scarred men, orphaned children, and land soaked with spilled blood? A queen of ramshackle cabins? What kind of king makes his queen sleep on the floor?"

"Don't be so dramatic. If you'll remember, I put it at fifty-fifty odds that I'd be queen of nothing and we'd both be dead right now, so this is a vast improvement." She stands from our spot on the floor and cracks her back, then smiles down at me, offering her hand to help me up. I don't need her help, but I take it anyway, standing with a shake of my head.

"How can you be so consistently positive about all this?"

She shrugs. "I'm happy." She repacks her bag, which doesn't take long because we slept in yesterday's clothes, and heads outside. I follow, confused.

"You're happy?" My voice strains on the words. "How can you be happy after everything that's happened to us? Everything that's in front of us."

The giggle she gives as she straps her bag onto Romulus is frustratingly simple. "Because I would rather be going through this with you than with anyone else on any world." She snorts. "When are you going to understand, Damien? We've already died together. We've walked the shadowpath hand in hand and faced a vengeful goddess. What's sleeping on the floor in comparison?"

I kiss her with enough vigor she has to arch her back. She's grinning ear to ear when I stop.

"What was that for?" she asks.

"For being the person you are. The queen I married. The love of my existence."

She snorts. "Are you ready to become someone else? Velis and Marquis, cousins from the west villages, fleeing certain starvation on their steeds, Scout and Atticus?"

I shake my head. "I was wrong to assume that anyone from the west villages was free to roam Tenebris. After what happened to Victus, I think our safest story is to claim we're citizens of the Borderlands. I believe Odette's people still have favor with the crown."

"Velis and Marquis, from the northwest Borderlands, then."

"And who shall I be?" Warbill strides from the cabin, looking younger and healthier than he did last night. His formerly stringy gray hair is full and dark brown now, although still peppered with gray, and pulled into a ponytail. His previously cloudy eyes are now a bright midnight blue, and the muscles of his shoulders fill out his threadbare shirt.

I turn to my old friend and fellow umbrae warrior with a questioning gaze.

"Did you forget I'm coming with you?"

"I didn't forget. I just wasn't sure your decision would survive a good night's sleep and a clear head."

He scoffs. "You need warriors. I'm a warrior. Don't let my appearance fool you, Damien. A few more meals and I'll be back to my old self. Plus, when New Stygarde isn't breathing down my neck, I've been practicing with Andromeda." He draws a sword from the scabbard on his hip, the light of the moon catching on the Stygian steel.

"You've kept her, all this time?"

"They tried to take her from me. It's illegal for me to have her. Bastards never thought to look under the three feet of ash in the cooking pit of my tavern."

"What about the children?" Eloise asks.

"I will care for them," Ariadne says, appearing in the yard with Zander and Zarissa at her side. "I cannot fight, but I can do this. We have meat and blood enough to last for weeks, and when it's gone, I will hunt. I've survived this long. The children and I will find a way to survive together."

"I can chop wood," Zander says, puffing out his chest.

"And I can make stew. I know what roots are good to eat. My father taught me," Zarissa says, nodding her sweet little chin.

"Then it's settled," I declare, before Warbill can change his mind. I do need him. I need every warrior I can find. "Warbill will come with us."

Eloise claps her hands. "Then you will be Valerian, brother of Velis and cousin of Marquis." She circles her hand, and Warbill's hair grows black, his nose thins to a point that echoes a bony chin, and his body stretches taller. With Eloise's hair dark and straight again, they easily pass for brother and sister.

"Not used to seeing you as a blond," Warbill says as his new whiskey-colored eyes scan me.

"Get used to it. We need to come off as extended family."

"Got it. Maybe I should come up with a pet name for you then, like runt or blondie. I rather like blondie. It suits."

I curl my lip at him. "We're too much for the rabble beasts with our cargo. You can ride Borus. Eloise is on Romulus. I'll walk or shadoweave."

"We'll take turns walking," Warbill says. "You're right, we shouldn't wear out the rabble beasts, but it's equally important we don't wear each other out. I'm not at full strength yet, but I can carry my own."

"I agree," Eloise says. "I can't shadoweave, but I can walk or ride Phantom. I think it's imperative we all stay at our best."

"Fine," I say, not bothering to point out to Eloise that she's maintaining our disguises and therefore should have the benefit of riding Romulus. I know her, and it's a battle I won't win. "Let's go. We're burning moonlight."

After saying our goodbyes to Ariadne and the children, we cut through the forest to rejoin the road that leads to the Borderlands and dark forest. We travel in relative silence for most of the day, all of us wary of attracting the attention of New Stygarde soldiers who might be policing Bolvet and the west villages. Only when we cross into the Borderlands do I breathe a sigh of relief. As far as I've heard, Odette's region has avoided the worst of New Stygarde's wrath, although she's paid dearly for it with her region's children.

"So..." Warbill says as we trade places on Borus, and he begins walking beside us. "Are you two always this entertaining or only in my presence?"

I grumble. "Just trying to avoid being the next one strung up in a tree."

"There's the dark, brooding prince we know and love."

"Don't mind him," Eloise says. "He's like this when he's happy."

"What's he like when he's grumpy?"

"No one's ever survived to tell the tale," she says.

I glare at each of them in turn. "Is that a tavern up ahead? It might be good to stop to eat and drink, perhaps listen for news of what's in store for us here?"

Warbill nods. "No place better to hear the local gossip than the local tavern."

Eloise gestures toward the quaint stone cottage with its steeply pitched clay roof and coiling smoke rising from the chimney. "I, for one, could definitely use a meal."

We gallop down the hill but slow when we see an entire herd of rabble beasts tied up in front of the place. I dismount and get a glimpse of the sign on the door. "The Road Raven: Welcome, Friends."

We look at one another and find a nearby tree to tie our beasts to, as the pole in front of the establishment normally used for the purpose proves to be full. "Perhaps this is a bad idea," Warbill whispers. "Could be silver coats."

I shake my head. "Look at the packs." I point to a roughshod bundle of pots and pans. "This is no army of soldiers. It looks like peasants fleeing their homes."

"Only one way to find out." Eloise heads for the door.

9

THE ROAD RAVEN

I push my way into the crowded tavern and am immediately overcome by the stench of smoke and unwashed bodies. All the chairs and tables are full, as are all the stools at the bar. I find Damien's hand and squeeze. People are crying, leaning into one another. Some have food and drink in front of them, but they're hardly eating.

"Welcome," an old man in an apron says to us when we reach the bar. "I'm afraid I can't offer you a table, but there is some soup left and some ale if you need it. I'm so sorry to hear about Covellton."

"New Stygarde must be stopped," Warbill says. And his guess is accurate, based on the bobbing heads around us.

"Burned my home, right to the ground, for no reason," an old woman on the stool beside us says. "I wasn't harboring anyone! We already gave them our children, now they take our homes. We've nothing left. Nothing."

"I'm so sorry," I say, resting a hand on her shoulder.

She pats my hand sympathetically. I remember my disguise and add, "For all of us."

Warbill hails the bartender with a wave of his hand. "Do you need help in the kitchen? I have experience. Ran a tavern up north."

For a second, I wonder if the barman will ask questions. After all, it's possible he knows his competitors and knows Valerian, as we are calling Warbill, is not among them. But the man only motions for him to come around the bar, and Warbill disappears into the kitchen.

Damien raises an eyebrow at me with that strange face that isn't his own. "I guess we're staying."

"Of course we are," I whisper, moving deeper into the crowd. It takes no effort at all to get people to tell their stories. New Stygarde marched in, just as they did in Bolvet, asked that the town turn us over. But of course, no one in Covellton was harboring us. Nevina knew this because she knew we were behind the rescue of the children. But the point was fear. The point was an excuse to occupy the Borderlands. And so, they burned the village and stole anything of value that the residents couldn't load onto their rabble beasts.

Damien and I listen and give as much comfort as we can. By the time the moon sets, I am heavy with the overwhelming weight of loss shared by this community, but I sense something different along my bond with Damien. He's angry. So angry, I have to use extra magic to keep his disguise in place.

"Take a deep breath," I whisper to him. "You're going to blow our cover."

In response, he says, "I'm going to find a place to make

camp in the woods behind the tavern. Bring…Valerian when his work is done."

I nod, knowing that he will do a lot more than make camp. Damien needs to blow off steam. I almost feel sorry for the trees that will receive the brunt of his wrath.

But I stay and I listen. I hold hands. I give hugs. I buy food for those who escaped with nothing but the clothes on their back, their quills left behind out of fear for their lives. And I help those who need it make beds on the floor of the tavern or on benches in booths.

Warbill joins me at some point and has to usher me out of the Road Raven. My concentration is slipping with my grief, my dark hair going curly and taking on a red hue. "You need rest. Let's find Damien."

We find him deep in the woods, lying on a blanket with his head on one of the saddlebags. We have no tent, but we do have bedrolls, and he's laid them out under the stars. I lower myself to the mat beside him and lay my head on his shoulder. What I'd like more than anything is a hot shower and a warm bed, but that's not to be. I hear Warbill lie down on the bedroll a few feet from us, and soon, the shade is snoring evenly.

Damien kisses me on the temple and whispers, "We will avenge Covellton."

"Yes, we will," I say, and then I'm fast asleep.

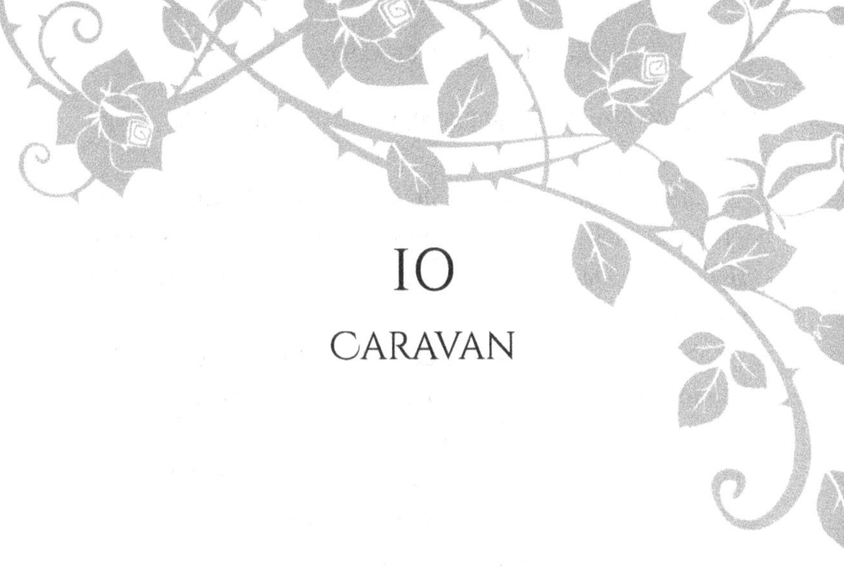

10

CARAVAN

DAMIEN

The next day, we ride in silence, my mind turning over the problem of this war in my head. We need more men. We can't win without more men. And every day we wait is a day another village like Covellton is burned.

"Do you see that wagon in the distance? I think that's the end of the Rivertoad caravan." Warbill points to a splash of bright red along the deep green horizon.

"Not far. If we hurry, I'm sure we can catch them," Eloise says.

"No." I tug on the reins, slowing Borus to a stop. "If they see us running toward them, they'll be on the defensive."

"Mr. Deep Thoughts is right," Warbill adds, with an obvious jab at my sullen mood this morning. "Rivertoads do not like surprises or overeager guests. Eventually, they'll stop for the night to make camp. If we continue in that direction, we'll happen upon them without any need for haste."

I nudge Borus into a slow walk again, and we cut across the field toward the end of the caravan of wagons. "If I'm Mr. Deep Thoughts, you're Mr. No Thoughts," I murmur.

Warbill snorts. "Was that a joke? Eloise, record this date for posterity. This moment may never come again."

She laughs the first real laugh I've heard from her in days, and I'm instantly jealous that it took Warbill to get it out of her. And then my jealousy is buried in a heaping helping of self-loathing that this war has completely ruined my sense of humor. "It must be easy for you to make others laugh, Warbill, given your natural appearance, but some of us need to exercise our wit."

Eloise laughs even harder, while Warbill takes a moment to puzzle out that I just called him funny-looking, and then he hits me with a lopsided scowl. "Two jokes in one day. He's truly going for a record."

"Should I stop now? Or make a reference to the size of your marriage material?" I ask him.

"Ah, but your queen mother would know all about that."

I'm going to kill him. I'm going to jump off this rabble beast and wring his bloody neck.

"Shh," Eloise says, raising her finger to her lips. "They're slowing down."

Sure enough, the bright-red wagon slows to a stop not more than a mile in front of us. Surrounded as we are by thick woods, it's hard to tell what's happening, but my ears pick up a flurry of activity.

"Looks like they're making camp. Everyone in character. It's showtime." I slow Borus's walk, and we creep up on the Rivertoad camp. By the time we've reached it, I see something I've never seen before. They've parked the wagons in a large circle and erected a tent between them. The sound of lively music drifts out from under the white canvas.

We dismount and secure our rabble beasts to a nearby tree, then walk toward the flap of the tent, propped open to reveal a dozen or more tables inside.

"Hold it right there, stranger." I stop when I feel the cold edge of a blade press into my throat and, out of the corner of my eye, see the glint of a second one pressed into Eloise's. Warbill, slightly behind us, goes absolutely still. "What brings you to our family?" the Rivertoad asks. He's a lanky specimen, with long, sandy-brown curls and a subtly hollowed-out look, as if he could do with a good meal.

"We've been traveling all day," I say, "And we need food and drink. We've heard you have a kitchen. We smelled roasting meat."

"Where are you from, strangers?" The voice is soft and ominously low.

"Covellton, northwest Borderlands," I say. They will have heard what happened there by now.

"Covellton." The man lowers his blade and gestures to his friend to do the same. Behind Eloise, a bald man sheathes the weapon he'd held to her neck. "We heard what happened there but held out little hope for survivors."

Eloise's eyes grow haunted as she adds. "There are always survivors, sir. The trick is getting them to trust you enough to share their survival. These days, I think it's safer to be from nowhere."

"Ain't that the truth." He rubs his nose. "Very well. You're welcome to share a table with us."

"Do you have a place for our rabble beasts?" I ask. Borus and Romulus will need tending.

"There's a pen built between the southeast spokes. So there's no confusion, the fire is free, but if you want food or drink, it will cost you. If you want to rent a wagon, that's available for a price as well."

"Thank you," Warbill says. "I'm Valarian, by the way. I didn't catch your name."

The man's smile fades. "I didn't give it." He and his bald compatriot drift out of the tent.

"Well, he was friendly," Warbill says.

"Do you blame him?" Eloise says. "They have to be careful, especially now."

We find a table next to a fire pit constructed out of freshly laid stones and take a seat. Rows of glass-encased candles are strung above our heads, casting the tent in a mustard-colored glow. An old woman with a handkerchief covering her hair and a full skirt decorated with a few stains of mysterious origin comes over with a pitcher of some kind of ale.

"Name's Maggie. Welcome to my hot pot. The ale will be five quill for the three of ya. If you want something to fill your bellies, ya best double it."

"What's on the menu?" Eloise asks.

"Stew," the woman says. "Couldna tell ya what kind it is, though. Whatever the boys could catch today."

I toss the quill on the table. "We'll take three and some bread if you have it."

"I does," she says through missing teeth. "I'd say you won't be disappointed, but we can make no such guarantees here. All we Rivertoads swear by is that you won't leave hungry." She turns to go, but I reach out and stop her.

"We'd also like to talk to someone about hiring… protection." My eyes meet hers, and although I have no doubt my disguise is in place, she seems to read my intent pretty clearly.

She leans in, her voice dropping. "Stay for the dancing. I don't handle that sort of thing, but I'll point out who does if they show up."

"Dancing?" Eloise grins, waggling her eyebrows at me.

"Yes, dear," Maggie says. "I'm sure a sweet young thing like you will have plenty of opportunity."

Maggie leaves me to scowl over that comment.

"Did you hear that?" Warbill says. "My sister might find herself a suitor tonight."

It's all I can do to stifle a growl.

But Eloise is already standing from the table. "I'm going to go guide the rabble beasts to that pen the welcoming party mentioned."

"I can do that," I offer immediately.

But she shakes her head. "Sometimes would-be suitors talk around a *sweet young thing*, especially when that young thing can do magic," she whispers. "Stay here. I'll be right back."

II

JAQUAL

ELOISE

Finding the pen so that the rabble beasts can run and graze proves harder than it should be. I've figured out the Rivertoad encampment is shaped like a wheel, and the nameless man who welcomed us into the tent said the rabble beast pen was between the southeast spokes. Only, there are multiple southeast spokes, and a girl leading two rabble beasts can't fit between the wagons to search for the pen. I try following one spoke to the end, thinking I can walk around the outside of the wheel, but after walking for a concerning amount of time, I suspect I'm in trouble. The caravan is enormous. No question the Rivertoads can harbor thousands of mercenaries for hire. There are thousands of wagons.

"There's a break every ten wagons. You're not far from the next one." Looking around Romulus, I spot the man who's offered the welcome advice and raise my eyebrows when he instantly reminds me of an actor from a pirate movie. He sports long, wavy black hair and eyes an arresting shade of violet. Tall and lean, with the type of tight, ropy muscles you get from constant movement, he has a manner of dress that fits right in amongst the vibrant wagons. His pants are a thick, dark material, but his long-sleeved white shirt looks thin as linen. The jacket he wears is colorful leather but pieced together like a quilt from scraps of more than one animal. Mismatched beads dangle from his ears, his neck, his wrists, one necklace displaying a painting of an oversized eye that rests over his sternum. Nothing of value. Almost as if he went shopping in the lost and found of a retirement home.

Somehow, on this man, it all works.

"Thank you," I say. "It's my first time enjoying your hospitality. I'm afraid I haven't figured out the lay of the land yet."

He saunters over to me. "Hospitality? You must be so new as not to have tasted the food or drank the ale."

I chuckle. "Honestly, I don't require much and am grateful for whatever we can get."

"We?"

"My brother, cousin, and I. We recently fled Covellton. New Stygarde," I say by way of explanation.

"I see. Well, then you're lucky to be alive."

"And to have made a friend who can show me to the animal pen." I slant him a pleading look.

A ghost of a smile turns his lips, and he starts forward, gesturing for me to come along. We fall into step. "You know, most inhabitants of the northern Borderlands don't think highly of Rivertoads. Are you sure you want to make a friend of one?"

"My grams always said to judge a rose by its blooms,

not by where it takes root, and if you knew my grams, you'd know she wasn't talking about roses."

He laughs. "You haven't known me long enough to assess my bloom."

"Don't underestimate the power of your stench," I say through a chuckle.

His laugh grows stronger.

"Anyway, I'm giving you the benefit of the doubt. If you rob me instead of leading me to the rabble beast pen, you will ruin my perception of all Rivertoads going forward indefinitely. Please don't. I'd really like a place to sleep tonight."

His laughter finally simmers down, and he points at a gap between two wagons that I wouldn't have seen without him there. I don't know how they've managed it, but the angle of the wagons makes my eye go right over the gap. Though, once I know it's there, I can't unsee it. I lead the rabble beasts, single file, through the opening and see the pen straightaway. Borus and Romulus practically dance once I remove their tack and the saddlebags.

I turn to the man, who still waits by the gate, as I hang the tack on the posts provided and move to hoist the heavy saddlebags onto my shoulders. "Well, you haven't tried to deprive me of my things after all, so I'd say your bloom is adequate to meet the bar of friendship."

"The night is young. I could be a danger to you yet." He opens the gate and grabs one of the bags, hoisting it onto his shoulder. Although I could use magic, to lighten the load and carry them both, I don't risk it and allow him to assist me. I'm supposed to be a common farmer after all.

"Thank you for your help."

He glances at me. "Oh, I'm stealing this. I just happen to be heading in the same direction as you."

I snort. "What do you want with my brother's dirty underwear?"

He laughs again. "What is your name, friend?"

"Velis."

"Velis? That hardly suits you."

I scoff. "Who are you to say a name suits or doesn't suit me? We've never met. I think my parents understood what would suit me far better than you could."

"Fair." He winks. "But you have too much fire now for such a common, airy name."

"What's your name?"

He studies me for a second, as if wondering if he should tell me, then says, "Jaqual."

I try the syllables of the unusual name out on my tongue. "*Zha-qu-ahl.*"

He nods that I've got it right. "Would you say it suits me?" He grins devilishly.

I instantly think of the Earth animal jackal and the similarities to his toothy smile and doglike presence at my side. "I don't see how I could possibly judge, but off the cuff, I'd say the name is perfect for you. You can tell your parents they did a very fine job indeed."

His smile falters. "That I can't do. My parents are dead."

Great. Nice work, Eloise. Way to ingratiate yourself to the Rivertoads by bringing up this man's dead parents. "I'm sorry—"

"Never mind it. I was left with the community as a baby. They named me."

"But if you were abandoned as a baby, don't you have —I only mean, were you raised by the entire community?"

He smiles a little wider. "I have a few families that I think of as mine, but yes, I am a child of all. And thank the goddess. There's no better life, especially now."

My thoughts wander to what it would be like to be raised by multiple families. I lost my parents as a teen, but at least I had Grams.

"What do *you* think of our caravan?" he asks me, shooting me a crooked smile.

I shrug. "I haven't tried the food yet, of course, but it smells edible. Plus, you're not starving, which is a major plus."

His smile falters, and he sighs at my reference to my village. "And the rest of it?"

"You mean the traveling and the wagons?"

He nods.

"I think when I was a young girl, I would have balked at calling a wagon *home*, but only a few days ago, I stood by helplessly as everything *I* called home went up in flames. Now, I wonder if there is wisdom in traveling light, in making roots in the wind and the dust of the road, in staying true only to each other and not to a single place."

He stops walking and gazes down at me with those arresting purple eyes. "That's a beautiful sentiment, Velis, and delivered from the heart." And that's when I see it. The eye pendant around his neck...*blinks*.

I stare at it for a moment, my eyes widening. "Your amulet. I could swear I saw it blink just now."

He snorts and walks on. "A trick of the light."

But I reach out for Phantom and send a tiny tendril of

magic toward the eye. The hair on the back of my neck stands on end as my fiery dragon magic meets another magic, one that tastes like cool water and smells of green grass. This is not the magic of the witches of Dimhollow or the shadow magic inherent among shades. This is something completely unique. Something I've never encountered before.

Jaqual slides a glance in my direction, and I retract my power, worried he might have felt my probing. Do Rivertoads have witches living among them? Have I made friends with the Merlin of this Camelot?

I am more intrigued than ever by this caravan and its people, but especially this man and his unusual magic. "Jaqual, you said you were found and raised by the Rivertoads, but have you always lived among them? Ever stayed in any of the regions for school or work?"

His eyes narrow on me, and I get the sense he's looking right through me. "The caravan is the only life I've ever known, and I'm grateful for it."

I can see the tent up ahead, smell the stewing meat. "Are you afraid New Stygarde could take it all away, as they did my home?"

His shallow smile doesn't falter on his lips, but it leaves his eyes entirely. "I'm afraid this is where I leave you, Velis." He hands me the other saddlebag, and I shift it onto my opposite shoulder with an exaggerated oomph and a bend of my knees. "Welcome to the caravan. Perhaps I'll see you again tomorrow."

12

DELAYS AND DISAPPOINTMENTS

DAMIEN

I'm halfway through my second pint of ale and feeling the effects of the Rivertoad brew when Eloise returns, spine bowed under both saddlebags. I shadoweave over to her and alleviate her burden, tossing them under the table near Warbill's feet.

"I'm relieved you've returned," I tell her. "I wanted to go looking for you, but Warbill convinced me to give you time. That you might be conversing with someone."

"Warbill was right," Eloise whispers.

"As always," Warbill chimes in in a throaty whisper.

I shoot him a sharp look.

Eloise sits down beside me at the table and slides her bowl of stew closer, picking up the spoon. "I did meet someone, although I now have more questions than answers." She takes a bite of the dish and hums. "Goddess, this is good."

I nod in agreement. For as much self-deprecating

humor as Maggie used about the dish, it's one of the best I've ever had. Warbill thought the same. "What did you learn?" I ask her.

"Well..." She tips her head to the side. "Rivertoads are shades, right?"

"Yes. Although I assume they're different from us, like the mountain dwellers are different. They've adapted to this life of constant travel," I say. Although in truth, I'm not sure exactly the differences. In battle, they seem more hesitant to shift than other shades. Sometimes, as in the case of Maggie, their dialogue seems less sophisticated. Other times, I hardly notice a difference in speech. The people under this tent seem taller, lankier than the people of Stygarde.

Eloise finishes another bite and rolls her lips. She squints at me as if truly baffled. "But do they have magic like witches?"

That raises my brows. "Not as far as I know. Why?"

She lowers her voice even further. "Because I met someone with magic, Damien. A type I've never encountered before, on Earth or Tenebris."

"A Rivertoad?"

"Yes."

We stop talking when Maggie arrives, wiping her hands on her apron. When she reaches the table, she sets one long gold key with butterfly wings in front of Eloise and a second silver one, smaller and less ornate, in between Warbill and me. "Seeing as how you've your bags under the table, I assume you'll be stayin' the night. That'll be ten quill for the two wagons."

"We prefer to stay together," I say.

But Maggie makes a face. "Not done here, lad. Married

wagons are only for folks who've said their vows and had the wheels blessed."

"But we're family," Eloise protests.

Maggie snorts. "Over fifteen is what you are, and among the Rivertoads, unless you're wed, women in one wagon and men in another." I don't argue. Eloise and I are supposed to be cousins and Warbill her brother. We can't claim to be married now.

Maggie taps the gold key and looks toward Eloise. "This wagon is outfitted for a woman. It's all yours for the night." She points her chin at me and then Warbill. "You two can stay in that one. It'll sleep two men comfortably. You'll find your wagons along the east spoke."

I dig in my coinbag and place ten quill on the table. Maggie sweeps it into her hand.

"The protection we inquired about..." I say quietly. "We're still interested in hiring some...help."

"Not tonight, Covellton," she says, calling us by our fictional origins. "I'm afraid busy men live busy lives. They don't keep a schedule these days. Stop in tomorrow night, and I may have more information for you." She drifts off toward the kitchen wagon.

"I guess we're spending the night," Eloise says, plucking the butterfly key from the table.

Warbill finishes his third ale and releases a burp that turns heads. "Best idea I've heard all day. I don't relish another night out in the open." She clears the table, and Warbill and I shoulder the bags.

"There's a gap every tenth wagon," Eloise says, leading us down the spoke and finding the wagon whose number matches that which is on her key. The exterior is a beautiful shade of violet, and through the small square window beside the door, I view an interior decor of ruby velvet, dark wood trim, and floral accents of pink and gold. She slips the key into the door and opens it. I move to follow her inside, rules be damned. But she stops me with an extended hand. "No. We follow the rules."

"Stupid rules," I mutter, wanting desperately to be with her tonight. Two nights ago, we couldn't be together because we slept in the same cabin as Warbill and Ariadne and the children. Then last night, we slept under the stars with Warbill not three feet from us. It pains me to miss an opportunity to be alone with her.

"I don't know why they follow this rule, or how serious it is to them, but we want to gain their trust. We're living in their world, borrowing their things—"

"Paying for—"

"I want to respect their wishes," she says firmly. "Goodnight, cousin."

Resolved, I back away from the door. "Goodnight."

"Sleep well," Warbill chimes in, already walking down the row toward our wagon. I catch up to him in a foul mood, a growl rumbling in my chest. "She's right, you know."

"What do you know about it?"

"I know that if there were strangers in my village, I'd be watching. They wouldn't see me, but I'd be there."

My eyes drift to the darkened windows of the wagons, and I frown. Of course the Rivertoads are watching. We still haven't done what we came to do. We can't afford to offend our hosts before we've even had a chance to speak to them about hiring their men. I meet Warbill's eyes and nod.

"Here we are," he says. He opens the door to a wagon

twice the size of Eloise's, with a bed on each end and a small kitchen in the middle. Warbill closes the door behind us.

"Do you think our disguises will hold while she sleeps?" Warbill asks.

"I have no idea, but it's worth taking precautions." I close the drapes on all the windows.

"What do you think she meant about the Rivertoad she met having magic? You ever heard of anything like that?" Warbill asks.

I shake my head. "Never. Although, they've always been mysterious to me. Weird, even. Maybe it was a trick to test her."

"Possible. But Eloise seems wiser than that."

I frown. "She is. I'll ask her for more details tomorrow when we're alone."

We get ready for bed and climb under the blankets.

"I'm not going to lie, Damien. This bed is the most comfortable one I've slept in in a long time. The food was decent and the music was merry. I'm tempted to join up with this crew and ditch your ass."

I stare at the ceiling, warm and comfortable aside from the lack of Eloise at my side. This wagon, although seemingly small on the outside, is surprisingly adequate. But my mind lingers on Warbill's words. "New Stygarde has given the Rivertoads their freedom because they've been useful to them. But the second they have what they want, they will close their fist around this community the same way they closed it around Bolvet. Brahm answers to Nevina, and Nevina answers to King Entrydal. The goal is and always has been for the dark elves to rule everything."

"How do you know?"

"Entrydal told Eloise as much when she was his captive. The king wants us either dead or acting as servants to his people. Taking our children was only step one. The next is to exterminate any who don't bow to his ultimate rule."

"Evil," Warbill says softly. "And it rings true to me."

"Bolvet didn't comply and it burned. Covellton complied and it burned too. This war isn't about governance or laws or order. And one day, even those who fight for Nevina in her silver coat army will realize they are only pawns in a game where the elves plan to wipe them from the board."

"You need to win this, my king."

"I plan to, Warbill. Or I swear I will die trying."

"Better dead than an elf's slave."

"I agree, old friend. I agree."

I3
WAGON

For the first time in months, I wake from a deep sleep, warm and cozy in a soft bed. Not too hot, not too cold. I spent the night dreaming about painting in my mother's studio in Harcourt Manor. In the morning light, I miss my hobby. It's been months since I held a paintbrush against a blank canvas. Will I ever have the sort of peace and space I need to create again the way I used to? So much has changed. My physical composition, my magic, my world. But inside, I'm the same.

No, that's not true.

I am not the same. When I left Tony, I was a child, barely brave enough to drag myself to the safety of my grandmother's home in order to escape an abusive marriage. I was a desperate woman willing to trade her own blood for someone to protect me. Today, I am powerful. I am brave. I am the protector. And, importantly, I am loved. Damien's love is a constant, a foundation to the tower of my confidence and self-esteem. I am worthy because I am loved. I am able to love because I was already worthy.

And still, my inner child cries out for a paintbrush.

A knock on my door startles me, and I make sure my disguise is in place before opening it. A teenage boy hands me a copper vessel that feels hot to the touch and a lidded basket that I hook on my elbow. "Your morning provisions, ma'am. The caravan will set off in one hour. I'm supposed to ask you if you're comfortable driving or if we need to supply someone."

"You want me to drive the wagon in the caravan?"

"If you're capable. We usually have to hook this one up to the next as it is normally unoccupied, but it would be easier on the rabble beasts if you were able to share the load."

I nod. "I'll drive."

"Excellent. I will retrieve your rabble beast."

I furrow my brow. "How will you know which one is mine?"

He laughs. "We know." He waves a hand and disappears. I open the lid of the basket. Inside is a small basin with a sponge, soap that smells of rose petals, and a towel quilted from scraps of soft, plush material. A metal canister contains a meal of something like oatmeal but with nuts, fruit, and small pieces of sausage. On top of it all is a packet of tea that wafts a scent I can only compare to chai—cardamon and cinnamon and other spices completely foreign to me. The copper vessel contains hot water—much more than I need to bathe. Clever River-toads. I'm meant to eat and drink first and then use the remainder of the water to wash. A marvelously efficient system from a people I'm swiftly coming to respect for their pragmatic approach to things.

I'm finishing my morning routine when I feel the wagon rock as the boy who visited before attaches the yoke to Romulus. I have just enough time to use the latrines the caravan erects in the woods before everything is deconstructed, filled in, and packed away. The boy helps me into the driver's seat of my wagon, a leather-upholstered bench built on springs, and shoves the reins into my hands. He's much too busy to answer any of my questions, which is just as well because, truthfully, there's nothing to know. When the caravan moves, Romulus seems to know what to do. Like a great, winding serpent, we set off to the east, before the moon has reached its apex.

We've been traveling about an hour when a column of shadow funnels into the seat next to me, and Damien's smoke and spice scent perfumes the air. He forms, still in his disguise. "Good morning, Marquis. What brings my cousin to my wagon?" I ask through a smile. Maintaining our ruse, even now when the caravan is in motion, seems a wise idea in a group that remembered which rabble beast was mine among a herd of hundreds of animals.

"Are you well, *cousin*?" The corners of his eyes wrinkle in a way that is pure Damien and weird to see on a pale, blond-headed face. "Feeling fatigued? Any reason we should abandon this route?"

It doesn't take our bond for me to understand what he's actually asking. He's checking to make sure I can hold the disguises we're wearing.

"I'm fine," I whisper. "All of this is hardly a burden. I could do it for days."

"I doubt that will be necessary, but for now, Valerian and I agree we should continue our mission, earn their trust, and propose an alliance."

I nod. "Have you noticed we're heading toward Aendor? If nothing else, we've found a safer way to make the journey."

"Safer?" His eyes shift right then left. "I don't think so. I think these people would sell us to the highest bidder if they thought we were worth anything. Trust no one. The only thing keeping us safe right now is our coin purse, and you'd best believe I slept with it under my pillow last night."

I frown. "Everyone here has been kind to me. They've given us no reason not to trust them."

He scoffs. "Yet."

"I think you should keep an open mind."

"Maybe," he says more softly. In silence, we ride together until the caravan begins to slow.

"I think they're stopping."

"Probably a scheduled break. I'll see you in Maggie's tent tonight." We say our goodbyes, and he shadows out from beside me.

It turns out that it is a scheduled break. The caravan stops every three hours. Young Rivertoads help the elderly with their needs, and someone comes by to check Romulus for signs of distress, including the place where the yoke rubs his shoulders and his feet. They offer the rabble beasts water and bring me a sandwich made from red wheat and a type of blood sausage. It's simple but delicious.

The moon is low in the sky when we halt beside a river, and this time, the boy comes back and removes

Romulus's harness. "Are we stopping for the night?" I ask him.

He nods. "You'll find everyone down by the river until the tent is set up."

"Should I help?"

The boy chuckles. "Maggie has a team and is very... exacting. She'd only shoo you out of the way."

"Understood." I give a soft laugh, easily picturing Maggie shouting orders at a small crew. I follow the crowd down to the river and join the people gathered there. Everyone is talking and laughing. Most have removed their shoes and are walking along the shore barefoot.

"Well, Velis, what did you think of your first day on the road?" Jaqual appears beside me, his smile as bright as the moon.

I answer truthfully. "Peaceful," I say. "I understand why you love it."

"Ooh? Pray tell, why do you think I love it?" He brushes a string of beads that dangles from his headband behind his shoulders.

Jaqual is the first and only person who has had any real conversation with me here. If I want him to open up to me and trust me with information about the River-toads, I need to authentically answer his question. So I think about what I experienced today and try to answer specifically. "The colors," I say. "All the brightly colored wagons carving their way through the green and the red of the countryside are like the first brush of paint on a canvas. I bet you love that, and I bet you love the community, how everyone helps one another and knows their role during the breaks. And I bet you enjoy how the scenery is never the same from hour to hour. A person could never be bored living among you."

When he doesn't say anything, I look over at him, and his amethyst eyes are sparkling. "I believe you may secretly have the soul of a Rivertoad."

I laugh. "Why are you called that anyway? Rivertoad?"

"It doesn't seem to fit, does it? Once you know what we're really like."

"My thoughts exactly."

"In our culture, toads represent adaptability because they are born in the water and then grow to thrive on the land, and the river is a symbol of the infinite flow of time. My people have been traveling these roads for thousands of years, longer than Stygarde has ruled and since before the dark elves of Willowgulch crawled out of the rocks they once lived under and organized a government. We are a creation of the goddess and are natives of Tenebris, as close to the land as any. We are Rivertoads, and although you might hear the name used in a derogatory way, it is who we are."

"Fascinating." I wasn't expecting to learn that Rivertoads were the indigenous people of Tenebris, or that they considered themselves the preservers of an ancient culture. The way Damien talked about them, they were thieves and hired guns. It's hard to reconcile the two views of their culture.

He pauses. "You mentioned the colors of the wagons reminding you of paint on canvas. Has anyone introduced you to the artist's conclave?"

I shake my head.

"I'll show you." A few minutes' walk downriver and Jaqual slides a paintbrush into my hand and positions me in front of a used canvas painted white. I'm in a circle of easels, a group of five Rivertoads painting riverside, three of them old and one young.

"Enjoy, Velis. Maggie's should be open in an hour." Jaqual waves his goodbye and disappears toward the wagons as I fight back tears at the joy of painting again. I dip the tip of my brush into the paint and get started.

"IT'S LOVELY," TERILLA SAYS, HER GRAY BRAIDS THE ONLY sign of her advanced age. Since she's a shade, I suppose she doesn't have to show her age at all, but she seems proud of her advanced years and grins at my painting of a wagon.

"Do you think? I'm out of practice." I painted my wagon blue to represent the river and filled the windows with stars to show how an entire universe could fit inside, a universe of culture anyway.

Terilla nods and tugs on my arm. "It's perfect, my dear. But you should come now. You don't want to miss dinner." I look up for the first time in I don't know how long and realize that we are the only ones left beside the river. "Oh no! My…cousin is going to be livid."

She pats my shoulder. "Go. It's my turn to clean up."

I thank her profusely and rush toward the scent of grilling meat and the warm sound of music. Inside the tent, Damien and Warbill are seated at the same table as before. Profound relief passes through Damien's expression when he sees me. I make my way around a crowded dance floor to reach them.

The Rivertoads may have a reputation for being hired

killers, but they also know how to party. In one corner of the tent, a band wails a lively tune with instruments that resemble a fiddle, a harmonica, and a bass, but are just different enough that I'm reminded this isn't Earth. Still, there's a classic rock vibe with a folksy slant. The singer could be a shade version of Stevie Nicks, although her voice is less throaty and more resonant.

I slide in next to Damien. "Thank the goddess. I wondered if we'd lost you along the road."

Warbill laughs. "I told him not to worry. I figured you'd made friends with the kitchen staff and been roped into helping bake bread or something of the sort."

"Actually, I was painting."

"Painting?" Damien looks perplexed.

"They have an artist's enclave that meets by the river while the tent is going up." I hold up my hand to show Damien the paint on my fingers. "Speaking of, I didn't see you tonight with the others. Where were you two?"

"We used the opportunity to investigate the caravan while everyone was distracted," Warbill whispers, his eyes shifting to Damien.

"Did you find anything?" I ask.

Damien scowls. "No. And still no contact to negotiate hiring their men."

Maggie zooms in and slides a bowl of stew in front of me. "Like it or not, it's what's on the menu," she says to me.

"Looks hot and brown. Good enough for me."

She laughs and takes off toward the kitchen, while Damien and Warbill look down at their own bowls, noticing that I have twice as much and mine looks a hell of a lot tastier. All our bowls were the same last night.

"Looks like my *sister* has charmed the Rivertoads," Warbill says, raising an eyebrow.

I take a bite, and it's positively delicious. "You know, Grams used to say you could catch more flies with honey than with vinegar. You two could be more personable. Make some friends."

"Why did she want to catch flies?" Warbill asks.

"I, uh… It's an expression. Like if you're trying to clear them from the room."

Both Warbill and Damien squint at me.

"Never mind. It was a bad analogy. These people aren't flies. Just be nice and make friends. It's not that hard."

Couples take to the dance floor, twirling by me in a way that reminds me of a combination of the waltz and swing dancing. I'm enchanted and tap my foot to the beat the entire time I'm eating.

"This is the most fun I've seen a group of people have in your world since we arrived in Tenebris," I say. "And that includes the Harvest Festival."

The illusion I've placed over Damien's face does not hide his bitterness. "In my people's defense, there hasn't been a lot to celebrate."

The Rivertoads must feel the weight of what's happening as well, but they find a way to come together despite all of it. It's beautiful to me. "Do you know this dance?"

"I vaguely remember it."

"Want to swing your cousin around the room, Marquis?" I say playfully.

He glances toward Warbill. "Only if your brother stays put in case our promised contact arrives."

Warbill leans harder on his elbows, his ale between his palms. "I'm not going anywhere."

Damien stands and holds out his hand to me. "Come. I'll teach you."

We join the others on the makeshift dance floor, Damien tossing me around as if I weigh nothing, swinging me between his legs and launching me into the air as he turns to the count along with the other dancers. Before long, we're laughing, and I feel lighter than I have in ages. When the song is over, I'm tempted to kiss him, then remember that we're supposed to be cousins and opt to put more room between us.

I almost jump when a hand lands on the center of my back. I turn to find Jaqual, dressed in a suit of purple velvet and a white linen shirt. He's covered in beads and the same necklace I saw wink at me before, the one with a large eye in the center of the flat stone.

"Do you mind if I cut in?" he asks Damien.

My mate has no choice but to bow and politely leave the floor. He's supposed to be my cousin after all, not some jealous husband. To make matters worse, the music changes, and I find myself slow dancing with my new friend.

"Did you enjoy painting tonight?" he asks me.

"So much. Thank you. I haven't painted since I lost my home. I was dreaming about it last night."

His eyes narrow and his smile fades. "That's right. New Stygarde left you homeless."

"Yes," I say sadly. It's not a lie, just not the truth he thinks it is.

"That dark elf cunt who sits on the throne is nothing but an extension of Entrydal's rule," he seethes, and it's the first time I've seen Jaqual without a smile on his face. "The elves have infiltrated almost every district with their tyranny. They steal children and turn any who resist to ash. And now, they're trying to limit my people's freedom, as if anyone in the history of time has successfully chained the neck of a Rivertoad."

"I agree, but what can we do to stop them?" I ask softly.

We sway to the music, and for a moment, his lips twitch and I think he'll make a joke, but he doesn't. "We've heard rumors along our travels of a prophecy," he whispers. "The one who tames the dragon will rule this world." He studies me, his gaze lingering long enough to make me uncomfortable.

When I sense the song winding to a close, I say, "Don't you think we might wait forever for such a savior? Maybe... Maybe we should be doing more to resist."

The corners of his eyes wrinkle. "It seems like you've put some thought into this."

I glance at Damien, who is watching me like a bird of prey from his perch at our table. "The truth is that my friends and I were hoping to hire some men to help us avenge Covellton. Do you know who we can talk to about that?"

He slants a knowing smile at me, a cunning smile, like I've somehow stepped into his trap. But how could I have? I've told him nothing. "You want to hire mercenaries to... avenge your burned village? You think you can take New Stygarde with mercenaries and a few townsfolk?"

The eye hanging around his neck blinks. What did he say about it being a trick of the light? "We have an idea—a way to help not just our village rebuild but all of Tenebris.

Would you like to have a drink together?" I tip my head in the direction of our table. "If you could connect us with your leader, someone who can discuss a coordinated effort—"

He cuts me off with a laugh and grabs my upper arm. The music stops. Everyone turns to stare at us. "You want to talk to the Rivertoad king about a coordinated response against New Stygarde? That's a lofty ambition for a simple peasant girl who's just lost her home."

"Release my cousin immediately," Damien says. When did he move across the room? Although my disguise still holds, and he looks like Marquis, his threat outweighs his size. The tip of Dawnbreaker is way too close to Jaqual's throat not to be perceived as a risk, and Damien manages the weight of the weapon in one hand, something a starving shade as slender as Marquis could never do.

Jaqual's gaze slowly drops from me to the weapon, and he releases my arm, holding up a hand between us. That cunning, lopsided smile is back. "Easy. You don't want to make trouble. Rivertoads don't take kindly to threats from outsiders," Jaqual says softly. "Especially not against their king."

"Their king?" I repeat, but I know instantly that he's referring to himself.

"And I'm willing to bet you are no helpless peasant girl." He glares at me, that eye winking again. Everyone is still staring. Everyone. Many of the men have drawn weapons that reflect the candlelight ominously.

I place my hand on Damien's blade and push it aside. "Put this away. He isn't going to hurt me."

Damien reluctantly slides Dawnbreaker back into his scabbard but never takes his eyes off Jaqual.

"Please forgive my cousin," I say. "We've been through so much trauma at the hands of New Stygarde, it's hard to tell friend from foe. I'd like to think you're a friend, Jaqual. Am I wrong?"

Jaqual's gaze slides from holding Damien's stare back to me. I raise my eyebrows, my hands clasped in front of my hips, my entire demeanor soft, warm, feminine. All the while the bond between Phantom and me tightens like a guitar string ready for me to pluck. I could have us out of here in thirty seconds if need be.

"Of course we're friends," he says through a smile. With a wave of his hand, he gestures for the others to back down. There's a clatter as the dancers put away their weapons. Slowly, the music starts again. Jaqual turns to Damien. "Your cousin suggested you're in the market to hire protection."

"More or less," Damien says.

Jaqual leans back on his heels, sliding his hands into the pockets of his breeches. "Stay another night in the wagons we've assigned you. I will send someone to you to discuss our fees." He offers me a bow, so much more formal than he was before with me, and his talisman winks in the candlelight. He strides from the tent, the other Rivertoads acknowledging him with a bow or wave as he passes.

"Way to endear yourself to the community, Damien," I whisper for his ears only as we stride back to the table. "We're supposed to be creating new allies, not forging new enemies. We have enough of those, in case you're keeping count. Holding a sword to the king's neck seems like a poor way to do that."

"He grabbed you."

"I was handling it."

"Did you know he was king?"

"Of course not."

"I did not like the way he was looking at you."

"Grow up. This isn't the eighth-grade cafeteria." I send Damien a sharp glare and slide onto the bench beside Warbill.

"You two sure know how to make friends," Warbill says and takes a long sip of ale.

14

MAXIMUS

DAMIEN

"I think we should stay together tonight. Come to our wagon. There's plenty of space," I say to Eloise. I don't trust this King Jaqual. Keeping us separate seems like a ploy to weaken us.

But Eloise shakes her head, and I know by her tone and the look she casts that it won't be happening. "No. It isn't done here."

I cast her an incredulous look.

"You want their help, right? Then we need to live by their rules when we're under their roofs. They've provided us food and shelter at a reasonable price. And I don't think Jaqual buys that we're peasants from Covellton anyway. He told me as much. So, the fact that he hasn't kicked us out of the caravan is all the hope we need that he's willing to talk." We reach her pretty violet wagon, and she pulls out the gold butterfly-winged key.

"Just plead our case. Try to keep an open mind. I'll see you in the morning."

She kisses me on the cheek, a quick peck that maintains enough distance to be appropriate for cousins, and then disappears inside.

"I hate this," I say to Warbill, dark waves of foreboding rippling through me.

"Don't waste all your hate on this," he says. "Something worse is bound to happen soon. Especially considering you threatened the Rivertoad king with your sword at his throat." He holds up our key. "Let's go settle in and await the fresh horrors that will inevitably be sent our way."

"You're a real barrel of laughs, Warbill."

"As are you, Sir Grump."

"I may have made a mistake agreeing to bring you with us," I grumble.

"Ah, good decisions rarely make for good stories."

I make a lewd gesture in his direction and step into the wagon, pacing the small space as Warbill throws himself across his bed. It's so late, I can see the silver edge of the moon threatening to rise for the day. We don't have to wait long. A knock on the door comes after only my third lap. I look over my shoulder at Warbill and then move for the door.

A familiar man in a patchwork tunic and breeches stands outside, a brown cape draped over one shoulder and a scabbard on his hip. His face is impassive as he says, "You are interested in hiring a sword?"

"Yes. Please come in." I open the door wider, and he enters. I know this man. He was once an umbrae under my command, but I can't say anything without revealing my true identity, so I keep my mouth shut and pretend I don't recognize him. I back up toward my bed but don't sit, opting to fold my arms over my chest instead.

The man positions himself at the center of the wagon with his back against the cabinets so he can see us both. "How many men do you need, and what are you willing to pay?"

"How many men do you have?"

"More than a peasant from the northwest Borderlands can afford."

"You have no idea what I can afford."

"Tell me more. How have you come by such a considerable sum as to think you can hire one mercenary, let alone many?"

I glance at Warbill, and he's smart enough to know what I want him to do.

"What is your name?" Warbill asks.

"You can call me Maximus. I am the chosen leader of the band of mercenaries you wish to hire."

"Commander of the Guard?" I ask.

"The Rivertoads have no guard. We are individuals who live by the sword, not nameless soldiers fighting for a power-swollen king."

"Yet you do have a king," Warbill adds, his brow furrowing.

Maximus chuckles. "I used to think like you." He shakes his head. "The one we call king is not like the one that sits on New Stygarde's throne. Things don't work like that here."

I wait for him to elaborate, but he doesn't.

"Maximus, my cousin Valerian and I have joined a growing insurgency with the goal of taking back New

Stygarde from Brahm and his dark elf queen. You must have heard about the men training in secret in Aendor?"

"One hears many things on the road."

"It's a sizable rebellion, but we need more men, and I'm authorized to offer a considerable sum."

"You don't want to hire mercenaries—you want to hire an army."

Warbill nods. "So I ask again, how many men do you have available for hire?"

The man scowls at a spot on the floor. "And if I told you a number, and you were able to pay the price, you would expect us to follow a simple villager from Covellton into battle?"

Warbill clears his throat, and I force my expression to remain unreadable as he adds, "Prince Damien is back. He's alive and working with the rebels."

Max snorts. "Rumor. Innuendo. I once fought under Prince Damien and saw him fall on the battlefield. But even if he were back, you'd be hard-pressed to get my men to fight for another son of Malek. Who's to say he'd be any better than his brother? We might be swapping one tyrant for another."

"Damien isn't a tyrant," I say, forgetting myself in my passion for the topic. "He wants a kingdom where everyone has a voice and the Rivertoads can remain free."

"You seem surprisingly knowledgeable of the ways Prince Damien intends to rule." He taps the hilt of his sword. "I can take your offer back to my men, but unlike the silver coats, each person has a choice to fight or not fight. We each set our own price, even if we work collectively. I can't tell you how many will entertain your offer, but I promise you, it won't be many. Rivertoads don't fight other people's wars."

"Don't you see what Brahm is doing? Don't you want a better Tenebris?" Warbill asks, growing defensive.

"It's only a matter of time before Brahm's hard-line tactics come to your wagon," I say. "And when it happens, it will be too late to stop him. He'll be too powerful."

Maximus stands up straighter. "My men and I will look out for our own interests. I won't stop any individual from bargaining with you, but I will not help you coordinate a large-scale enlistment. Good luck to you." He turns to leave.

"Wait! What about your king? Will Jaqual speak with us about this?"

Maximus looks at the ceiling and then at me. "I thought you wanted men, not political relations."

"Both," I say.

He snorts. "Fine. I'll let him know you'd like to talk. Good luck to you." He pushes through the door and disappears into the night.

"Well, that went over like a wingless bird," Warbill says. "Sounds like we'll be lucky to have any men join our cause. And what was that all about a different type of king and each man having his own choices? I swear the Rivertoads are from another planet rather than another community."

I grunt. "This conversation isn't over. There is hope yet."

15

THE BIG REVEAL

ELOISE

I've just made myself a cup of tea on the small potbellied stove that warms my wagon when my gut tightens and Damien's scent, like leather and rain, invades my nose. I get the sense that he's upset, that maybe his meeting hasn't gone as he wished. I take my mug and move for the door, planning to check on him and Warbill. But when I open it, Jaqual is there.

"Oh, hello," I say. "What brings the Rivertoad king to my humble wagon?"

He flashes a lopsided grin. "Maybe I just needed a friend. Although I wonder about our status as such, given that your cousin almost slit my throat."

"He didn't mean it. We've been brutally mistreated, as you know. He thought you were hurting me."

"I wasn't kidding about needing to talk. Were you heading somewhere?"

"Just going to ask my brother if he'd like some tea for

the morning. I had all of it in my saddlebag. But it can wait. Would you like to come in?"

Silver light rises behind the trees, casting shadows, hollowing his cheekbones and making his teeth gleam as he shakes his head. "It isn't done. You have a maiden's wagon. But I will take a cup of tea if you're offering. Out here, please. We can watch the moonrise."

"The moon is rising, and I haven't even slept." I sigh. "I'll get the tea." I retreat inside the wagon, wondering why even the king won't enter it, and pour him a cup. Then I return to his side, handing him the steaming hot mug. He turns his face toward the first silver light until his eyes gleam and the stone around his neck winks. And that's when I feel it, *magic* coming off him in ripples that dance across my skin. Jaqual has real power, a power I don't fully understand. Power that feels different from the witches of Dimhollow's or the dark elves's. This is something I haven't encountered before.

"What are you?" I ask in a whisper. I can't help myself. The cool morning air on my cheeks makes me feel alert, vibrant, reflective. Jaqual is a mystery I need to solve.

"The king of the Rivertoads," he answers evasively. "I thought we settled that earlier tonight."

"Something more, though. That amulet around your neck winks occasionally. I don't think it's a trick of the light, as you've said. I think it's enchanted. What is its purpose?"

He narrows his eyes on me, like he's trying to see into my soul. "It helps me see through lies," he admits forcefully. "Now, I have revealed who I am, *Velis*. Will you reveal your true identity—or make me use my abilities on you?"

Oh. He knows about my illusion. But how much? Only that I am not who I say I am? Or can he see right through my spell? I swallow hard, not knowing where to begin. "I'd prefer if my brother and cousin were here. This conversation won't be an easy one."

He snorts. "The two men traveling with you are no more your brother and cousin than they are from Covellton."

"Why are you here, Jaqual, when you promised to speak with them tonight about the price of your mercenaries?"

"I sent them a mercenary to inform them about our mercenaries. They don't need me for that conversation. Why did you think I'd want to discuss anything with them? I don't know them. I don't know you, to be sure, but at least you've attempted a relationship."

"I'm sorry about that. I—"

"Stop apologizing for your compatriots and tell me who you are and what you want from us."

I look down at myself and then at his amulet, which winks again. "You can see through my illusion, can't you?"

His violet eyes twinkle. "Beautiful red hair. I'd love to see it without the haze of your magic getting in the way."

I see no benefit in prolonging the game and draw back my magical representation of Velis, although I keep Damien's and Warbill's up. I lift my chin and straighten my spine. "I am Eloise Hymir, rightful queen of Stygarde. It is my great pleasure to make your acquaintance, King Jaqual." I offer him a slight curtsy.

A smile spreads slowly across his lips. "Holy goddess in the Darklands. Hymir? You have already wed the resurrected prince?"

"We are wed and mated. Damien is alive and well, the rightful heir to the throne."

"All this time, New Stygarde has been needling me for any information about your whereabouts, and you've been here, right under my nose."

"We need your help to take back this kingdom. Join us, Jaqual. Ally with us and help us end this nightmare that's befallen Tenebris."

Silence fills the space between us, our warm mugs clasped between our hands, as if we were just friends talking over morning drinks rather than leaders discussing the ways of our world. He sips from his mug and then stares at me, waiting.

"Well?" I ask.

"I'm waiting for the punch line."

"The punch line?"

"I'm sorry, I assumed you were joking. You want the Rivertoads to ally to help you put Damien Hymir back on the throne? Goddess, the rumors said Damien's mate was from another world, but I assumed your husband would have brought you up to speed on the history between the Hymirs and the Rivertoads, Eloise. Allow me to edify you. There is no way in the Darklands that we will be helping you put another Hymir on the throne."

I shake my head, my hackles rising. "Damien isn't part of that history. He isn't his father, and he definitely isn't his brother."

His violet eyes flare, and shadows bleed off the edges of his form. "I don't care if he's the secret baby of the witch queen of Dimhollow, I will never purposely put another Hymir on the throne."

I sip my tea to slow my thoughts because I'm very

close to losing my shit. "You know that Brahm and Nevina are a sock-puppet government for the dark elf king, one that threatens your people's freedom, threatens the future of every shade in Tenebris, and yet you would allow their tyranny to continue rather than help Damien take back what is his? You cut off your nose to spite your face, Jaqual."

"Damien is not the only option. You're blinded by your relationship with him. If you were neutral, you'd see that a leader elected by the people would be a far better replacement than another Hymir king."

"You want the next ruler of Stygarde to be voted on to the throne?" Coming from Earth, I'm not opposed to this idea, although it feels like a betrayal of Damien to admit it.

He stares between the trees at the rising moon. "You asked about my amulet. I suspect you can sense its magic. Most shades can. I will tell you something that few know about me, Eloise. When I was abandoned as a baby, I was left in a basket of the sort constructed by the witches of Dimhollow, and I had this eye around my infant neck."

A tingle travels the length of my spine. "Are you part witch, Jaqual?"

"Your guess is as good as mine. I suspect half. My magic isn't particularly strong. But I do have one remarkable gift that is unique among my kind."

"The ability to see through illusion?"

He scoffs. "The ability to *see*. The truth. The future. I have dreams, Eloise. Ones that come true."

My palms are starting to sweat, and I set my mug down before it slips out of my hands. "What have you seen about the future of Tenebris?"

He licks his lips. "I saw myself, standing on the veranda of Stygarde Castle with a dragon by my side. As I told you, we hear many things along our travels. I heard tell of a prophecy out of Dimhollow, one that confirms my vision. They say the one who tames the dragon will rule this world."

"And you think that's going to be you?" I ask incredulously.

He nods. "Centuries ago, before the prophecy was ever dreamed or shared, a war was fought over a dragon, and both sides thought if they were the one to capture her, they would rule Tenebris. Neither did, and the dragon died. Do you know what I've come to understand since then?"

"What?"

"The dragon is a metaphor. If you observed our caravan from the sky, our chain of wagons would appear as a dragon winding its way across the land." He points to himself. "We are the dragon, Eloise. The Rivertoads. My people. And the one who brings us all together, the one who unites us, will be the one who tames the dragon. I have united the Rivertoads. I am their elected king. That is why I will never help you or Damien Hymir back to the throne. The only solution is to destroy it. The people—the dragon itself—should rule."

I find myself staring at Jaqual as he speaks, unable to blink, mesmerized by what he's saying. And when he's finished, I try to process it all. He's a prophet, just like Aurora was, with the gift of sight. Both channeled similar visions concerning the future of Tenebris, visions that could be construed differently based on one's perspective. Catarina had assumed her mother's vision was about

Brahm and Nevina. She was wrong. So is Jaqual. He has no idea that he will never tame the dragon because she's standing right in front of him. Not a metaphor, not a caravan, but a woman. I am the dragon. And I have already bound myself to Damien.

Still, I come from a world and a place where democracy is the rule of law. I agree with his ideals. But ideals won't solve this problem. Ideals won't protect the children who are even now being drugged and worked to death as slaves for the pleasure of the crown. I need to show Jaqual the truth. It's the only way to win him to our side.

"There's something I have to show you," I say. "Something you need to know." I back up a few steps. Ariadne made me this outfit. Pants and a corset that shows my tattoo, all covered in a dazzling jacket that makes the entire thing look like a dress when it's fastened. I unfasten the clasp.

"What are you doing?" he asks, shaking his head. "You cannot seduce me into helping him, Eloise. I am not so desperate or so lacking in morals."

I turn my back to him, and at the same time, I summon Phantom. Sweeping my red curls over one shoulder, I nudge the jacket off and down to my waist, revealing my tattoo. I look at him over one shoulder as Phantom forms in all their white-scaled glory in front of me and spreads her wings.

Jaqual drops his mug. It shatters on the ground, the tea soaking into the earth. It looks as if he's stopped breathing. His eyes widen as Phantom lowers their head and sniffs him, their teeth as long as he is tall and each as sharp as the weapon at his hip.

"I am the dragon, Jaqual," I say. "It's not the caravan.

Your vision showed you the future, but not one where you rule. It's one where you help us. You're in the castle because you are our friend."

"No," he mumbles, shaking his head. All the color has drained from his cheeks.

"You may be right that someday the best outcome for Stygarde...for Tenebris...is to be ruled by the people. But the only way we'll successfully reach that end in the future is by taking the power back from Brahm and Nevina now. And the only way we'll be successful at doing that is if we work together."

His mouth hangs open, his eyes fixated, not on my bare back but on the dragon who watches him over my shoulder. I slide my jacket back into place and fasten the belt.

"This changes everything," he murmurs.

I offer him a shallow smile, confident that he'll help us now that he understands. We can move forward. "Then, you'll fight with us?"

"Let's go talk to your prince," he says with a swing of his chin that tells me he's in. "I assume the one who brought his sword to my throat and threatened to run me through is actually Damien Hymir."

Phantom fades away, and I turn on my heel to stride toward Damien's wagon, not bothering to disguise myself again. There's a spring in my step. If we have the allegiance of the Rivertoads, we can win this war. We reach the wagon where Damien and Warbill are staying just as a tall man in a strange uniform exits. I see Damien behind him and drop his and Warbill's disguises as we approach.

"Eloise—"

"Jaqual knows who we are," I explain. "And he's here to discuss his alliance."

Damien swings the door wide, but Jaqual stops me before I can enter the wagon. "Out here, please."

Damn, when Maggie told us that men and women who are unmarried can't stay in the same wagon, I had no idea they were sticklers for that rule in all cases. But it's a small enough ask, considering the stakes. Damien and Warbill join us in the treelined clearing outside their door.

"Damien Hymir, let me introduce myself formally. I am the Rivertoad king, and I have authority over four thousand trained mercenaries. I think it's time we talk about taking back Stygarde."

Damien's eyes narrow. "Then you'll join the rebellion?"

"On one condition." A cunning smile cracks Jaqual's face, giving him the appearance of a fox rather than a dog. My stomach clenches as my intuition kicks in. "I'll lend you every man under my command to fight New Stygarde at your side, but I require one thing in exchange."

"What's that?" Damien asks in a low growl.

"Your wife."

16
RAGE

DAMIEN

My hand balls into a fist, my molecules pulling apart into shadow. Warbill places a steadying hand on my shoulder. "I'm sure we misheard you, Jaqual. Surely you know better than to threaten a shade's mate."

I glare at Jaqual as Eloise comes to me and stands by my side. Her lip curls in the way it often does when she doesn't know what to make of something or someone. She lifts her chin, her glare sliding down her nose at the Rivertoad king.

"You did not mishear me, and there is no mistake," Jaqual says. "The one who tames the dragon rules this world. She is the dragon, and if you want my men, you will give her to me. Not as my wife but as my prisoner." My growl echoes around us, and he adds, "And I will return her to you the moment we win the war and the people elect a leader. Once the Rivertoads are free, she will be free. It's a simple bargain, Hymir."

I glare at Jaqual but then I shift my attention to Eloise, and the look I see on her face makes me lean back on my heels. There was a time in the beginning when my jealousy and possessiveness might have led me by the nose. Not today. Not anymore. I am no longer the newly mated shade I once was, and I see the scene of us standing in the clearing in front of our wagon as if from a distance. Then I laugh until everyone is staring at me like I've lost my mind, even her.

"What exactly do you find so funny?" Jaqual asks.

"*You* asking *me* to hand over my mate. Your first mistake, Jaqual, is thinking that Eloise is mine to give. She may be my mate, but I don't control her, and I do not own her to lend or give away in exchange for your men." Eloise gives me a grateful and self-assured look, and I know that I'm onto something. "Now, you could ask her to stay with you in exchange for your men, and she might consider it because my wife, my mate, my queen, has a deep love for this kingdom and a penchant for self-sacrifice, but you could never hold her. Make no mistake, she is the most powerful being among us."

Jaqual's eyes fall on Eloise. "Well? Then I pose my offer to you, Eloise. Will you stay with me in exchange for an army capable of flipping this kingdom? Will you be my leverage to ensure your mate doesn't go the same way as his brother?"

Eloise glares at the man, her green eyes hard and cold. She's bound to me. I trust her. But the longer she doesn't speak, the more I worry she might actually be considering Jaqual's proposal for the state of the kingdom. I can't fathom such a thing. To be without her, even for a day, would be torture. To know she was here, with this man, even if we were planning the same war and her absence was only political—I couldn't stand it.

I trust her.

I don't trust fate.

"No," she says decisively. I hide the tremble in the breath of relief I release. "Damien is right. I am my own person, and I make my own rules. I will not offer myself to be traded or possessed. You're a smart man, Jaqual. You saw what I am, and you know the prophecy. You also know what will happen to your people if you do nothing. The writing is on the wall. A decade from now, your children will work in a dark elf mine, and you'll ask yourself what you could have done to stop it. And you'll remember this conversation. You'll remember how you knew New Stygarde was stealing children, drugging them, and making them slaves all over Tenebris, and you thought you could outrun that fate. And you'll know you were wrong."

He scowls. "Rivertoads have always taken care of their own."

Eloise shakes her head. "You think that your tradition of traveling can save you from being ruled by them. But they don't care about your traditions. And they don't care about your freedom. New Stygarde has a pattern of oppression. First, they'll restrict your mobility, then they'll restrict you economically. Then, once you've watched families who've counted on you starve to death despite your best efforts, they'll attack, burn your wagons, and execute your leaders on trumped-up charges, and there will be no one left to help you."

Jaqual's amulet winks.

"Am I lying, Jaqual?" she asks.

He growls. "The Rivertoads will never fall. Our caravan was born with this world and will only die when the world dies with it."

Eloise glances at me and snorts. "Shall we tell him, Damien, how long the journey between life and death can be?"

With a smug curl of my lip, I say, "You wouldn't believe how long. Made longer by every life for whom you are responsible."

The amulet winks and Jaqual winces. "Then I'm afraid we're at an impasse. You are free to rest in the wagons until we pull up stakes. You have about four hours."

"Thank you, but no," I say. "We'll be going now."

Eloise nods. "I'll get my things."

Warbill grimaces. I can't imagine he relishes facing a day's ride with no sleep. But he obeys like the true umbrae he is. "I'll fetch the rabble beasts."

Once they both leave us, Jaqual turns to me. "Your father never once reached out to my people, Hymir. That toxic blood of yours is why this world is in danger to begin with. Imagine believing you could cure a poisoned land by pouring on more poison."

I shove past him toward the door to the wagon. "Imagine believing the poison won't kill you while you watch everyone else who drinks it die." He sneers at me in response. "My blood isn't poison, Jaqual. Maybe it was once, but that was a lifetime ago. My father never reached out to the Rivertoads because you were too busy keeping his son drunk on cheap wine to come to the negotiation table, and too obsessed with traveling to speak to him about the peace you took for granted."

"A narrow view of the circumstances—"

I hold up a hand. "Dwelling on the past won't fix this world or the future. We know what caused the problem. Reach out if you want to be part of the solution."

He closes the space between us and faces me, eye to eye. "Don't hold your breath."

"Your prerogative."

"Just tell me one thing," Jaqual says through his teeth. "How did you ever win the dragon to your side?"

I scoff. "It's a simple act, but one so beyond your abilities, I have no fear of sharing it with you. I love her. I won her because I love her."

I don't wait for him to say anything more. This time, I blend into shadow and leave him to his own.

17

HARD KNOCKS

ELOISE

"No matter how many times you tell me that shades don't have to sleep every night, it won't help me stay on this beast. I can barely keep my eyes open." We've been riding for hours. Damien seems obsessed with putting the caravan as far behind us as possible. I've watched Warbill's head bob several times on the back of Borus, and I'm convinced he's sleeping while sitting up at this point. "Had I known you would deprive me of sleep, I might have stayed with Jaqual."

Damien forms from the shadows beside me and scowls. It was a low blow, but a girl's got to do what a girl's got to do. "Fine. If I remember correctly, there's a safe house about a mile from here…if it's still there. Warbill. Warbill!"

Warbill startles awake. He was asleep, the lucky bastard. "Yeah?"

"Does the safe house at Barrel Pines still exist?"

He nods, slowly looking around. "I think so, although it's been years, you understand. Not too far from here."

Damien snorts. "Lead the way."

We've been following two ruts in the underbrush that could be called a road if one were feeling generous, but Warbill takes a hard left into a trackless wood. Romulus snorts at the seemingly impenetrable thicket, the branches of the trees too low and tangled to move through, but Warbill and Damien use the shadows to bend branches to allow us passage. The rabble beasts' paws tangle in the dense foliage, requiring we pause to free them. Above us, old growth chokes off the moonlight. Our progress is slow. Tedious. The air is suffocatingly close.

When the forest finally opens again, I inhale deeply in relief, thankful for the room, the air, the light. A shack comes into view, surrounded by a deep layer of dead, undisturbed leaves. It's clear this safe house hasn't welcomed any recent visitors.

Damien opens the front door, and a blast of stale air invades my nostrils even before I dismount. Romulus sneezes and shakes his head. "It's safe," he says.

I'm so tired, it could be a rat-infested cave, and I'd happily sleep on the stone floor. I dismount and remove Romulus's tack, setting him free to hunt in the surrounding woods, and then I enter the tiny cottage. I'm relieved to find there are two beds with bedding folded and stacked at the end of each, although everything is covered in a thick layer of dust. A fireplace and a stack of old wood await us on one wall with a cauldron on an arm that can swing over the fire. Out the back window, I see the outline of a small outhouse beside a hand pump for water.

Warbill sidles up to me and rests his hands on his hips, scowling at the accommodations, as Damien begins stacking wood for a fire. "I think the back of Borus might have been the better option."

"Ye of little faith," I mutter, drawing on my bond with Phantom. I mumble the spell they feed me and snap my fingers. A breeze starts near our feet, sparking with magic as it slithers around our ankles, kicks up dust, and spirals, corralling the dirt in a cyclone of power. The mattresses and pillows give up years' worth of grit that joins the cloud of filth. Both mattresses fold in half, cover themselves in sheets and blankets, and return to their frames, dressed in perfect corners with blankets layered cozily on top.

The tornado of magic sweeps all the dirt and grime and insect husks up the chimney, blowing out whatever obstructions have built up there over time. A storm of leaves and sticks, along with flapping, bat-like things, falls toward the backyard beyond the window.

Finally, with a flick of my fingers, the logs Damien has stacked ignite.

Damien steps back from the growing blaze and slants a smug grin in Warbill's direction. "In case you were wondering why I almost ran Jaqual through for daring to touch my woman." He takes me into his arms and spins me around.

"She is easy to have around, I will admit," Warbill says, drifting to his side of the room.

Moments later, I'm under the covers, tucked into Damien's side. It takes me precious little time to fall asleep.

THE GRANDFATHER CLOCK IN THE CORNER OF THE PARLOR of Harcourt Manor chimes one time as I bring the cup of tea to my lips. I breathe deeply of Grams's rosewater perfume mixed with the scent of the fire and the soft feel of the green velvet sofa beneath me. And then a pale face fringed in black bangs leans into my field of vision, her eyes blinking from behind black-rimmed glasses. "Fuck yeah!" Maeve says. "I thought I'd never catch you sleeping."

I set down the cup in my hand and pull my best friend into a hug as a laugh bubbles up my throat. "Oh, I missed you so much!"

"Then why haven't you come to see us? Do you have any idea how bad your parents' Hitch and Cast spell tastes? I've been drinking that shit night after night, trying to reach you. I finally tried it during the day, and here you are. Are our timelines out of sync?"

"No, I'm sleeping during the day today. And honestly, things have been so busy, I haven't been sleeping much at all." I give her a rundown of what's happened in the month since I saw her last and watch her face grow more and more concerned.

"If you're heavily outnumbered and things aren't safe for you on Tenebris anymore, why not come back home? Harcourt Manor is big enough for all of us, Eloise, and the heat is officially off you from everything that went down with Tony and his goons. As far as the police are concerned, you'd put the house up for sale and were living in New York for months before the shootout on your lawn happened."

"You managed that?"

"Easy enough with a little magic. Anyway, there's no reason you can't move back, especially now that you're a shade."

I sit back down on my grandmother's old sofa and fold my hands. "Despite everything, I don't want to."

"Why not?"

"Damien is the rightful king of Stygarde, and I am the rightful queen. Our people need us."

"His people."

"Our people. I'm not from there, but I see how they're being treated. An entire world at the mercy of a spoiled brat and his evil wife. And if I'm being honest, I have a vendetta to settle with her father as well. I will not give up, and I will not allow Damien to either, not to those evil bastards."

She sighs and folds her tattooed arms. She's wearing a sleeveless purple mock turtleneck with a full skirt sporting a pattern of purple Scottie dogs. So Maeve. "What will you do if you don't have the soldiers necessary to win this war?"

I study my fingers. Damn, I need a manicure. "I have to find more support. There's no other way." I lift an eyebrow. "I don't suppose the Gowdie family would help us?"

"Will the Gowdie witches help a family of shades? That would be the day." She snorts. "But you know *I'll* help you when the time comes. As long as you can open a portal for me to get there, my magic is yours." She drums her fingers on her biceps. "I'm more powerful than I look, but unfortunately, I can't replace thousands of men."

I squeeze her hand, so thankful for her friendship, it

brings me to tears. "Why were you trying to reach me anyway?"

She blows out a breath, her red lips spreading into an uncharacteristically wide smile. "I asked Ren to marry me, and she said yes."

"What?"

"We're getting married!"

"You are?" I squeal, remembering all that Ren did for me when I was in Night Haven. If there were ever a person who was as close to a best friend as Maeve is to me, it is Ren. "I can't believe how lucky I am to have both of you together!"

"I wish she could be here. Hard to cast two people into a dream. She has to wake me up if I stay in too long."

"Right, of course."

"Anyway, the wedding is in a week. We both want you there. Do you think you can make it? We're going to tie the knot at the old sawmill."

I glance down at my teacup and notice it's almost empty. We're running out of time. "If I'm still breathing and we're not actively at war, I'll be there."

Maeve frowns. "My goddess, you're serious."

"Unfortunately, yes."

A hint of anger bleeds into her expression. "You know who you should ask to help you? Cassius and Morpheus. It's their fucking world."

I narrow my eyes. "That's actually a great idea. I'm the key. I can bring them to Tenebris if they're willing to fight."

"Sounds like a nice side trip for you...after you come for the wedding." She laughs.

I glance down at the ring of tea at the bottom of my cup. "I love you, Maeve. Congratulations."

"I love you t—"

I wake in the tiny cottage, tucked into Damien's side, and blink as my brain processes that I did, in fact, see my friend tonight. That was no ordinary dream.

And Maeve's suggestion is the best idea I've heard in a long time.

18

AENDOR

DAMIEN

The closer we get to Aendor, the more I worry about what we will find when we arrive. Every village we pass has been raided by New Stygarde soldiers. Every person we meet seems reluctant to even talk to us about what happened. In our disguises, we blend in perfectly with the people migrating or trying to rebuild, but there seems to be no end to the destruction. If this has happened in the Borderlands, what will our destination look like? Brahm and Nevina can't have made it easy on Tempest when we went missing. The coastal territory would have been the first place the crown would have looked for us.

To top off my concerns, Eloise is keeping something from me. She's been quiet since we left the cabin. Contemplative. Down the bond, I can feel there's something she wants to ask me, but she's not quite ready to broach the subject. And I'm not ready to prod either.

What if she's changed her mind about Jaqual? What if she wants to fall on her sword, sacrifice herself for the greater good, as she has so many times before, to improve our chances of success?

I scowl and slump in the saddle as I consider it.

Beside me, Warbill picks up on my sour mood. "You two are in rare form today. Did I miss a wagon of dead puppies, or has something else turned your personalities into black holes where all good humor goes to die?"

"I miss the days when you were starving to death and were too weak to share every thought that pops into that drink-addled brain of yours."

"Drink-addled? Did I miss morning cocktails?"

"He's worried what we'll find when we reach our destination," Eloise chimes in, raising an eyebrow. "And so am I."

Warbill scoffs. "Oh yeah, we're totally fucked. But we were fucked either here or there, so best to accept the inevitable with a smile on our faces."

I turn my head to face Warbill and force a smile.

"Goddess, that's frightening. I'll stick to the scowl."

Eloise chuckles.

It's a few hours' ride more until we reach Wickham Wood and enter Aendor through a narrow mountain passageway that borders Dimhollow. A single uniformed guard polices the border, and I'm relieved that he's wearing the blue uniform of Aendor and not Nevina's silvery white.

"Only one man?" Eloise says. "During a time like this?"

"Few know about this passage, and fewer still would risk being this close to witch territory. People fear this area just as they fear the forest."

If we'd had the option to send a raven letting Tempest know we were coming, I would have. It's been weeks since we communicated. The last message I received from her was when we were under the protection of the mountain dwellers, and I have no idea what to expect tonight. But reaching out through the shadow network is out of the question. Every shade in the area would feel it.

"Identification?" the guard mumbles.

"We're spice traders, visiting Aendor for the market."

He studies me more closely. "What type of spice?"

"Thanesia's own," I say, invoking the name of the goddess. "A spice fit for the true king."

Now, he meets my eyes. "Enter. We need more of that flavor in Aendor."

The gate rises, and we ride through. "Thank the goddess that still worked," I mumble. "It's been a while since Tempest gave me that code."

"Thank the goddess you remembered it after those morning cocktails," Warbill says.

Eloise chuckles.

The rocky terrain that marks the base of Mount Perilon gradually blends into the red sand beach as we near the coast. "The lord and lady of Aendor stay in the Palace of Dawn at the other end of the city. We'll find Tempest and Thane there. If we follow the coast, it will take us through the port, and then we can make our way to the capital."

"Wow, the red sand against the blue water and the purple moonset is stunning," Eloise says. "I've only ever been here in an alternate reality, during my trial with Valeska. This is so much more."

"The most beautiful view in Tenebris," I say without a

second of hesitation. Stygarde Castle and its surrounding grounds are beautiful, but they don't hold a candle to this.

"I'd have to agree," Warbill says. "I'd do anything to have Bolvet back to its former glory, but even I must admit, the view has always paled in comparison to this one."

We take it in for a few seconds more, and I catalog this moment, this profound and indescribable experience of looking out on an unbroken horizon, as one more reason we must win this war. The dark elves can't have this. They can't take this from us.

"We should keep going," Eloise says. "We haven't eaten, and we've been riding all day."

I nod. She's right. We have to keep up our strength. I can see our journey has weighed heavily on Warbill, who seems to sag in his saddle. I cluck my tongue, and we set off for the city. We reach the port as the moon sets. All three of us dismount, leading our rabble beasts through the congested marketplace. A fist-sized lump forms in my throat at the state of things.

At one time, this marketplace was the envy of every territory, with ships docked at long wooden ports and a central market brimming with the freshest fruits and vegetables, the most beautiful jewels from our world and others, and any spice or root one could dream of. Textiles that begged to be touched billowed in the sea breeze. The colors and textures brought the region alive. One could obtain anything here.

Now, the docks have all been burned, as has the large open-air building with its many tables used for trade. Exchanges are still happening, but the goods arrive by dinghy, and the traders are operating directly out of the cargo boxes. The entire beach smells of char.

"Goddess, it's worse than I ever expected," Warbill murmurs. "Do we even know if Tempest is still alive?"

His fears are well justified. "I don't. My last message to her was not returned, but of course, she would have sent it to the mountain dwellers using Dimhollow's ravens."

"It's like walking through a funeral," Eloise mumbles.

"I have to agree, little bird."

"Let's hope no one we know is in the coffin," Warbill adds.

We exchange glances and hasten our steps. It's full dark by the time we reach the Palace of Dawn. Aendor's castle isn't quite as large as Stygarde's but is just as beautiful, constructed of slabs of pink quartz from the mines of Perilon. It gleams in the moonlight as if it's made of glass. But although my memory recalls candlelit windows and acres of blooming gardens, the windows are dark now. The front torches are extinguished. The garden is noticeably overgrown. Although, a spark of hope ignites in my heart that it hasn't been completely untended. A few blooms are still in place, and weeds grow sporadically around the base of the plants but haven't outgrown them altogether. The gardener's duties have been neglected for a matter of weeks rather than months.

I lead Borus around back but find no one in the stables, no guards, no signs of life. All the doors are locked.

"What now?" Eloise asks.

Warbill answers for me. "Now, we take our disguised selves to the local pub and inquire about the happenings of the last several weeks. Mark my words, if you want to know something, you ask at the tavern."

"The best plan I've heard all day is the one where we sit down and drink a beer," Eloise says.

We all journey to the center of the territory, encouraged by an increase in activity there, and find a pub called the Maiden's Voyage, where a somber man in a filthy shirt serves us ale.

"Sir, if you don't mind my asking, what happened here?" I try my best to sound simple, like a man who grew up on a farm in the Borderlands.

The bartender looks over his shoulder then steps in close to the table. "Same as what's happened everywhere. That blond harlot on the throne come burn everything down looking for Prince Damien and his mate, assuming we're hiding them here. If he were here, you bet your ass we'd be helping him, but he's not. Fucking Banias ruined half the territory looking for him, though. We were blessed by the goddess that the fire didn't reach the Maiden."

"What happened to the lord and lady?" Eloise asks. She clears her throat and adds, "We passed the palace on the way here, and it looks abandoned."

"They're not dead, if that's what you're asking."

The man takes notice when we all breathe a sigh of relief.

"What brings you three to the territory anyway?" the man asks.

"If someone would like an audience with the lord and lady, where would they go to find them?"

The man's face grows impassive. "I'm just a barkeep. Wouldn't know anything about that."

"We're spice traders," I say. "Thanesia's own. A spice fit for a king."

The man rubs his stubbled chin. "I'm afraid I can't help you with that. But...if you need a place for the night, I have a few rooms upstairs. Best view of the harbor."

"We'll take two." I toss a gold quill on the bar.

He picks two brass keys off the rack behind him and slides them across the bar to us. "Upstairs. This one—" he twirls the slightly larger of the two between his fingers "— is to the door at the end of the hall. Make sure you visit that one first." He hands it to me with a wink.

We abandon our unfinished beers on the bar and climb the steps to the second floor. Eloise's still-disguised hand slips into mine as we walk down a long, narrow hall to a heavy wood and metal door that looks as if it belongs in a dungeon rather than an inn. I slip the key into the lock.

"Nothing foreboding about this situation at all," Warbill mutters.

I press a finger to my lip and slowly swing open the heavy door. We all step into the dark chamber beyond, where it takes my night vision a few seconds to adjust.

The door slams behind us, and a pair of swords presses into our throats. "You'd best tell us what you know about spices."

Candles flicker to life in the antechamber, and I look into the face of a man I once knew very well. "Lord Thane?" I tug Eloise's hand, and she drops the spell disguising us.

"Prince Damien!" The older shade lowers his sword and slides it into its sheath, then motions for a younger man who I don't know to do the same. Thane's gaze darts between me, Eloise, and Warbill. "Thank the goddess! Welcome to Aendor."

19

THE RESISTANCE

ELOISE

The one called Lord Thane embraces Damien and then Warbill. He approaches me next, stopping a few inches from me with his arms held wide in invitation. I don't know the man, but I move into the friendly embrace without hesitation. Lady Tempest is a confidante and a good friend to me, and she's best friends with Damien's mother. If this is her mate, he must be a worthy shade.

"Allow me to introduce you all to Percival. He's one of our newest umbrae, a former citizen of Zephrine," Thane says.

"Call me Percy," the man says—a boy, really. I get the sense from his demeanor that he's closer to a teenager than an adult.

Percy secures the door behind us, and Thane gestures for us to follow him deeper into the building.

"We train in secret and move via a network of tunnels

that connect our buildings. Unfortunately, as a coastal community, we can't build underground because of the flooding risk, but we've made use of interstitial space."

"Interstitial space?" I'm embarrassed to admit I don't know what that means, and I wonder if it involves magic.

Lord Thane smiles kindly. "When we designed the capital of our territory, we had streets that ran between the backs of buildings, places for deliveries and refuse removal."

I immediately picture an alleyway in Richmond.

"We built over those streets." He opens the door, and I see what he means. We are standing on a stone road, but it's completely boxed in, like a warehouse, with no windows and no doors. Lamps burn at regular intervals. This isn't like an alley; it's like Night Haven, a completely secured world existing in a place between places. "To make sure the silver coats wouldn't find us, we limited access points. The ones that do exist are well protected, with gateways like this where we can pick off intruders."

Damien points at a slit in the wall. "Arrows?"

Lord Thane raises his chin proudly. "They're watching us. Although I presume they've recognized you by now and are sending word—"

"Eloise!" Tempest rushes through a door at the end of the passageway and swings me into a violent hug. "Damien!"

"Aunt Tempest. Thank the goddess." Damien embraces her with a kiss to her cheek.

"Is that...?" Tempest's gaze sweeps to our third.

"Warbill, my lady."

She hugs us each in turn. "Thank the goddess you

made it here safely. Word has reached us that the silver coats have been excessively cruel in their zest to find you."

"They have been. Thankfully, Eloise kept us disguised the entire time," Damien says.

"Come, I'll give you the tour. Lord Undaku and Lord Prandle are leading exercises in the training facility, but I'm sure Lady Odette and Lady Eudora will want to join us for a meal. You must be hungry and exhausted."

"They're all here?" I ask, surprised the leaders from the Borderlands and Zephrine would abandon their people in such difficult times.

Tempest pauses her steps, her expression losing some of its characteristic optimism. "If they weren't here, they'd be dead. Even Thane and I must hide here." That's why the Palace of Dawn looks abandoned. The lord and lady of Aendor are as much fugitives as we are.

Our eyes catch and hold, and the pain I see in the older woman's gaze is heartbreaking. What must she have endured since last we saw her at the Harvest Festival?

"Tempest," Damien says softly, breaking the unspoken conversation passing between us. "You mentioned a meal. We are famished, but also, our rabble beasts and saddle-bags are still tied up in front of the Maiden's Voyage. They'll need tending."

Percy raises a hand. "I'll do it. We have a secured stable as well. I'll have the bags brought to your rooms."

"Thank you, Percy," Thane says.

The young umbrae hastens toward the door we entered through.

Tempest gestures deeper into the compound. "This way."

As if headed for a royal ball, Thane hooks his elbow

into hers as they lead us through another guarded gateway and into a training facility the size of two football fields. There's a sparring arena, an obstacle course, a strength training corner, and an entire section for weapons training. But the most exciting part to us is the men. Thousands of men. And they are warriors.

"How many?" Damien asks.

"Seven thousand ready to fight," Thane says. "We gain more every day from the villages, but it takes time to rebuild their strength and train them. Most are starving farmers or shopkeepers who have never held a sword."

I see the disappointment on Damien's face, but it's Warbill who speaks. "Seven thousand is a lot. But we've heard New Stygarde has fifteen thousand, some of them the barely grown children of the villagers. Dark elf magic makes them puppets for Nevina."

"I'm afraid you've heard correctly. We don't know the exact number, but that is the estimate our spies report. They can no longer fit them all in the castle dormitories. They have them in tents on the grounds."

My stomach roils at the reminder of what New Stygarde is doing with shade children. I need to talk to Damien about my visit with Maeve. I've held off because we haven't been alone in days. Some decisions we have to weigh in private. Some abilities I'm not ready to share openly, even with Warbill, and this is one of them.

"As much as I'd love to finish this tour, I have to rest," I announce, inviting Tempest's concerned perusal. "Using my magic these last few days to disguise all three of us has drained my reserves."

She places her hand on her cheek. "Damien, you

should have reminded me that Eloise's magic is what saw you across Tenebris."

Damien's eyes meet mine, and an entire unspoken conversation passes between us. "I believe the fatigue of traveling has made me careless. Would it be possible for the two of us to rest before the remainder of this tour?"

"Of course," Thane says. "We've prepared a room for the two of you, and one for Warbill as well."

"Make mine among the other soldiers," Warbill says solemnly. "I plan to train."

Thane nods. "Welcome, umbrae. We are grateful to have you. Come with me, and I'll show you to the barracks. Tempest can take these two to their room."

I hug Warbill goodbye, and we part ways. "Thank you for making this journey with us," I tell him.

"You're welcome, my queen. I'm sure you'd never have made it without me to lighten the mood. Would have slit your own throat with no one to talk to but this one." He points his thumb at Damien.

Damien gives a slow eye roll. "Don't strain something reliving your glory days."

Warbill directs a lewd gesture his way, and then he and Thane disappear through a door in the east corner of the facility.

"I'll show you to your room." Tempest leads Damien and me through a network of passageways to a building that must once have been part of an inn. The rooms are opulent suites, with full bathrooms and sitting and dining areas, along with a king-size bed.

"I'll have your bags sent up. We can speak at breakfast about next steps. We need your leadership, Damien. Now more than ever." She hugs each of us and then departs.

The door is barely closed behind her when I turn to Damien. "We need to talk."

"I've sensed as much since we left the caravan."

"I wanted to wait until we were alone."

His scowl turns into a rippling darkness that courses under his skin and curls off the edges of his form. He prowls toward me until we're toe-to-toe. I'd be intimidated if I didn't know with all my heart that he'd never hurt me. "Then talk."

"We need more soldiers. As big as the resistance is, even with the mountain dwellers, we won't have enough, not with elf magic involved."

In a flash, he grips my neck. Not to choke me, but to keep me in place. I lift my chin, holding his diamond-hard gaze. He strokes his thumb from the hollow of my throat to the tip of my jaw. "Do not ask for my permission to return to Jaqual, little bird. Don't you know that I will give up my crown and let this kingdom fall into chaos before I will ever hand you over to him."

"I thought you said it was my choice?" I raise an eyebrow, knowing that I'm goading him, but loving the possessive heat I see in his eyes.

"It is your choice. It will always be your choice," he says through his teeth as if he resents every syllable. "But I will *never* give you my blessing. Had you stayed with him, I'm not sure I could have survived it." His shadows wrap around me like cool ribbons, binding me, threading us together.

I place my hands on his neck, feeling his pulse. "Don't you know that you can't ever trade me or give me away?" I tangle my fingers in his hair, grown long during our adventures. "I don't stop being yours because I'm in a different building, Damien, or on a different world. I will always be your mate at any distance."

He bends his neck and brushes his lips over mine. "I'd much rather we be in the same space at the same time," he says in that low, gritty drawl that always reminds me of the *shiff* of a just-lit match. "The exact same space, at the exact same time."

He kisses me possessively, and a deep, carnal need rises within me to match what I taste on his lips. It's been over a week since we've been alone. A week of road filth and the smell of rabble beast. A week of barely serviceable beds. A week of Warbill within hearing distance.

"Those are some filthy thoughts I feel along our bond, Damien. Do you need a bath?" I take his hand and pull him toward the bathroom.

"I thought you wanted to talk," he mutters.

"It can wait."

"Thank fuck."

I figure out the tub, which is harder than it should be. There's a lever that opens a foot-wide spout, and hot water pours in, filling the basin in seconds. It takes more effort to slide it back into place, but by then, Damien is at my side and places his hand on mine to help me.

"Thanks," I try to say, but he cuts off the word with another kiss. This one deeper, hungrier. He shifts into shadow and reforms in the tub, leaving his clothes in a pile near my feet.

"No fair. I still have to do this the old-fashioned way," I say, stripping off my jacket and going to work on my corset.

"You're a witch with a dragon's magic, little bird. If you're struggling with your ties, just burn them off."

I gasp in feigned indignation, grasping at my nonexistent pearls. "And wreck one of Ariadne's masterpieces? Not on your life." I wrestle it off and toss it all over a nearby chair. He growls as I straddle his hips and sink slowly into the hot water. "Mmmm."

He eases me around so that my back is to his front and reaches for the soap, lathering it between his hands. "One day, you will have more dresses than you can count, designed by Ariadne herself when she isn't half starved and lusting for your blood. I swear it. Closets of shoes and jewelry." I take a deep breath and sag against him. The truth is, I care very little about any of that. He seems to notice my lack of enthusiasm because he pauses with a soapy hand on my shoulder. "An art studio, like the one in Harcourt Manor. A place you can create, with a balcony so you can look out on the beauty of your kingdom."

"Now you're talking," I say breathlessly.

"We'll rehabilitate my father's dusty library. You can fill a section with books from your world."

"An art studio and a library. Now I think you just want to get laid."

He strokes over my breast and my belly in a slow, languid way, his lips finding the back of my ear. "Oh, little bird, if you only knew how much I want you, every minute of every day. What I would do to make you happy."

He lathers my back, my arms, my neck. The hot water warms me to the core, and the slick glide of his hands makes everywhere we touch sensual, slippery, weightless. He slides them along my sides, over the peaks of my breasts, the flat of my stomach, the mounds of my ass. His lips brush against my ear, and I hear him inhale as his palms slide along my inner thighs, spreading my legs.

"You're not tired of me yet?" I chide. "My incessant challenging of your notions of safety and security hasn't pushed you over the edge?"

His chest rumbles with his laugh. "Saving your life is a hobby I just can't quit."

He exhales as he courses his hand down my side to my hip and then tucks it between my legs. His fingers just barely brush my clit before traveling up again, kindling a deep ache low within me. Slow, even strokes. They might be soothing if their friction weren't driving me mad. He brushes between my legs again, and I lift my hips, chasing the sensation and sending a wave sloshing against the side of the tub.

His low, teasing chuckle fills my ear. "Needy little bird. I hope all this pent-up sexual desire isn't thanks to a certain Rivertoad king?" He exposes that last part as if it's a festering wound he needs cleaned out.

I grab his wrist. "No. If I'd wanted to stay, I would have stayed. You were right. The Rivertoads are manipulative. The second Jaqual knew I was the dragon, he wanted me for himself. He wants to rule from Stygarde's throne. If I'd have stayed with him on his terms, he'd have effectively tamed me and fulfilled the prophecy. You belong on that throne, Damien. No way was I going to fall for that crap."

He circles my waist with his arm and pulls me close. His hard length presses against my bottom, but he stills his hands. "I know you said it could wait, but if it is not a desire to stay with Jaqual, what has been bothering you since we left the caravan?"

I shift so that he can see my face. Has he thought my

silence was about Jaqual this entire time? "Not since we left. Since we slept. I do have something to talk to you about, but it's not Jaqual."

He trails his wet fingers over my neck and shoulder. "What is it, then?"

"Maeve used the Hitch and Cast spell to reach me last night in my dreams. She's marrying Ren, and she wants me at the wedding. It's in one week."

"You should go, but I can't go with you. Not now. Not when there's so much to be done."

I nod. "I thought you'd feel that way, but there's something else. When I told her we need men, she suggested something I hadn't thought of before, something I think we should try."

"And that is?"

"What if we asked Morpheus and Cassius for their help?"

Damien frowns. "Morpheus won't come. He's sworn his allegiance to the triune."

"You don't know that. He might change his mind when he realizes his mother and father are in danger. I have to ask."

"Cassius will want to help," Damien concedes. "But he answers to his coven masters. If Sabrina and Tobias refuse, he is bound."

I lick my lips, almost afraid to say this next part aloud. "I plan to ask Sabrina and Tobias directly for military support, not just for Cassius himself but some of his men. If I could bring a vampire army through the key to fight for us—"

"Is that *possible*?" he asks in a low voice, as if the prospect had never occurred to him. He rinses the soap from my back with water from his cupped hand and skims his fingers over my tattoo, my sigil, the physical reminder of my power.

"I'm not sure if the coven master, Sabrina, will agree to it, but I believe I am capable of it. The key symbol would have to be the biggest I've ever activated, and I'd have to hold it open while everyone came through. I'm strong enough, though. Stronger than I've ever been. If she agrees to send her warriors, I will do what it takes to bring them here."

He rinses the other side of me, smoothing the last of the suds off my skin.

"You don't like the idea," I say.

"I like it far better than you staying with Jaqual in exchange for his mercenaries."

"So then, you're supportive of the idea. When I travel to Earth for this wedding, I will visit with Morpheus and Cassius and ask them for help."

"Yes," he finally says. "Please be careful, my little dragon. Your world is a long way away, and I don't think I can do what I must do here without you."

I take his face in my wet hands. "You won't have to. A few days. That's all."

A low rumble begins in his chest, and his lids lower over his diamond stare. He grips my lower jaw. "If we must spend time apart, I'm going to need a dose of you to hold me over, little bird."

I lift one corner of my smile off my fangs. My voice is a low croon as I say, "Then take your medicine, mate."

He rises to sit on the edge of the tub, his massive erection jutting between us. The way he's looking at me, hungry, wanting, with that soul-deep need I can feel down the bond, I know what he wants.

In our relationship, most of the time, he's felt like the predator and I, the prey. Not long ago, he even fed on me. But here, now, he's flipped the script. He wants me in control. And I think I understand why. With everything that's happened, with his jealousy of Jaqual so fresh in his mind, he wants to feel how much I want him. He wants to experience the full force of my desire.

Goddess, if that's what he needs, I will give it to him.

I rise onto my knees and grip his thighs, pulling myself closer. The water only comes up to my belly button, and droplets bead off my peaked breasts. Damien's gaze drifts over the slope of my neck, the curve of each of my breasts, my torso, and the surface of the water, where the rest of me is lost beneath the refraction of light. Then his gaze rises again to my mouth.

The rumble of his purr grows louder, and the swollen head of his dick weeps for me. I lean over and run the flat of my tongue along the underside of his shaft and swirl it over the sensitive tip. The taste of him is pure ecstasy. Our mating means that we are each other's special recipe, a match made by the goddess. The salty sweetness of him only makes me want more.

He curses under his breath and grips the side of the tub. I'm reminded of the first time I did this, in the kitchen of Harcourt Manor, when it was the sides of the chair he was gripping. Different place. Different circumstances. But he feels just as vulnerable. I suck his cock to the back of my throat, taking him as deep as I dare.

His moan is all the encouragement I need. I start to move, drawing back slowly before taking him in again. I hollow my cheeks and suck hard, bringing my lips almost to the tip, swirling my tongue, before driving him to the back of my throat again.

The growl that tears from him is more animal than shade. He releases his hold on the tub and sinks his wet fingers into the back of my head, tangling them in my red curls. I raise my eyes to meet his as he begins to match my movements, thrusting to the back of my throat until my eyes water from the intensity. I don't let up. I move faster, alternating suction with licks and swirls. I cup the heavy weights at the base of his shaft, rolling them in my palm.

His balls tighten and he roars. Hot jets hit the back of my throat, and I swallow him down, my body reacting almost to the point of orgasm from the experience of feeling him come. This is Damien, though. Once he's finished, he's far from done.

He sweeps me from the water, spins me around, and braces my hands against the wall behind the tub. He hooks his fingers and lifts one of my knees, bracing my foot on the ledge. Before I can draw my next breath, he's inside me from behind and reaching around my hips to circle my clit with his strong, capable fingers.

Our joining isn't gentle. His thrusts come full force, his bigger body wrapping around me, driving deep and fast as his arm holds me tight against him and his fingers rub with exacting circles of pressure.

I shatter into a million falling stars. Or, should I say, falling shadows? I feel myself come apart, something I've been trying and failing to do for months. And then just as naturally, just as organically, I come back together.

"Good girl," he whispers in my ear, and as always, the praise sends a jolt through me I can't explain. My knees tremble, and he holds me there, our hearts beating in unison.

After several minutes, when I've caught my breath, I turn in his arms.

"Did I...break into shadow?" I ask, still unable to believe it.

"Yes," he says. "Spectacularly."

"Why can I do it now and not when I want to?"

He shrugs. "Strong emotions make it easier. You can do it. You just need practice and motivation."

My mouth opens wide on a sharp yawn. "Damn. I'm not practicing anything tonight. It feels like my battery is on empty."

"Shifting does that to you in the beginning. Here, let me help you." He cleans me up and then sweeps me into his arms to carry me to the bed. I'm still a little damp when he slides us between the crisp white sheets. I'm asleep the second my head hits the pillow.

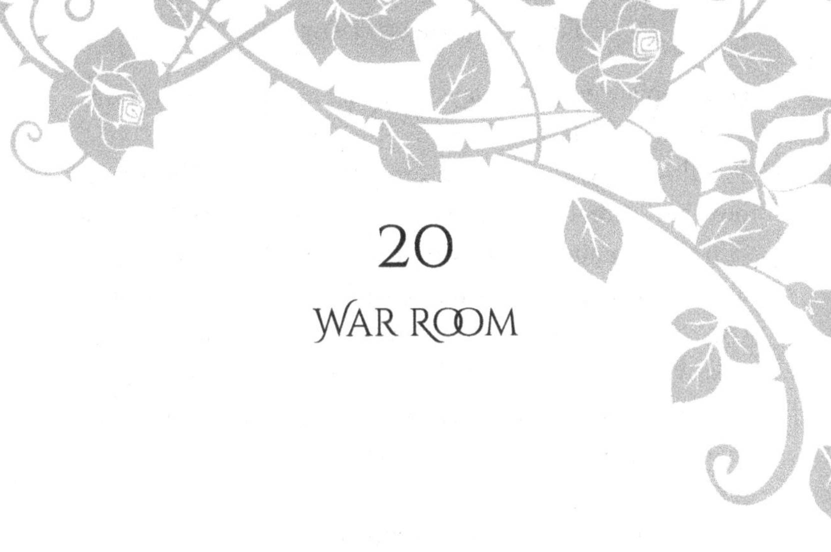

20
WAR ROOM

DAMIEN

Ten thousand men. The next morning, I stand at the end of the resistance's war table, a tactical map of Tenebris spread out before me. White pegs denote where our spies report New Stygarde has stationed troops. Two thousand in Willowgulch, Thane tells me—mostly dark elves, based on his surveillance. Five thousand around Stygarde Castle. Another three thousand patrolling the west villages, the Borderlands, and even Aendor, although Stuart at the Maiden's Voyage and other spies around the port are good about sending word when they spot the silver coats in the area.

Our possible plan of attack is depicted with black pegs. Our east flank would attack from the forests of Aendor. Our mountain dweller regiment would come in from the west, taking advantage of the secret underground tunnels to leverage the element of surprise. We contemplate various ways to split up the units, various strategies of attack.

Ultimately, though, we are outnumbered. No matter how we spread our troops, no matter the strategy, we don't have enough warriors to take New Stygarde, especially considering the silver coats' access to elven magic. Our vulnerability is still the Borderlands that bisect Tenebris. Without our having a regiment in that area, New Stygarde and Willowgulch have uninterrupted territory that runs from north to south. We cannot win. Our defeat is an inevitability.

I spend the morning monitoring the rebels as they practice inside Aendor's training facility. These people are the best Tenebris has to offer. Some, like Warbill, I know from my time here. But the younger shades, ones who earned their stripes after I was taken, are just as capable. These men move fast, strike hard, and are ready for battle.

New Stygarde's soldiers may be less motivated than these men, less loyal. But Brahm and Nevina will use the rebel's own children against them. In some cases, their own brothers and sisters. Will these warriors be able to kill their own when the time comes? Under different circumstances, we might be able to spare the young shades poisoned by Nevina's magic. But with such a shortage of fighters, any hesitation is a death sentence.

Heavy with dread, I return to the war room. It's impossible. It will be a bloodbath.

"Where is that better half of yours?" Thane asks, noticing my sour mood.

"I could ask you the same."

"Tempest usually helps cook in the kitchen this time of day. It takes a lot to keep these men fed and a lot more to do it without drawing the attention of New Stygarde. Tempest buys meat straight off the ships, before any of it is registered in port. She's the only one stealthy enough and with enough sway to keep it all our little secret."

I'm thankful for his honesty and feel I can be honest in return. "Eloise is preparing for a journey to investigate some additional options to help us. Magical options."

"The rumors are true, then. She's a witch and a shade?"

"She is."

"Tempest said you spent time with the witches of Dimhollow and that your mother claimed Eloise was the dragon."

I sigh. "One of the wise witches, Aurora, saw a future on her deathbed where a son of Malek would rise up to defend them with a dragon at his side. Eloise was born with dragon's blood in her veins and has resurrected the dragon from the bowels of Mount Damocles."

"But that would mean...?"

I meet the man's eyes. "Yes, the very dragon we fought the war over."

"By the goddess, Damien, an actual dragon? I thought Tempest was speaking metaphorically when she said your mate *was* the dragon."

"Eloise *is* the dragon. It's her magic that animates the beast. Without her power, the dragon would be nothing more than a pile of bones."

"If she's one of them, can she convince the witches to help us? A legion of witches would greatly increase our chances of success."

"No. She is a witch but not of Dimhollow. She comes from Earth."

"Then the witches of Earth."

"It doesn't work like that. She has no coven. Not like you think."

He frowns, bracing his hands on the table and leaning over the map. "Then we are doomed. We don't have enough men. Even with the thousand or so you say we can count on from the mountain dwellers, we don't have the numbers for an offensive against New Stygarde. Considering what you told me about the Rivertoads, I don't see any scenario where we can win this war."

"I agree. I've tried every strategy. We don't have a chance unless Eloise comes through for us."

Thane turns to me, raising an eyebrow.

"Eloise and I have an idea. It's too early to share the details, but give us time. We may have a viable plan soon."

"It can't come soon enough." The older shade scrubs the back of his neck with his burly palm. "Ever since the Harvest Festival, New Stygarde has been ramping up their patrol of Aendor. All it would take is New Stygarde cutting off interdimensional trade, and they could starve us out. We can't hunt, ourselves…not the amount it would take to feed them all. And I'm sure you can imagine how financing this facility has drained our coffers. I'm truly not sure how much longer we can continue like this."

"We have to. You said it yourself. We do not have enough men. Unless we find a way to capture the Borderlands and fight our way north and south simultaneously, New Stygarde and Willowgulch will be impossible to break. They'll use our own people against us."

"I know you don't trust them, but the Rivertoads are uniquely positioned in the Borderlands. If they joined us, we'd have a chance."

"Not happening," I mumble. "Jaqual offered his men

only in exchange for Eloise, because he thinks if he has her, he has tamed the dragon and will become King of Stygarde."

Thane hesitates a moment, then lowers his voice to a whisper. "Have you ever considered that if Jaqual asked for Eloise, as you've mentioned, maybe she could influence him… Use her magic to charm him into doing what we want."

"It's. Not. Happening." I meet his eyes so that he knows I'm serious. "I refuse to use Eloise as a bargaining chip for a promise from a man I don't trust, who rules a people who don't contribute to our society in any meaningful way. We will find another option."

Thane nods. "I understand. I wouldn't give up Tempest to save our world either. I'd let the whole thing burn if it came down to it."

I stare at the military map in front of me, my arms crossed defensively against an impossible scenario. "I didn't return to Tenebris to run from my soulless brother and his wicked dark elf bride. I wasn't born of my king father and then trained for decades to fight as an umbrae warrior to bow to the dark elf king who captured and tortured him. Eloise is the dragon, and we will take back Tenebris. If this world burns, we burn with it."

His barrel chest rises and falls with his exhale. "I admire your passion, Damien. You remind me of Malek in all the important ways. You'd make a fine king. I admit, my own passion has been ground down under the weight of time, disappointment, and loss. Watching Aendor burn and being helpless to stop it was a particularly low point. It's good to have you here, breathing new energy into the cause. We all need that."

I nod, understanding what he means, how I felt when I left the castle, the loss of my home, the split of my family. The wound still rankles. And just like a slow-to-heal, infected limb, one can be tempted to cut it off to stop the spread. But I have to have faith.

"We will find a way, Thane. Aendor will be yours to rebuild again. We will have peace. We will have freedom for all."

He runs a thumb along his bottom lip, studying the map. "It will be a relief to have you on the throne, listening and responding to the needs of the people. The voice of Stygarde has been ignored for far too long."

I hear echoes of Jaqual in the man's words, and I hate that the notion once again sounds reasonable. This time, hearing it come from one of my father's oldest friends helps it find purchase in my soul. After everything, the voice of the people will need to be heard. They will need to feel in control. And when I am king, I will find a way to make that happen.

21

THE KEY

ELOISE

"Be careful, little bird. I know you can protect yourself, but I fear how long you might wait to do so, if you believe the pain you suffer will serve your purposes."

I kiss Damien, skimming my palms down his chest. He's right, of course. I do have a penchant for self-sacrifice and, admittedly, self-sabotage, if I believe I'm helping the people I love. My relationship with Tony was the perfect example. I allowed him to prey on me because, in the deep grief of my parents' passing, I believed I would do my grandmother a favor by marrying myself off. I was so wrong. To some extent, what I was doing was risky and selfless, but it didn't mean I had to fall on my sword or dance with the devil.

I'd like to think I've learned my lesson.

"I will be careful. No matter what happens over there,

I'll make sure that I'm back here, in one piece, in a few days' time."

He presses a kiss to my forehead. "Go. Tell Maeve and Ren congratulations from me."

I pick up the silver-and-gold-wrapped box that contains our wedding gift to them and step into the symbol. I'm wearing one of my favorite Ariadne designs, a purple gown that perfectly contrasts with my green eyes and bright-red hair. It's comfortable enough to run or fight in, but glamorous enough for any formal occasion. I don't need to bring anything else. I came here with nothing. All my things are still in Harcourt Manor. I hug the box to my chest and draw on the bond between Phantom and me.

You know what to do this time, right? Before we ascend to Earth, you must abandon the bones of the dragon in the underworld and return to the grandfather clock. There are no dragons on Earth.

My grandmother's voice speaks for my ancestors. *We've got this, darling. We know better what to expect.*

My eyes meet Damien's as I trigger the key spell, my mind focused on my parents' stillroom in the attic of Harcourt Manor. It's the first time I've used the key since we came to Tenebris and my first time in the Darklands since we traveled to the shadowpath and faced Thanesia. I recognize the goddess's realm, with its deep-water blues and forest-green darkness, as I pass through her door and through her version of the netherworld. I say a prayer to her, aloud, just in case she can hear me, thanking her for safe passage and wishing her well. I swear the air vibrates in response.

I pass into the ashy red glow of Earth's underworld

without delay or discomfort. I've been in darkness so long that the crimson light stings my eyes, and I blink rapidly toward the version of Harcourt Manor that exists here.

I reach out for my bond with Phantom and feel it come apart as if a braid were unwinding into its separate components. A shimmer of light, and my grandmother manifests on the porch. My grandfather appears next to her, my mother, my father, and then a legion of Harcourts whose names are lost to time fill in around them. All of them are gray-scale, newsprint versions of themselves with pinprick pupils that glow silver from smiling faces. I have more relatives than can fit on that porch or in that house, but that doesn't matter. A soul takes up no space.

Pressure builds within my body, and I wave goodbye. A thousand gray hands wave back, some of them passing through walls to say their farewells. I turn my attention straight up and begin to rise, a bubble zooming along a straw. I land with a pop inside the key symbol in the attic of Harcourt Manor, my old attic. It's discombobulating, first the sensation of rocketing upward, rising like a cannonball shot toward the sky, and then an abrupt fall that buckles my knees. I land in a sort of lunge, one hand braced on the floor under me and the other gripping the small box.

Breath coming in huffs, my skin clammy and moist like I'm fighting a fever, I wipe sweat from my brow and slowly stand, smoothing my dress. Things in the attic have changed. The bookshelves and worktable still stand where they were before, as does the red velvet chair, but three large tubs labeled "Christmas" are stuffed in the back corner, and a dozen or more types of herbs are hanging from a new rack affixed to the ceiling. Maeve must be using the space for her own magic.

But then, what did I expect? She owns the house now. This is her home. Without her magic, she couldn't have made the Hitch and Cast potion to visit me in my dreams. Still, it's weird when I step over the white border of the symbol and hear running steps coming up the stairwell.

"El?" Maeve's voice calls, and then she's there, the smiling face of my best friend framed in walnut paneling. I set down the gift on the table and brace myself as she hurls a hug my way. She's just as I remember her, blunt-cut of black fringe, heavy dark-rimmed glasses, tattoos covering every inch of the pale skin of her arms. We cling to each other with the sort of fervor you only experience when you are prepared never to see someone you love again, but you get one last shot. My vision goes blurry with joy.

Maeve is my ride or die. Always has been. Always will be. It's as if our time apart never even happened.

"How did you know I'd arrived?" I finally manage when we break apart.

"The grandfather clock started ticking again. It hasn't worked since you left."

"Oh. I had to use it as my anchor since the dragon I use in Tenebris doesn't exist here."

"Dragon? I thought your anchor was a fox?"

I offer a light laugh. "We have a lot to catch up on."

She grabs my hand and tugs me toward the stairwell. "Well, come on. Ren is downstairs preparing dinner. She even has some blood warming for you."

"Oh, you shouldn't have troubled yourself. I can eat anything now, as a shade. Although, blood is appreciated."

"Goddess, I forgot. You can enjoy the full meal, then. The woman is a phenomenal cook. It's part of the reason I put a ring on it." We both giggle, and an unexpected warmth kindles in my chest. Maeve has never been much of a giggler. We've laughed together before, yes, but there's always been an untouchable sullenness about her that matched her black wardrobe. Now, she's brimming with joy. Although black is still her wardrobe staple, she's painted her nails a bright kelly green, and she has a light in her demeanor I've never seen before.

Maeve is in love. Really in love. And I couldn't be happier for her.

"Good. I came hungry."

Maeve opens her mouth to say something else but doesn't have a chance.

"Is she here?" Ren shuffles into the hall outside the kitchen, and I can't help but gasp. We met when we were both blood slaves in Night Haven. She was thin then, almost waifish. Now, those days are long behind her. The long hair we were all forced to keep in Night Haven is gone. Ren wears it bobbed now, her naturally brown color toned a deep, shiny mahogany that flips out flirtatiously at her jawline. Her face is fuller, as is her figure, and the added meat on her bones suits her well. But beyond her physical appearance, she's glowing, just like Maeve.

She squeals when she sees me. "Eloise! My God, it's been months." We embrace, and before I know it, we're all sitting in my old parlor—I'm relieved they haven't changed a thing—catching up over plates of roast chicken and a savory rice pilaf. Maeve wasn't kidding when she said Ren could cook. It's delicious.

Slowly, methodically, I give them both a synopsis of what's happened since I left. Maeve knows some of it, but both women gasp when I tell them about facing off against Thanesia and becoming a shade. And when I fill them in on Brahm and Nevina's tyranny and what they're doing to Stygarde's children, Ren tears up.

"So, you can be in the sun now without it killing you?" Ren asks.

I nod. "It doesn't feel great and it weakens me, but it won't kill me."

Ren shakes her head. "You've been through so much."

I meet her eyes. "So have you." A silent exchange passes between us. Ren was once a drug addict who joined Marabella's to work as a blood whore in exchange for a place to live and the forced discipline to sober up. It worked for her. It helped her survive. But by the time she was healthy again, her family had disowned her. She'd stayed in Night Haven longer than necessary because she didn't have anywhere to go. Once I killed the vampire queen, Valeska, I'd invited Ren to stay with me, but I was gone by the time she arrived.

Lucky for both of them, Maeve was here to open the door. Pure serendipity.

"My mother and my sister are coming to the wedding tomorrow," Ren says. "Can you believe it? Dad didn't RSVP, but I'm still hopeful he'll show."

"Whether he does or not, you look so good. So happy. You made this life for yourself, and if they'd give you half a chance, they'd be so proud of the woman you've become."

"Thanks, El," she says. "You know I never would've left if I hadn't been blessed with your friendship. Seeing how brave you were and having your encouragement, it meant everything. It means everything."

"I'm so happy that something I said helped you, but honestly, everything that you've improved about your life, you did on your own and under your own strength."

She shrugs, a blush creeping up her neck. "You don't give yourself enough credit, El. After you killed Valeska, you changed everything for the people of Night Haven."

"Oh?" I have no doubt Valeska's death shook up the governance of the coven. That was always the plan. But could things be that different from before for a community of vampires?

"George is coven master now."

"George? Master of Night Haven? I thought they broke up the nest into independent covens?"

"They did. Night Haven is much smaller than it once was but quadruple the size of Liberty coven. He's got to be the most powerful vampire on the East Coast. And you are the reason."

I try not to think about how George sired me by having Marabella feed me his blood in the protein shakes she served me, without my consent. While he did immediately free me from the sire bond following my transformation, it was still a dick move. I always liked George, but I don't think I could ever trust him again.

"How have the changes been received by the masses?"

"You can ask him yourself. He and Marabella will be at the wedding tomorrow."

"You invited them?" I shove another bite into my mouth, wondering what it will be like to face those two after all this time. Now that I know what they'd planned for me all along, I find it hard to reconcile that with the fact that Ren intentionally invited them to the happy occasion. It all worked out for me, but it might have ended differently. I deserved to be in on the plan. I deserved better than what they did to me. And although I can't claim that what they did, they did out of malice—in their minds, I'm sure they felt like they were helping me, albeit in the only way that was sure to preserve their interests—I have no desire to break bread with them.

Ren must notice the mix of emotions that course through me—betrayal, anger, and also resolve—because her own face echoes all of them. "Marabella used us," she finally says. "She created a system designed to make it nearly impossible for us to buy our way out. But she did help me. I'd still be in the gutter without her. And in the end, she used her position to do what was right for all of us."

"Because what was right for all of us was also good for business," I murmur.

"There is that." She laughs and takes another sip of tea, but I don't miss the way Maeve's scowl betrays her feelings on the matter. "I just felt like she was too big a part of my life not to invite her. It surprised me when she accepted our invitation."

"Anyway," Maeve adds. "It's done. She's coming. And to accommodate our vampire and shade guests, the ceremony will begin at sunset tomorrow evening."

"Great. Um, I hope it's okay if I stay for a few days. I have some business to attend to after the wedding."

Maeve pushes her glasses up her nose. "Stay as long as you like. We have your old room all set up. However, we are leaving on our honeymoon right after the wedding, so you'll be on your own."

I nod. "I'll make sure to lock up before I go." On a whim, I reach for the box I brought. "Since I won't be here when you get back, I thought you might open your gift."

Ren takes the small gold-and-silver box and, with a happy glance at Maeve, pulls one end of the bow and makes short work of the paper. But when she lifts the lid, her face falls.

"What is it, Ren?" Maeve rises to look inside.

"I know it seems weird, okay? But there's a reason—"

"A vial of your blood? You gave us a vial of blood for our wedding?" Ren asks, looking mildly disgusted.

Maeve snort-laughs.

"It's enchanted, okay?" I say, laughing. "If you dribble it on the key sigil upstairs, the portal will bring you to me, wherever I am in the universe. I don't suggest coming now, considering my world is it war, but someday, it could be the trip of a lifetime."

Maeve brightens and hugs me, hard. "I love it. It's like the world's most universal plane ticket."

Ren seems less enthusiastic but gives me a warm "thank you" before unloading the box on Maeve.

SLEEPING IN MY OLD ROOM THE NEXT DAY BRINGS BACK memories. Before I left for Night Haven, I watched the sunrise beyond the cliffs that border this property with only a blanket over my shoulders. I thought I was saying goodbye to the sun before I risked everything to save Damien. I never expected to come home again. I was ready to die to save him.

Once again, I'm ready to die for him, this time to put

him back on the throne. I guess the more things change, the more they stay the same. Maybe Damien is right that I am terrible at self-preservation.

I no longer need a blanket for warmth, but walking out to the cliffs this morning is out of the question. I watch the sunrise from the shadows, thankful for the angle of the house, which gives me a decent view of the sun's ascent, while allowing me to stay safely and painlessly behind a panel of curtains. I remember sunrises—dozens of them—but this one hits differently. It's a spectacular show from a planet I once took for granted.

As I close the drapes against the morning light and lie down on the bed that was once mine for my day's slumber, the strongest wistfulness washes over me. I can almost hear Grams's footsteps in the kitchen, smell her perfume. Memories spark like exploding fireworks in my mind—painting with my mother, swinging from my father's arms as he spun me in the yard, eating pizza and watching movies with Maeve, Grams's famous chocolate chip cookies at a small worn table with mismatched chairs.

This is no longer my home, and I don't wish to move back here. Those memories are yearnings for a place and a time that no longer exist. But it also makes me realize how Damien and I have nowhere to call home right now. The place we sleep each night changes often. We may share hope for a future home, but nothing is certain. Nothing is ours. Maybe there never will be a place for us again.

This war we will wage against New Stygarde is not just to overthrow a tyrant and save Damien's people; it's also a war to reclaim his home. As I lie in the bed in the house where I was raised, I see everything so clearly. Damien once helped me fight for my home, and now I'm helping him fight for his. But everything changed when I became his mate. My home is wherever he is. His people are my people. His world is my world. Fighting New Stygarde *is* fighting for home. My home as well as Damien's.

I have to find a way to persuade Cassius and Morpheus to help us.

Before sunset, I snap awake like I'm hardwired to the rising of the moon. I dress in one of the floaty, feminine dresses I find in my closet. This one is royal blue and accentuates my pale skin and bright-red curls. I step into a pair of stilettos I haven't worn in over a year and catch my reflection in the pedestal mirror in the corner of my room. I am dressed like a human, but no one could mistake me for one. My green eyes give off their own light, and my complexion is the color of starlight. But it's my body that gives me away more than anything. I'm lean but solid, and when I move, it's silent and smooth as gathering shadows. Grace bound to unmatched power.

Ren and Maeve are already at the old mill getting ready, so I run the short distance to the venue and blend into an eclectic crowd gathering among rows of white chairs. Humans, witches, and vampires are in attendance, although not exactly commingling at the happy event. Ren's relatives stand in a tight circle, eyeing the other guests with obvious curiosity. I wonder how much she's explained to them about the supernatural world.

Maeve's relatives with their raven-black hair and deep brown eyes would be easy enough to identify by looks alone, even if most of the women weren't wearing dresses that expose their skull and crossbones tattoos. The witches move slowly, their gait off-balance ever so slightly, their skin marred with imperfections—a dry patch here, a blemish there. They are so obviously human.

No such imperfections slight the vampires. While their bodies come in all shapes and sizes, their skin is pale and smooth as glass, and when they move, it's with the surety and grace of a veteran ballet dancer. I take a seat on Maeve's side of the aisle, next to a young witch who scoots to the far side of her chair when I sit down. She whispers to her mother, "Why is she sitting on our side?"

I suppress a smile as her mother looks me up and down. Intentionally, I twist to gaze over my shoulder, giving her a full view of my tattoo.

"See," the mother says, pointing to my back. "She's a witch too. Just a different kind than us."

"Why does she look like one of them?"

"I don't know. Hush. It's about to start."

When I turn back around, I catch a glimpse of George and Marabella three rows ahead of me on the opposite side of the aisle. George meets my gaze, and I frown, pretending I don't see him.

Maeve is waiting at the end of the aisle, dressed in a tuxedo-style suit with a purple floral jacquard jacket and satin peak lapels. She's worn her hair up for the occasion and replaced her usual square black glasses with a cat's-eye design in a print that matches her jacket. It's all wildly Maeve's style while also looking stylish and elevated. She's stunning. Our eyes meet, and I place my hand over my heart.

A string quartet starts to play, and her eyes shift from mine to the head of the aisle. I stand with the rest of the attendees. All eyes fall on Ren, stunning in a spaghetti-strap ball gown that is formfitting to her waist and then juts out at the hip with layer upon layer of floor-length tulle. The white material is threaded with silver to reflect the moonlight, and she floats down the aisle an ethereal beauty, a bride awash in stars. When the officiant leads the couple through their vows, I see tears on both women's cheeks. Their happiness is infectious, and I find myself overwhelmed with warmth and joy until the second they descend the aisle, hand in hand.

Afterward, all of us filter inside the rustic, restored building where the non-vampires in the group get in line for the bar. I decide a lemon drop martini is exactly what this day calls for and step in line myself.

"You look good, Eloise. It's nice to see you." George stands beside me, having popped up out of nowhere like a spot of black mold. The witches in line with me take a step forward or back, putting as much space between themselves and us as possible without losing their place.

"Funny, you still look short, fat, and devious," I deadpan.

He snorts. "That's fair, all things considered. Hey, we should talk. We never got to put things right between us after what happened."

"You're scaring the other guests, George. Besides, we have nothing to talk about."

"I think we do. I think I never had a chance to truly apologize for how things went down."

"Apologize for making me your pawn in a game I had no idea you were playing? I heard it's worked out well for you, by the way. You slid into Valeska's spot quick enough."

A wrinkle forms along his brow, and his eyes narrow to slits. "As I recall, you were playing a game too, and my help was what gave you an edge. Considering I can hear your heartbeat, I think we can both agree it worked out for you as well."

I slant a glare at him, just as I reach the front of the line and order my drink. When the bartender slides it into my hand, I turn from the bar and curse. George is still there. I guess it's time we had this out. With a quick tilt of my head, I lead him out the back of the sawmill, to where a giant wraparound porch offers stunning views of the mill wheel that squeaks with every turn under the pressure of the water that flows toward the Rappahannock River. It's decorative, as this place hasn't been used for milling since the fifties, but the creak and groan of the old wood is undeniably soothing.

I need all the calm I can get as I whirl to face George. "What is it you want to say to me?"

He scratches the side of his stubbled jaw. George isn't what anyone would call a looker. In fact, his closest celebrity doppelgänger is Danny DeVito. He's balding and portly, not what anyone would expect from a vampire. But the woman who sired him didn't want him for his looks. He's wicked-smart and good with his hands. Rumor is that George can fix anything, including, it seems, an out-of-control vampire queen.

"I want to apologize for not telling you what Marabella and I had done, for not asking for your consent. I was turned without my permission. I knew the evil thing I was doing, but there was no other way. No other fucking way, Eloise. Do you understand that?" He holds out his hand, palm up, and shakes his head.

My nostrils flare as I catch his scent. He's not lying. "I thought you said vampires couldn't change. It sounds like you're growing a conscience."

He lowers his outstretched hand and rocks back on his heels. Human body language, purposely slow. He's trying his best to put me at ease.

"Look, somehow I should have told you what it meant that you'd had my blood and I'd had yours. I really like you, kid, and I believed in you. I thought you could best her, and you did. You saved us all, the entire coven, and we owe you a debt of gratitude. That's all I wanted to say. I hope you understand why I did what I did, and I hope we can be friends."

Until this point, I hadn't thought whether I could forgive George, but as I search my heart, I realize I already have. I'm a shade, finally Damien's equal. And while George isn't fully responsible for that transformation, his blood kicked it off. Being a shade is what I was always meant to be. I feel it in my bones and every time I use my magic. How can I blame him for helping me become who I am? And still, the darkest part of me awakens in his presence. George isn't innocent, and my shadow heart wants reparation for what he's done. And as the darkness within roils and homes in on the opportunity he's opened for me, I strike.

"A debt of gratitude, you say? In that case, you may have my forgiveness on one condition. I need your help."

"What kind of help?" he drawls suspiciously.

"I need men. Soldiers. Warriors." George's nose crinkles, and I barrel on. "All the problems you had in Night Haven, I have in Tenebris. I saved your world—now it's time for you to return the favor."

"You want me to lend you vampires to fight in your world? Fight what exactly?"

"An evil queen, not unlike Valeska. She's a dark elf, as sinister as they come. She must be stopped. But as of now, Damien and I don't have the muscle to take back the kingdom."

George glares at me for a beat and then starts laughing, low and deep. "Let's pretend I lent you these men, Eloise. How exactly would you get them to..." He draws out the last word, circling a bent knuckle between us.

"Tenebris," I chime in. "It's another world, like Earth, but the atmosphere is safe for vampires. Safer than here, actually. There, it's always night. They divide their time based on the rising and setting of their moon."

He makes a dismissive noise deep in his throat. "How exactly would you transport these soldiers to this night world of yours?"

I clear my throat. "I'll open a portal. As it turns out, I'm a talented witch."

He snorts. "Of course you are," he says with a note of disbelief. "Okay, kid. For shits and giggles, how many men do you need?"

"How many do you have?"

"Don't be cute." He picks at something on the side of his thumb.

"Five thousand."

Silence, like an exclamation point, is followed by the rise of both bushy brows. "You're serious?"

"You asked what I need. That's what I need."

"I don't have that many to give, doll. The armies of Night Haven were split when you vanquished Valeska. Liberty coven has some, and Night Haven has a few more, but nowhere near that amount, and I can't leave the coven undefended."

"How many can you lend me?" I ask again. "To appease your debt of gratitude?"

He thinks for a minute, rubbing his chin. "A thousand."

A buoyant ray of hope bobs through me. It's fewer than we need but more than I ever expected, considering the source. I hadn't even thought to ask George for help and probably wouldn't have if Ren hadn't invited him. But his yes means even more to me, because if George can say yes, then so can Morpheus and Cassius. A yes means everything.

"Two thousand," I counter.

He rubs his chin. "I have to check with Marcel, but it's as high as I can go, Eloise. Two thousand. No more."

A warm smile spreads across my face. "Done. I forgive you."

He blows out a deeply held breath. I reach out a hand and give his a few firm shakes.

"You know," he says, peering at me through the corner of his eye, "I always saw the darkness in you."

"The darkness in me? You think I'm evil?"

"No! No. You, of all people, should know that darkness doesn't equal evil. All of us have a shadow self, Eloise, a part of ourselves we conceal in the deepest darkness of our spirit. What we conceal says a lot about a person. Someone like Damien made a show of being outwardly callous, when inside, he was secretly kind and capable of loving you. I'd like to think I'm that kind of man. That my shadow self is selfless, but maybe I like power a bit too much to claim that entirely. But you...you came across sweet and helpless the first time I met you, much too pretty to be a killer. Though, inside, your shadow self is ruthless, not in an evil way, but in a loving one. You'd kill for the people you love, and you'll play whatever game you have to to end the injustice you see on this world. You were never a meek little mouse, Eloise. And now your shadow self is so big and strong, it's shining through your skin."

"My new shadow self thinks you should shut up about it already," I say with a laugh. "I've grown and changed. It doesn't make me any better or worse than who I once was. I simply have different options."

He huffs. "If you think so, you must be a true leader, doll. Never lose that. It'll keep you grounded."

The door behind him opens, and Marabella, dressed in a low-cut red gown, steps out onto the deck. "Is she going to kill me if I join you?" she asks, one hand on the door. Her heart hammers in her chest. I remember too well what it was like to be a vulnerable human.

"Not if you move out of my way." I glide past her, through the door before she has time to blink. "I want to dance."

22
TRAP

DAMIEN

Convincing Thane to wait for Eloise's return before making any strategic moves isn't particularly difficult. What choice does he have, given our circumstances? If we attack New Stygarde with the men we currently have, we will lose. There's no other way to spin it.

Days pass. We train, but morale is low. Everyone knows our odds. Everyone hears rumors of how their homes have been ransacked by silver coats. Everyone wants to do something.

In the war room, we stare at the map of Tenebris. "What if we were able to sneak an explosive into the camp?" Thane asks.

"Before we left New Stygarde, we learned Nevina set up a magical boundary around the castle, along with a military boundary. A talented warrior might get lucky and sneak in, but if they trigger her spell, they'll have a hard time getting out again. If they're caught, our entire operation will be in jeopardy. No explosive at our disposal is strong enough to take out enough men to make it worth our own."

We both turn as the door flies open and Tempest rushes in, covered in blood. A bad feeling lands in the pit of my stomach.

"You're hurt. Damien, fetch the healer!" Thane takes her into his arms.

"I don't need a healer," she says, throwing him off. "My wounds have already healed. Most of this is from the stag."

"The stag? I thought you were obtaining meat for the kitchen, not wearing it," I say, relieved she's not hurt.

She groans, balling her hands into fists. "I took Stuart with me to meet the ship delivering our provisions. When we returned, we opened one of the crates in the safe room, like we always do, just to make sure our shipment hadn't been tampered with."

"Wise. It wouldn't be beyond reason for the enemy to hide in one of the crates."

"Exactly. Unfortunately, we proved the need for our protocols." The look she gives us is devastated.

"No..." Thane says.

She turns toward me. "We aren't trusting around here and always test the shipments in a secure location below the Maiden's Voyage. I open them with a long crowbar and shift immediately, while Stuart guards me from the opposite side, daggers ready. If we hadn't been on our toes, one of us could have been killed. As it was, Stuart was left with an incredible mess to clean up, and the entire shipment had to be destroyed."

Thane closes his eyes and runs a hand over his face. "No food for the men."

"How much do we have in store?" I ask.

"Enough for a week at least, if we ration," Tempest says.

"Is it possible to send a contingent into the forest to hunt?"

She shakes her head. "The entire city is crawling with New Stygarde soldiers. Thank the goddess we've already received our supply of weapons from Mount Damocles, or I'm sure those shipments would be a liability as well. Brahm is convinced you have to be here. He knows I have a soft spot for you. They've searched everywhere else. Even the witches of Dimhollow allowed them to look for you in their village once you were long gone and they'd hidden your mother and sister. Banias has been searching for us, Thane and me. If he finds us, he'll question us, and his methods will not be merciful."

I pace the room and then grab my sword and sheath and head for the door.

"Damien, where are you going?"

"To follow my wife's advice and try to make a friend," I mumble.

"What?"

"An idea. Maybe nothing. Maybe something. If Eloise returns while I'm gone, tell her to wait here for me."

"Damien?" Tempest reaches for me. But I shift and surf the shadows before I change my mind.

I ARRIVE AT THE RIVERTOAD CARAVAN AT MOONSET AND snake my shadow form under the wagons and between the narrow canvas walls of the tent. I wait and I watch. Rivertoads come and go, singing and dancing and eating Maggie's food. Hours pass before I see Jaqual.

No one would mark him as a king. He blends in with the others, his clothing tailored but made of scraps of leather, sewn together as if nothing could go to waste, with those cheap strings of multicolored beads in his hair, around his neck, around his wrists. And the eye, waiting, watching, on top of his shirt. He doesn't favor any single group of his people. It fascinates me. No noble class. No social hierarchy. He mills from table to table, talking with everyone, singing when asked to, dancing when the mood strikes him. And I notice something else, something I noticed the first time we were here. He does not drink the ale.

His eyes remain as sharp as his weapons.

He is the first to notice me when I form inside the tent. And when he approaches me, his hand is on his blade. The music stops, and every Rivertoad in the place turns to stare. "I thought we'd said everything there was to say to each other, Prince Damien, or have you decided to trade that lovely bride of yours after all?"

I refuse to take the bait. Offering a shallow smile, I meet the man's eyes and speak to him as an equal. My voice is low, steady, and respectful as I say, "King Jaqual, please excuse the interruption. I've come to seek your counsel on an important political matter. I know our people have not always shared the best of relations, but I hope to change that. Will you meet with me?"

His sneer fades into a teasing smile, until he sees I'm

serious and matches my expression. He trails three fingers through the air, and the band starts up again. "Follow me."

We walk to one of the wagons near the middle of the western-facing spoke, and he shows me inside. It's a moderate wagon with a purple and red interior. At first, I assume it's a random one he uses for meetings, but his scent is everywhere. "Do you live here?"

He glares at me. "Not up to your standards?"

I raise my brows. "I was simply surprised you'd show me where you live. My standards these days top out at wherever my brother isn't trying to kill me, which makes this wagon better than any castle. Would you like to sell it to me?"

My attempt at humor is wasted on him. He crosses his arms. "In fact, your brother's men have nosed around my camp quite a few times, looking for you. I allowed him to search the wagons once, but I refuse to be subjected to the constant monitoring he wants to impose. His commander found my mercenaries could be incredibly uncooperative when their space wasn't respected."

I snort. "I'm learning never to underestimate you, Jaqual."

He rubs the back of his neck. "You didn't come here to flatter me, Damien."

"No." I take a deep breath and think of Eloise. "I don't think you ever wanted my wife."

His gaze locks on mine, and he goes absolutely still. His violet eyes turn hungry, and I realize my mistake too late. He moves in close, backing me against the cabinets along the far wall of the wagon. "Then have you come to offer yourself?"

I clear my throat as his hand closes around it. I

swallow against his palm. "What I meant was that you wanted the dragon, not the woman."

He does not back off. His nose comes closer to mine. "Do you want the woman, Damien?" he asks softly.

"I do," I answer.

He backs up a step, a look of disappointment on his sharp features, and spreads his hands. "Secret's out. I have no use for Eloise, other than advancing my political agenda." He picks an apple from a fruit bowl on the small counter, tosses it into the air, and catches it. "To be fair, it was never a secret. Any Rivertoad could tell you I have no interest in women at all."

Once again, I've allowed my jealousy to get in the way of common sense and diplomacy. Have I learned nothing from my time in Night Haven and Eloise's relationship with Marcel, Everald, and George? Am I a slave to my mating instincts like some adolescent boy who can't control his temper?

"I owe you an apology," I say with utmost sincerity.

He snorts and eats a slice of apple off his knife. "Don't bother yourself, Damien. I didn't take your rejection to heart."

"No. Not that. I'm afraid you were right about my father, about the old biases that existed between us. I wanted to believe that how my family—how the kingdom, really—treated your people was deserved. And I think the way I jumped to the conclusion that your intentions for my wife were no better than King Entrydal's had everything to do with those biases. I see now that I was wrong."

"What did King Entrydal do to Eloise?"

I draw a deep breath. He wouldn't know the details, although I'm surprised there are no rumors of her time in captivity. "He abducted her, tortured her, almost killed her," I admit. "I was able to get her out, only because I had help from the witches of Dimhollow."

He gives a low whistle. "He is a bastard, that one."

"So, you see, I am not one to trust the intentions of any man when it comes to my wife. And what I said was true about her. She makes her own choices and is more powerful than any of us. But all that doesn't excuse my reaction. I should have acknowledged what you were trying to achieve as a king."

"You should know that king is a poor name for what I am. Rivertoads don't have castles, and we don't have royalty. The name for what I am among my people is *calla die*. In our language, it means "Wise One," and it is an elected position. Never mind that anyone who was actually wise would avoid the role at all costs."

"Truer words have never been spoken," I say with a laugh. Despite everything, I like Jaqual. "What a mess this kingdom has become."

"Is this why you came?" he asks more forcefully. "To apologize and nothing more?"

"No. Although it would be reason enough. I came again to ask for your support. I need your help to overthrow my brother and his dark elf queen."

"And to put you on the throne," he says through his teeth. "Don't forget your true goal."

I swallow. Here we go. "Not necessarily."

He leans forward from where he's perched on the edge of his bed and places the half-eaten apple carefully in his fruit bowl. "Tell me more."

"What if I agreed to an election? All citizens of Stygarde would vote for who should lead it. If I am elected, I become king and vow to rule more justly than my family before me. If you, or anyone else, are elected, I will step down peacefully and allow you to rule."

He squints at me. "You would allow me, a grimy River-toad, to rule from your father's throne and sleep in your mother's bed."

"Yes," I say quickly, knowing I would. "What good is coveting a palace or a throne if I'm not alive to enjoy it?"

He scoffs, the amulet around his neck winking. "You're lying. There's no way in hell a Hymir would voluntarily give up the throne."

I gesture at the amulet. "You know if I'm telling the truth."

He shakes his head. "You may believe it now, but when the war is won and you are standing on a bloody battle-field, you will change your mind. You will justify it by saying you can't allow a Rivertoad to rule the kingdom. You'll betray my people as generations of your kind have before you."

"What could I give you to prove my intentions?" I squeeze my eyes closed. "Aside from my wife."

"But you see, Damien. She is, and has always been, the only thing that will bind you to your word. I knew it the moment you held the tip of your sword to my neck and I smelled your mating scent. I will treat her well. She will live among us, and I will return her once you've kept your promise. It is the only way."

"It is an impossibility. She is the dragon. We will need her to fight with us. She can't do so if you have her in a cage."

He draws back, looking offended. "I mentioned no cage."

"Then how will you keep her?" He gives me a tired look. "You trust her word. If she promises to stay, you'll believe her."

"Finally, the resurrected prince is catching on." He clutches the eye around his neck. "This gift of mine allows me to see the heart of people, and I know she will keep her promises."

"But not me?"

"I don't trust what it tells me about you."

I scoff. "I won't ask her to stay with you."

He picks up the apple again and slices off another piece. "Then good luck to you. I hear Brahm and Nevina are becoming more aggressive with their pursuit. At this rate, there won't be a cottage in this kingdom left unburned." He takes the slice between his teeth.

My stomach sinks. We're running out of time. "How long until he burns your wagons, Jaqual?"

He scoffs. "He wouldn't dare."

"The citizens of Covellton told us that's what they believed about the Borderlands. They did everything the king and queen asked, and still, their homes were destroyed. Do you know what they couldn't do? Do you know what no shade in this kingdom can do? They couldn't become dark elves. Make no mistake, Jaqual, once my brother knows you are no further use to him, he'll wipe every wagon from the face of Tenebris."

Jaqual says nothing, but I don't miss the way his complexion pales. I slip out the door and surf the darkness back toward Aendor.

BAD WITCHES' CLUB

ELOISE

I should have asked Maeve for her key to Bad Witches' Club before she and Ren left on their honeymoon. I've never been here without a supernatural chaperone— and never when I wasn't human. I don't even know how Damien and Maeve got their keys. Do you pay a membership fee? Are you issued one by your coven? In any case, I realize the key is important as I arrive in the unlit parking lot of the club that, to me, looks like a nondescript warehouse from the outside.

The door to the place is locked, and unlike Damien, I don't have enough control to shadow my way through it. I resort to pounding on the door and screaming Morpheus's name. It doesn't take long for a scrawny redheaded man to open it for me. The foyer beyond him is just as I remember, an empty room with a single bare bulb swinging from the ceiling. The man adjusts his round glasses on his freckled nose, looking every bit the part of an irritated librarian. His shoulders hunch, as if he's spent too much time over a book today.

"Shh." He places a finger over his lips. "Can I help you with something?"

"I need to see Morpheus."

The man's eyes shift left then right, his nostrils flaring. A brief look of confusion tightens the corners of his eyes. "There's no one here by that name, miss. This warehouse isn't even in use yet. You have the wrong place."

"Look, just tell Morpheus that Diana Harcourt's daughter is here to see him."

The man scowls. "I said, you have the wrong address. Move along."

He begins to close the door, but my hand shoots out and stops it. His nostrils flare again, his notice of my speed and strength causing those brown eyes of his to squint. "Do you have a key?" he murmurs, so low that a human would never be able to hear it.

"No."

"Send in your application with payment, and your key will be mailed to you if you're approved."

"No time for that, unfortunately." I shove past him and dart through the fake back wall before he can utter another syllable. The steady thump of reggaeton reaches my ears, and then my mother's mural of the dark queen, her head tipped back in a dramatic laugh, comes into view. The mural is surrounded by purple smoke, just as I remember.

I intend to head for the dance floor and Morpheus's office beyond, but I find my coat cutting painfully under my arms and my feet bicycling through the open air before I can take another step. Peeking over my shoulder,

I see the redhead has caught up with me. He's no scrawny librarian anymore. This man, while sharing the freckles and glasses of the one who greeted me, is an ogre of a beast, at least three feet taller than I am, and holding me off the floor by the back of my jacket.

I struggle and kick, but neither his grip nor his muscled hold gives. "Put me down! I need to speak to Morpheus. Goddess, damn it!"

He plods back toward the wall. He's going to throw me out! Unacceptable.

Smack. I hit the floor as if he's dropped me, but by his growl, I suspect I shadowed through his fingers. Shit! Why is it I can always do it when I need to, but not when I want to? The cool slither of the shadows inside me remains, and I try to hold them, try with all my intention to shadoweave to Morpheus's office, but the sensation proves fleeting. All I manage is to scramble to my feet and dodge his lumbering grasp.

By this time, my screams have invited spectators. A half ring of vampires has formed in the entrance to Bad Witches' Club, and their murmurs and laughter seem to enrage the ogre. He charges toward me again.

"Never mind, Grog. I'm here," Morpheus says, the scar on his face more pronounced with his scowl. Then again, the shade is almost always scowling.

I smooth the wrinkles from my jacket. "It's about time. Goddess, did you ever consider a receptionist? An intercom system?"

He sighs. "My office, Eloise. Now."

"Gladly." I stride to his side.

His nostrils flare the moment I'm within smelling

distance. "You're a shade," he says, although it sounds as much like a question as a statement.

"We have a lot to catch up on."

He glances at the audience we've attracted, and his frown grows more pronounced. "Mind your own business, or I'll strip you all of your keys."

The crowd disperses as if he dropped a stink bomb.

A moment later, I'm sinking into one of two chairs across the desk from him in his office. I'm again struck by how much the decor in here reminds me of a local bank. I feel like I'm about to ask for a personal loan rather than an army of men. It throws me off, and I try to remember the speech I'd prepared to win him to our side.

"Rumor has it you were made vampire during your confrontation with Valeska. Can you explain to me how it is you are now a shade? I didn't think it was possible."

"I descended to the Darklands and faced off with Thanesia. She granted me a beating heart as a reward for successfully walking the shadowpath to her door."

Morpheus tips his head skeptically. "If you didn't want to tell me, Eloise, you could just say so."

"Magic. It was dark magic."

He nods as if that is an acceptable explanation. Never mind that it's a complete lie.

"Congratulations, by the way, on vanquishing Valeska and saving your mate. I have to admit, my money was on Valeska, but it was a bet I was happy to lose."

"That's a favor that would be easy for you to repay," I say, hoping this conversation goes the way of my last.

"A favor to whom?" he asks, clearly not taking the bait. "You faced those trials of your own free will and won back your mate. I owe you no favors."

Shit. The hard way, then. "Nevertheless, I need a favor from you now. From your whole triune."

He groans. "Why do I think I'm not going to like what you have to say? Why are you here without Damien?"

"Something terrible has happened to Stygarde," I start. I go on to tell him about Brahm and Nevina and about how his own mother and father, Tempest and Thane, are leading the resistance. I make sure to point out the theft and drugging of the kingdom's children, and end with Damien's plans to take back the throne. "We're close, Morpheus, but we need more warriors. Without more men, Brahm's soldiers outnumber ours. And unlike us, who value every soldier, Brahm is prepared to force his people to slaughter their own loved ones to stay in power."

If I thought his expression was sour before, the look he gives me now is positively infuriated. "That fucking menace. How dare he pollute the Hymir line with a dark elf whore?"

"Then will you help us? I have the magic to bring you and however many men you can spare through a portal to Tenebris to fight."

He rubs two fingers along his temple. "I understand why you asked me, Eloise, and you must know that I long to help. It has been centuries since I've seen my mother and father, but that doesn't mean I don't care what happens to them. If the elves have a stronghold in Stygarde, things are bad, indeed."

"You won't regret helping us. You can change the outcome of this war," I promise.

But he shakes his head. "I can't help you."

"What? Why? You just said—"

"When I accepted the triune bond, I agreed to put the lives of the witch and shifter I'm bound to above all others. My triune is my family now, and as Tenebris is another world and what happens there does not directly threaten our territory or position, asking them to endanger themselves for me would be illogical and foolhardy. Going alone and putting myself at risk threatens the triune. I am magically bound to put them first, Eloise. Always. My answer is no."

My blood heats. I can't keep the tremble of fury from my voice as I say, "You'd let your parents die to spare having to ask your precious triune for a favor?"

"It's not a favor. It's a potential death sentence."

"How? You're immune to the effects of sunlight, and so are they. The dark elves are less a threat to you three than any soldier."

He grits his teeth. "We have vulnerabilities. Our natural lives are protected, true, but we aren't invincible. This isn't our fight. Tenebris is no longer my world."

I stand, knocking over my chair, and lean across the desk until I'm right in his face. "And how about Damien? Is he still your friend? You'd let him get massacred to spare your own hide?"

"Careful, Eloise. No one attacks me in my own house. You are very close to crossing a line."

I look down and realize I've gripped my dagger. I slide it back into its sheath. "Ask them, Morpheus. That's all I want from you. Just ask the triune if they'll help us. Offer them a future favor. Surely having a pair of shades at your disposal is worth something."

"The answer is no," he says flatly, refusing to meet my eyes.

"Then send some of your men! That ogre guarding the door could fight."

"I run a bar, not a kingdom. I have bouncers, not an army." This time, his eyes do meet mine, and his expression is tired, ancient. "The answer is no. Tell Damien I'm sorry."

I flip him my middle finger. "Tell him yourself."

I fly through the door and back into the thumping music of the club, my heart pounding with resentment. But before I reach the exit, a hand lands on my shoulder. Morpheus. He hands me a gold key. "I can't help you on Tenebris, but if you decide to flee, to return here, you're welcome in this club."

I close my fingers around the cold metal. "Wonderful, Morpheus. I'm sure Damien will want to come dancing after he watches everyone he loves get slaughtered."

His eyelids flare, and I swear I see some real emotion pass through his expression, but it's gone just as quickly. "Goodbye, Miss Harcourt."

"Mrs. Hymir," I correct. "Damien and I were wed by the witches of Dimhollow months ago. You're speaking to your rightful queen."

He bares his teeth in surprise and then makes a show of an exaggerated bow. I head for the door, the key biting into my palm.

24

TRY, TRY AGAIN

ELOISE

Two thousand men. That's all I've gained from this trip unless I can convince Cassius to help us. I'm no child when it comes to rejection. I've heard no before. But the way Morpheus turned me down leaves me shaken. The way he seemed to disregard the fate of his own parents and completely close the door on my request unsettles me. The entire flight to Chicago, I think about it, turning the dials of it in my mind like a cryptex I can't crack.

It's twilight when I make my way to Cassius's door, the changing colors of the leaves on his street reminding me that it's fall. It's been almost exactly a year since I sought him out the first time. If it weren't for Cassius, I never would have known how to descend to Night Haven or have freed Damien from Valeska's clutches. I can trust Cassius. He'll do his best to help me. I know he will.

But when I knock on his door, no one answers. I call

his name, loud enough that a shade would hear me, even if he were sitting on his rooftop patio. But no one answers. I focus my hearing on the interior, blocking out the noise from the street. I smile when I hear what I think must be a mouse nesting somewhere inside. But there are no footsteps. Nothing else breathing within these walls.

I take a deep breath and descend the steep set of steps to the sidewalk, passing through the wrought-iron gate to hail a cab on the street. I remember how to access Lamia coven; it's just going to be more difficult than I expected to get in.

The bar called Boss Miller's is just as crowded as the day Cassius brought me here. That November night, my human heart was beating so hard and fast that I'd hardly acknowledged the crowd, and I'm thankful I was able to recall the name from the depths of my shade memory.

As I navigate the throng of bargoers, the slightly sweet scent of human mixes with the earthier one of witches and the acerbic tang of vampire. My new senses can easily sort these smells, and I wonder which of them is sorting me. I'm too far from my anchor in Harcourt to disguise myself, but the glasses I wear dim my glowing eyes. It's not enough to completely disguise my otherness to anyone but a human. All I can hope for is that my presence is forgettable.

A vampire as large and fit as a rugby player glances over her shoulder at me as I move into the stairwell at the back of the bar. Too casual. Too slow. She's trying to pass as human, but she's overcompensating. When I hear the bottom of her beer hit the bar and her stool shift, I hasten my steps. I don't want any trouble, and goddess knows the last thing I need right now is more delays.

At the bottom of the long flight of stairs, I find the same metal door I encountered before when Cassius brought me here. No handle or keyhole, just a silver panel the size of a thumb that will sample my blood and open if the coven has cleared me. The coven hasn't cleared me, but I pray feeding the mechanism my blood will raise awareness of my presence. And if I can get inside, I can reach Cassius. I press my thumb to the panel and feel the prick. The wound heals before I can bring it to my mouth.

I smell her before I see her. The vampire from the bar has moved into the stairwell with me. "That door's off-limits. Nothing back there but the HVAC."

Slowly, I pivot to face her. Her nostrils flare. "My name is Eloise Harcourt." If she's heard of me, it will be by my maiden name. "I'm here to see Cassius. It's an emergency. Can you get me inside?"

Her eyes widen, and her nostrils flare again. "Goddess. Fuck. Fuck! Are you *the* Eloise Harcourt who killed Valeska?" She glances over her shoulder as if to check who else might be listening.

"The one and only." Her reaction is not what I expected, but I'll take it. I guess my reputation precedes me.

"Wow." Her eyes spark with acknowledgment. "I heard you were turned, but…" Her nostrils flare again. "What are you?"

"You wouldn't believe me if I told you." I point my thumb at the door. "So, can you help me get inside?"

Her smile widens, showing her fangs. "Hey, would you autograph my dagger?" She draws a six-inch blade from the interior of her leather jacket.

"Sure. Ah, do you have a Sharpie?" I'd sign her ass if it meant getting to the other side of that door.

"Wait here." She zooms up the stairs at super speed, and I hear her have a quick conversation with the bartender. She returns with a black Sharpie, and I scroll Eloise Harcourt across her blade in big, looping letters.

"Can you let me in now?" I ask her, pointing at the door. I frown when I see a group of vampires gathered at the top of the stairs watching us. A man in front meets my eyes, smiles and waves nervously.

"It's very nice to meet you. All of you," I say kindly. "But I really need to talk to Cassius."

Behind me, there's a metal-on-metal scrape as the door finally opens, and the dark ebony skin and glowing amber eyes of my trusted friend come into view. "Eloise, what in the name of the old gods are you doing here?" he asks through a gleaming white smile.

"Making friends?" I spread my hands toward the gathering onlookers.

"My apologies, but master Sabrina is waiting," he says to them, pulling me inside and locking the door behind us. "Honestly, Eloise Harcourt, I'd have thought you'd know better than to call unnecessary attention—" He draws in a deep breath. "Fuck me, you're a shade!"

I flash him a slow grin. "Yep. I'm also married to your best friend, so it's Eloise Hymir now."

He draws me into a firm hug. "Congratulations. But why have you come alone? Where's Damien?"

Another vampire edges around us to get to the door. "Can we go somewhere more private? There's something I have to tell you."

"Yes. Actually, your blood triggered a security alert, so

Tobias and Sabrina know you're here. They're waiting for us in their quarters."

"Great," I say, some of my anxiety bleeding through to the word. Meeting with the master of Lamia coven and her dragon mate would make anyone's stomach flip. And although I expected my visit would eventually lead to this, I thought I'd have some time to get used to the idea, maybe run things by Cassius first. I take a deep, fortifying breath as he leads me through the underground vampire den they call the Star to their subterranean apartment.

"If I'd known you were coming, I would have met you," Cassius murmurs.

"I stopped by your house at sunset, but the only thing inside was a mouse. I think he's nesting in your kitchen cabinets."

"Gerbil. His name is Mike."

"You bought a gerbil?"

"It's nice to have something alive in the house when I come home. When I have time to come home—I stayed here last night because we had some trouble with a band of werewolves on the Indiana border. Nothing too serious, but I wanted to make sure my men made it home safely before sunrise."

"I would have called, but…"

He snorts. "I understand. It's not like Tenebris has great cell service."

"I no longer even have a phone, and I'm sorry to say I didn't memorize your number."

"But if you're a shade, you can reach out using the shadows." I feel a cool vibration at the base of my neck and jump away from his side, startled. "Sorry. I assumed Damien would have taught you."

"He's trying. I don't have control yet. Not like you do."

He studies me for a beat and then seems to figure it out. "Damien and I have always been this. We learn these things as children. You've had only… How long have you been a shade?"

"Going on three months."

"Give it time. It'll come."

I shrug. "Sure. I have plenty of time. A few days, at least," I say sarcastically.

"Days?" He frowns.

A human dressed in a cop's uniform opens a thick vault door for us, and I enter the now-familiar apartment where Sabrina and Tobias live. The sound of the piano meets my ears, then stops abruptly when we're announced. The next second, a lanky redhead is pulling me into her arms, her blond dragon mate waving to me from behind her. "Eloise, it's been too long. And, oh! You've gone through some changes!" Her eyes sparkle with wonder as she takes me in. She darts a glance to Tobias.

For the next hour, we sit in their parlor, and I recap everything that's happened since the last time I sat in the same chair, in the same place, asking for help. It's the fourth time I've told the tale in three days, and I notice I'm getting better at it. I end with my plea for help. "We can't win this war without more warriors. I'm here to ask you for a favor, to ask you to send troops to fight on our behalf."

Tobias winces and rubs the back of his neck. "That's a bigger ask than you might think, Eloise."

Sabrina leans back in her chair and crosses her legs. "What my mate means is our coven is spread thin right now protecting our territory. We don't have many men to spare, and if we send them to Tenebris, they aren't available here if things on the border graduate from harmless tension to full-scale conflict."

"More than that," Tobias says, the tenor of his voice bringing me back to the night his brother visited me and fed me his blood. The two brothers carry the same grittiness in their tone, like their throats are lined with embers. "Dragons like me come from a place called Paragon. Our kingdom follows a prime directive to avoid interfering with the political outcomes of other worlds. While we do have a trade agreement with Tenebris, we never meddle in our partners' governmental affairs."

I snort. "You would allow these tyrants to rule and enslave our kingdom's children over a moral principle not to interfere? What, like you are a scientist, watching colonies of bacteria kill each other under a microscope? You Paragonians are above it all?"

"That's not what I said."

"But it's what you meant. What do you think will happen if King Entrydal wins this war? Do you think he'll stop at Tenebris? Your brother Nathaniel witnessed firsthand the extent of the dark elf's cruelty. Entrydal told me that he doesn't consider any being superior to dark elves. His goal is to rule or annihilate every other creature. Mark my words, Tobias, he will not stop at Tenebris."

The dragon shifter runs a hand through his short blond hair, casting a look in Sabrina's direction. "I do not speak for Paragon. I abdicated my role in political affairs when I married Sabrina, but I can tell you this—the same issue you had crossing from Earth into Tenebris would exist for any dragon from Paragon attempting to inflict their rule on a citizen of Tenebris. We are ruled by the goddess of the mountain. You are ruled by the goddess of night. According to our mythology, those two aren't bosom buddies. I might be able to convince the king of Paragon to risk political fallout and assist in a foreign war, but angering the gods is another thing altogether."

I let out a long sigh. "I think Nathaniel shared some of this with me. Although, at the time, I'd lost so much blood, I thought he might be a hallucination."

"He was real and is horribly worried about you, and I don't think he'd mind my saying that, if things were different between the two kingdoms, he would have busted you out of there himself. But the fact is, nothing is simple when it comes to our two worlds. If I open a portal to transport Lamia vampires to your world, as I am a former prince of Paragon, it will be seen as an act of war between the two kingdoms. I can't put Paragon in that position."

I shake my head. "You won't have to open the portal. I will. The same way I opened the rift that brought me here for this visit. I am the key, Tobias. I can open the door between worlds at my will. If you don't want to risk being involved, don't be. Send Cassius and whatever vampires you can spare."

He and Sabrina exchange looks, and then both of their faces turn unreadable. But Cassius's jaw tightens. "Master, I...must return to Tenebris with Eloise." I do a double take, my eyes bulging as the weight of his words hits me. "My parents, Jozius and Faurine, still live in the Borderlands, not far from Covellton. Their land will be in the war zone. I must help Damien win this war. I will resign if you require it of me, but I must go."

My shoulders sag in relief. A warrior like Cassius is worth many men, and his support in this moment means everything to me.

"You will do no such thing," Sabrina says quickly. "I will not accept your resignation. You may take a thousand men of your choosing and return to Tenebris with Eloise, but I expect you back here when the war is won."

One thousand. It's not nearly enough but is better than nothing. And having Cassius is priceless. "Thank you. Thank you both." I clasp my hands in front of my chest and try my best to look grateful. At least it's something.

But Tobias's handsome face is scowling like he ate something bad. "I think Sabrina and I agree that no one should underestimate you, Eloise. War is unpredictable, even under the best of circumstances, and I'm sensing you don't have the best of circumstances. If things don't go as planned, I want you to know you and Damien always have a place here among the Lamia coven."

"I appreciate that." Although I know Damien and I will never take them up on the offer. We will die before we give up this war. We can't abandon our people. We will fight for them to the death. And with adding only three thousand vampires to our count, that death is looking more and more inevitable. I blink back unshed tears and swallow the lump in my throat. "I'll coordinate the portal with Cassius."

I stand and give them both a shallow bow. Sabrina and Tobias respond with a silent tip of their heads.

"I'll see you out," Cassius says solemnly. It's so quiet, it feels like a funeral. But then, everyone in this room knows I'm on a suicide mission. I leave the apartment, a dead woman walking.

25

HOMECOMING

DAMIEN

I return to Aendor with a stag over my shoulder, the largest beast I could find. Although I'm careful to reenter the city through the darkest shadows, I know it's a risk, and I'm relieved that I make it from Wickham Wood to the compound without interference. But I could not return empty-handed, not after my second attempt at getting the Rivertoads to help us failed so valiantly. One stag will not go far to feed thousands of hungry men, but it is something. The least I can do now.

"Thank you, Damien," Tempest says. Thane thumps me on the shoulder.

"It's with a heavy heart that I must tell you that my visit to Jaqual, while well received, did not result in his alliance."

"Damn Rivertoads," Thane seethes.

I shake my head. "He's doing what he thinks is best for his people. He's wrong, but I could not convince him."

Tempest frowns. "Then we wait for Eloise." She exchanges worried glances with Thane and me.

It's been five full days since my mate left. She will return. I must have faith in that. I must trust in her strength and discretion. But every day she is gone, my mood sours further.

I lead the troops through drill after drill, knowing I may be training them to fight to the death, watching old friends like Warbill and new friends like Percy train to exhaustion for a war we cannot win. And I lie awake at night fighting the notion that this is for me, for my power, for my rule. But if this were only for me and my family, I would call it off now. This is for Stygarde. This is for the children.

"Again!" I yell as we move into our fifth hour of drills.

Warbill rolls his eyes toward the ceiling. "Who knew that training for war would literally require fighting a war? Goddess, man. You'll send us all to the Darklands with these exercises!"

"Are you questioning my methods, old man?" I grumble.

He wipes sweat from his brow. "Simply hoping to survive another day."

Before I can answer him, purple light shoots from the center of the sparring area, sending every soldier scattering away from the energy it's throwing off. I shade my eyes and draw Dawnbreaker.

"Elven magic?" Warbill yells over the buzz coming off it.

"I don't know!" I yell back.

Swords drawn, we wait for the attack, but it's Eloise who appears, holding out her arms at the center. This is no ring. It's the key symbol! And she's not alone. My jaw drops as Cassius steps through the light, followed by a stream of vampires. A hundred! No, a thousand. And more. I recognize some of the men from Night Haven. They keep coming, the shades in the room having to move back to give them space.

They're still coming through when Cassius sees me and rushes to my embrace.

"Brother! You've come to our aid."

"It's been too long," he says.

"How many?" I sputter.

"A thousand from Lamia and two thousand from Night Haven."

"Night Haven?"

"George. He lent her his men as well. They're all vampires, but they're trained."

I turn my attention back to my mate and the symbol, to the parade of men who pour out of it. "Is she strong enough?" I mumble, but no one hears me.

"Goddess, bless us all!" Tempest yells, arriving at my side and greeting Cassius. "She's saved us! Damien, Eloise has saved us all!"

I'm not listening. I leave their side and walk straight for her, stopping at the edge of the spell and seeing the strain on her face, the sweat that drips from her temples.

"Eloise?" I call. She doesn't seem to hear me.

The last batch of men runs through the portal, and the light dies like a fizzling fire. She sways on her feet, and I rush forward to sweep her into my arms. "Bed," she whispers.

I kiss the side of her head, fighting back the burn in my eyes. "Always so eager."

"Very funny," she says sleepily. "I never took you for a necrophiliac."

"The term is somnophiliac. You're not dead. You're simply passing out."

"Don't count your chickens..." she says. "I'll need food and blood. I'm so weak."

I hug her tighter to my chest and increase my pace, shoving past a blur of nameless faces. "I've got you, little bird."

She rests her head against my chest. When we reach our room, I tuck her into the bed and promise to have everything she needs here when she wakes. Her eyes are closed as she says, "Three thousand."

"Cassius told me. You did well, little dragon. More than we ever expected."

"Not enough," she mumbles.

She's right. Our army is now eleven thousand strong to their fifteen thousand. Even with this help from Earth, we are vastly outnumbered, and no vampire will ever be as strong as a shade. We're outpowered too. I kiss her temple. "Don't worry about anything right now. Just rest."

Her breathing evens out, and I know she's asleep.

Once I'm sure she's sleeping peacefully, I return to the war room, where I find Cassius, Thane, Undaku, and Prandle huddled over the tactical map on the war table. Their faces tell me they see what I see.

"You're sure? Fifteen thousand?" Cassius asks.

"All of our intelligence confirms that number," Thane says.

"Some of them are our children, barely old enough to hold a sword, and enchanted by elf magic to fight," Undaku adds. "Our soldiers from the Borderlands may find themselves battling family they know and love. The emotional weapon New Stygarde is wielding against us makes up for any advantage we have in experience."

"The west villages have contributed fewer children than the Borderlands, but we are weaker. The price my people in Zephrine paid for not sacrificing their children was starvation. Many have not yet fully recovered," Prandle adds.

I turn to Cassius. "You have no other men to spare?"

As always, his voice is cool and unruffled as he answers. "Your mate did her best, but you must remember, these are not my men. They are the Lamia coven's. My master was generous to send the number she did. And George—"

"George." My brow tightens. I still don't know what to make of him.

"We are lucky to have the gift of his men. He could not come himself because they're still restructuring Night Haven, but he sent them with strict orders to follow my commands."

I frown. My little bird truly left no stone unturned. I hate that she had to face George alone. That couldn't have been easy. "It's not enough. We are still at an enormous disadvantage," I say.

He meets my eyes. "Eloise was unable to tell me what has happened to my parents."

I shake my head. "I don't know. I'm sorry."

But Thane raises his brows. "They are alive, Cassius. Safe, and living in the Borderlands in hiding."

I watch my friend's shoulders sag in relief. "We will find a way, Damien."

"I wish I could be so confident."

He lifts his chin and rests a dark hand on my shoulder. "Good will always triumph over evil. Love will always triumph over hate. You know this is true. You and I have seen it play out again and again."

"Over time, yes. But on the backs of fallen heroes. I'd very much like our men not to be the heroes who fall."

He nods sadly and removes his hand from my shoulder. "I'm afraid that every generation is faced with a cause that calls to their heroes, and this time, the voices might ring for us."

"I should get back to Eloise."

"But there is no time to waste. We must start training together to bring the vampires on board," Thane says.

"Cassius can do it," I say. "He knows everything I do and more. I need to care for my mate."

Thane bows his head, and they all stare after me as I rush from the room and return to Eloise. Someone has brought her a meal as I requested, but she's still asleep. I sink to my knees beside the bed, and I pray to the goddess for a way to win this war.

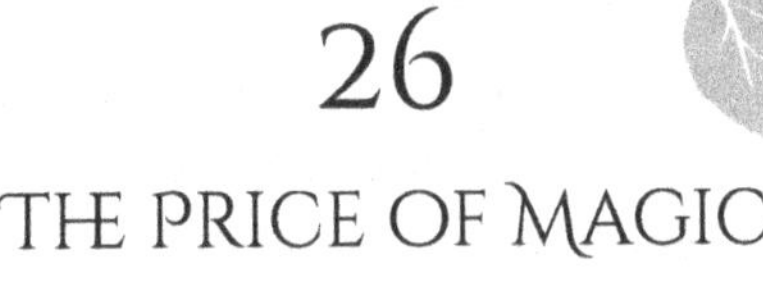

THE PRICE OF MAGIC

ELOISE

I wake to the scent of freshly baked biscuits, coffee, and blood, all swirling with the familiar dark spice of my mate. I'm not sure how long I've been asleep, but he's kneeling beside the bed, eyes closed and head rested on his folded hands as if he's fallen asleep praying. I place a hand on his and shake.

"Damien?" He opens his eyes and blinks at me. "Come to bed. You don't look comfortable there."

"I was praying."

"For me? I just needed some rest."

He massages the bridge of his nose. "For an answer to our situation. I was worried for you as well, but the sound of your heart gave me peace."

"We still don't have enough men, do we?"

"No."

Hearing him acknowledge it aloud makes it all the more real for me.

He stands and walks to a tray of food that has appeared while I was sleeping. Loading a plate, he brings it to me, along with a full goblet. "You should eat. You must keep your strength up."

As much as I want to continue this conversation, hunger takes control, and I down all the blood at once, then gobble everything on the plate. Holding open the portal was harder than I expected. I'm relieved that I was capable of transporting the soldiers and that they could come now. It gives us time to prepare and time to recover before we attack. But it's still not enough.

Think, darling, comes Phantom's voice in my head. *You have soldiers, but you also have magic. Might there be a way we could help you?*

I chew my food slowly, carefully. *Perhaps we could somehow shield our troops.*

Too many, Phantom says. *We could do a single unit if they were in the same location.*

I swallow and rub my head.

"I went to see Jaqual while you were gone."

My brows shoot up, and I turn my full attention on Damien. "You're lucky he didn't have you killed the moment you entered his territory. We didn't exactly part on great terms."

"The conversation went better this time."

"Better, how? Did he agree to help us?"

"No, unfortunately. He considered it, but he wants an election if we win the war. I tried to promise him one, but he doesn't trust me."

"That's why he wanted me. Not because he *wants* me, but because he knows you would follow through if my life were on the line."

He runs his fingers gently through my hair. "I told him it was out of the question. We need you and your dragon to fight this war. I know he couldn't hold you. You're too powerful. But I don't trust that he wouldn't abuse your good nature."

"Fair. It would be an unnecessary complication. He'd expect me to stay with the caravan, which would mean I couldn't protect you. I can't promise him my physical presence, and that's the only thing he trusts."

"I think you're right about that, little bird." Damien crawls into bed beside me and stares up at the ceiling.

"But the rest of it, the election, is that something you're willing to barter? It would mean there's a chance it's not you on the throne."

A muscle in his jaw twitches. "My mother, the queen, still lives among the witches. My sister too. It pains me to think of them losing their home all over again. But here we are, Eloise, at the crossing point, and the bridge is about to wash out from underneath us. Better that Stygarde be Stygarde with a Rivertoad on the throne than the Hymirs remain in power. If Jaqual would have agreed to help us, I would have allowed the election and stuck to my word."

We can make it so, Phantom answers when I send a thought in their direction.

Damien groans. "I know that look on your face, little bird. You have an idea, and why do I think I'm not going to like it?"

"We—my ancestors—have a binding spell. I have a way we can magically ensure your compliance with Jaqual's terms."

That muscle in his jaw pops again, and he scowls at me. "I don't relish binding myself or you to a Rivertoad."

"He would be bound to us as well. He and his people. Neither of you could change your mind without consequences."

He releases a heavy sigh, his eyes drifting closed. "We need his men. If he'll go for it, I will too."

I turn on my side and watch his profile. "I should be well enough in a day or two. I'll return to the caravan and propose the option to Jaqual."

"I'll go with you."

I clear my throat. "If what you say is true, and he trusts me, maybe I should talk to him alone first."

Damien doesn't open his eyes, just frowns into the darkness. "You'll go first. I'll give you a few hours and then catch up to you."

"Okay." I'm not sure his being there is the best thing for our cause, but I know he won't stay away. Besides, if Jaqual agrees, I'll need Damien for the spell.

"If he agrees, that brings us to fifteen thousand. We have a chance, although Undaku mentioned something today that I'm afraid will be a significant challenge."

"What's that?"

"The children. Many of the shades in the units, especially the ones from the Borderlands, will be fighting their own offspring, drugged by Nevina to be killing machines. Every one of them knows they could come face-to-face with someone they know, but I'd be a monster to think any of the warriors wouldn't hesitate. That hesitation, coupled with our reliance on vampires who cannot shift, could be the end of us."

The cursed children have bothered me since my time

in the castle. The problem is, Nevina used a gumdrop to track my every move for months. She can track the children as well. Without getting my hands on the magic used to control them, I can't study it to find an antidote. "If we could recover one of the children, Phantom and I might be able to study their blood and formulate an antidote for the elf poison keeping them under Nevina's control."

He nods. "If we were able to obtain a child for you, how long would it take you to analyze their blood and develop an antidote?"

I reach down my bond with Phantom and ask my ancestors. My great-great-great-aunt Sara was the best with potions, and I relay her answer. "Five days. Maybe a week, depending on the complexity of the antidote and the availability of the necessary ingredients."

His disappointment expands like a held breath. "She'd track us. We might be able to set you up in a safe house, but she'd inevitably reach you before you were finished. Not to mention, we're running out of time."

A chill runs the length of my spine, and my voice comes out like a thin squeak when I ask, "What do you mean?"

"Tempest has been having food delivered from outside our realm to feed the troops. They've been careful to have the crates unaccounted for so that there would be no record of the number or amount included in the deliveries. Because they weren't using food from Tenebris, there was no way for New Stygarde to surmise that Aendor was feeding seven thousand men here. But the last shipment was detected and compromised. One of the crates exploded, injuring Tempest. The entire shipment had to be destroyed."

"Is she okay?" I clutch my chest, worried for Tempest.

"Yes, but there are now New Stygarde soldiers stationed in Aendor. Brahm and Nevina's soldiers are inspecting every crate that comes in, under the guise of protecting the public. We only have five days' rations now that we have more men."

"Goddess, we don't have time for an antidote."

"No. We barely have enough time to implement a rational war plan."

I sit up and pull my knees into my chest. "Are you saying we're going to war, ready or not?"

He repositions himself to look at me. "Yes."

My hand finds his, and we thread our fingers together. "We have the prophecy and the goddess on our side. We're going to win this, Damien."

His tentative smile breaks my heart, and I know what he's thinking. There are many ways to interpret the prophecy, and the majority of those ways don't require our survival.

27

A BARGAIN WITH THE RIVERTOAD KING

ELOISE

R ivertoads are travelers. My understanding from my personal experience and everything I learned from Jaqual and Damien is that they traditionally travel up to thirty miles per day, crisscrossing Tenebris without exception for weather or season. I'm surprised, then, to find the camp not far from where we left them last. A few conversations over ale at Maggie's and I learn why. As we suspected, New Stygarde and Willowgulch are severely restricting where Rivertoads can move freely. Maggie tells me that the caravan had to double back before any of them could "pay homage to the sea," which, I learn, is an incredibly important part of Rivertoad culture.

"Has the goddess sent me a beautiful hallucination, or has the dragon returned?" Jaqual asks as he enters the tent. I haven't bothered with a disguise. Why would I? This meeting is all about being open and honest with each other.

I raise my glass, smiling brightly. "I have returned, and not only for Maggie's stew and ale."

"It's for my sense of humor, isn't it? You're hungry for more of my irresistible charm and jovial exuberance?"

I snort. "Well, it certainly isn't for your dancing."

The table beside me falls into raucous laughter. He moves closer to me and whispers, "You know, the soldiers of New Stygarde would make me a rich man for bringing you in. They've been here almost daily, asking for information."

"And yet none of them is here breaking bread with your people." I glance around the tent and raise an eyebrow.

"They're not welcome," he confirms.

"All the riches in the kingdom aren't worth the price of your freedom," I say.

"No." He smooths the arm of his patchwork velvet jacket. "And still, they take that from me."

"Can we talk?"

He nods slowly, then gestures toward the exit. I follow him down a row to an impressive wagon, but he stops me before I can enter.

"Aren't you afraid of being alone with a man in his wagon?" he asks. "I might try to take advantage of you. If your mate knew, he'd likely melt down into a swirl of shadows."

I laugh. "Have I ever told you the story of how I posed as a blood whore to take down a vampire queen?"

He jolts, his eyes narrowing as if he's waiting for the punch line.

"Here's the CliffsNotes. Oh hell, you don't have those

here, do you? Here's the short summary—they all ended up bowing down to me or meeting the business end of my blade, as will you if you try anything. And as for Damien, he knows I'm here. Besides, you won him over the last time he visited you. He thinks of you as a friend now. Poor schmuck."

"Is that true?" His eyes narrow.

"The friend part? Absolutely. I don't know what went down between you two, but he's turned into one of your biggest fans. Honestly weird for me."

"No. That you were a blood whore?" Jaqual seems completely disgusted by the idea.

I nod. "I used to be human. Um, that's like the witches here. People fed off me for money."

He curls his lip. "How did you become a shade?"

"Faced the goddess in the Darklands."

Our eyes lock and hold. The amulet around his neck winks at me. He knows I'm not lying.

"Nevertheless, we will stay outside the wagon," he states clearly. "Unmarried men and women do not inhabit the same wagon."

"Never?" I ask. I remember Maggie saying it wasn't done, but a meeting is far different from an overnight.

"Never," he says with a quirk of a brow. "So, what did you come all this way to talk to me about? If it's about my men, I think Damien and I said all there is to say."

"You said you'd lend us the men in exchange for me, and that he could have me back once there was a fair election to determine the next leader of Stygarde."

He folds his arms. "That's right. And I also told him, I don't trust him to keep his word. It's a moot point.

Damien suggested you can't stay with me because they'll need you to fight. You can't comply—therefore, my men remain off the table."

"What if I could guarantee that all parties would be held to our agreement?"

He rocks back on his heels. "How?"

"Magically." I lift my chin another inch. "I can cast a spell binding myself to you until the promise is fulfilled."

He studies me for a few long seconds. "What does that mean, specifically? You'd give me power over you?"

I sigh. "Not exactly. Damien and I promise to hold an election within ninety days of the end of winning the war. If we don't do that, it triggers the spell, and you can call me to your side. I will be forced to serve your will until Damien relents. If he breaks his promise, you get me."

"You'd do that? Does he know?"

"He knows. He's agreed to this plan because he has no interest in breaking his promise to you. He will hold the election if you agree to help us."

The eye in his amulet winks, and I can see hunger in Jaqual's eyes like a fish ready to snatch the bait. He wants this election and believes that it will be him sitting on the throne when all is said and done. I can't guarantee he won't be. It's a possible future that both Damien and I have to be willing to face. The prophecy says that the one who tames the dragon will rule. Logically, that would be Damien, because, as my mate, he has tamed my heart. But prophecies are vague and slippery. This agreement could be seen as a sort of taming of me.

"What happens if New Stygarde wins the war?"

"The agreement dissolves."

"What happens if you die in battle?" he asks.

"The magic dissolves, but Damien will follow through."

"And if Damien dies with you?"

"If we both die but win, you're on your own, Jaqual. You'll have to elect a leader anyway. Raise your gods-damned hand."

"What if I die?"

"The magical agreement dissolves."

"Unacceptable," he says, and I'm truly surprised by the passion he places behind the words.

"I'm a powerful witch, but I can't resurrect you from the dead just so you can be elected king."

He bats away my words with a flick of his narrow fingers. "I don't care if it's me, Eloise. I care that there's an election. I will not be party to an agreement that dissolves upon my death. Should I die, you must be compelled to have the election anyway."

I reach out to Phantom and have a mental conversation with my great-great-great-aunt Sara. "It can be done," I say. "Instead of binding myself to you, I can bind myself to the promise. If you provide the men, and I mean all of the men, Jaqual—you must compel your mercenaries to fight for us as a requirement of this agreement, or it's null and void."

"If I say so, they will fight to the death."

I nod. "Then the spell will drain my life-force and eventually kill me if Damien does not comply with the specifications we set out for holding the election."

His amulet blinks, and I can almost feel his magic scanning me for lies. But I'm not lying. I can do the spell. We need his army. The only thing we have to lose is Damien being named King of Stygarde, and that is a possibility he said he was willing to live with if it saved his people.

"Well?" I prompt when the silence seems to go on and on.

Jaqual rolls his eyes toward the starry sky above us. "I need to talk with the heads of each of the Rivertoad families. Unlike Stygarde, we believe in consent around here. My position and my biology bless me with the magical ability to force my assassins to fight, but I won't do it against their will. They have to agree. I need a few days."

"You have twenty-four hours," I say, turning away from him. "I can't be away from our camp for any longer than that."

He groans. "I don't know if it's possible."

"How many are there?"

"Sixteen. One for every spoke on the wheel."

It comes together for me like the pieces of a puzzle. "Are the heads of the families the head of the spoke and all the wagons in line behind them their descendants?"

He tips his head back and forth. "Being biologically related isn't a requirement to be part of a family, but otherwise, you have it. Each family head speaks for every wagon in their spoke."

"So sixteen conversations and sixteen yeses between us and this agreement. I have faith in you."

He rubs his temples, lips flattening. "Fine. You can use the same wagon you did before for the night. I'll come and get you when I have an answer. We can get the key from Maggie."

I follow Jaqual back toward Maggie's tent but psychically ask Phantom to deliver a message to Damien. *Our conversation was well received, we're close to an agreement, and*

I'll be staying the night at the Rivertoad camp while Jaqual thinks it through. I sense the dragon launch into the air, and then they're gone.

By the time Maggie provides me with the butterfly key, Jaqual has excused himself to follow through on what I presume will be a long night of conversations. I head to the violet wagon for some much-needed rest. I'm still recharging my batteries from bringing the vampires through the portal. Even though I slept well the last two nights, I'm wiped.

Since I've been here before, I find it easy to locate the wagon and haul myself inside, wondering for the first time what family's protection I'm officially under in this spoke. I undress completely, carefully stacking my weapons on the small counter. It feels incredible to be free of the weight. As before, the space is small but cozy, and I crawl under the red velvet blanket naked, snuggling into a surprisingly comfortable mattress. I drift off quickly but jolt awake when a cool shadow wraps around my waist.

"Shh. Eloise, it's just me." Damien forms, his vast size seeming to fill the wagon.

"What are you doing here?"

"I said it was okay with me for you to negotiate the election, not for you to spend the night alone. I came to stay with my wife."

I chuckle. "Okay, but good luck fitting into this tiny bed with me."

"Oh, I'll fit, little bird, even if I need to slide inside you to do so." He removes Dawnbreaker and then the rest of his clothing. Cool shadows wrap around my body, and my inner darkness seems to respond, my shadows fitting inside his. Somehow, we both end up in the small space, me mostly on top of him and propped up by the wall. It's tight but not uncomfortable.

He trails his hand down my spine and cups my ass. I throw one sleepy leg over his hips and straddle him, feeling the hard length of him pressed against my center. Lazily, he squeezes my upper thigh. "Are you tired, little bird?"

"Not tired enough to say no to this." I kiss along the underside of his jaw, feeling warm and loose and as if nothing exists in the world other than the heat of his body beneath me. He lifts me, and with a swift angle of his hips, slides into me, drawing a deep breath as we join. I interlace my fingers with his on either side of his head as we start to move. Our lips brush. Deeper. He sweeps his tongue into my mouth, the rhythm of our bodies moving against each other in the way of well-practiced lovers.

This lovemaking is soft, gentle, a tangling of souls in the night, a pinpoint of light in an otherwise eternal darkness. The wagon rocks with us as we crescendo, coming together, climaxing in unison as if everything we are is one and this mating is an orchestrated dance for the gods. Holy. Sacred. Soul-bound.

When it's finished, we curl onto our sides, his bigger body wrapped around mine. "The future King and Queen of Stygarde make cracking use of dog-sized bed," I say in my best news reporter voice.

"We don't know that," he whispers. "Depending on how this all goes down, we may have no titles at all. We may become renegades very happy to make use of any bed that's above ground."

He means, we'll be lucky to be alive. "Well, you did

once say you'd be happy to build a home for us in the wilds of Dimhollow. I'm sure the witches would be amenable to that plan if we survive."

He burrows his face into my hair and whispers, "I don't care where it is. Wherever you are is home."

I drift off, feeling exactly the same way.

28

SACRILEGE

DAMIEN

At moonrise, I wake to a knock on the wagon door. I open my eyes to find myself nose to nose with my mate, our bodies tangled in a ridiculous pretzel of interlocking limbs and mingled breath.

What a life I've given Eloise. Far from royal accommodations, this bed is a joke. It's a torture chamber. By some miracle, though, her face is serene. My queen seems perfectly happy and perfectly unconscious, a glittering thread of saliva running from the corner of her mouth to the mattress, the tips of her fangs poking white from beneath her full upper lip.

Another knock and I shift into shadow, dress quickly, and open the door. Jaqual waits on the other side, frowning in obvious disappointment when he sees me. "Don't look so disappointed, Jaqual. I understand that Eloise is the more appealing of the two of us, but it is both of us who are pursuing this arrangement with you."

He snorts. "Actually, that wince you saw was because I'll have to smudge the wagon with burning sage after you're gone. This is a maiden's wagon, Damien. In our culture, masculine energy isn't allowed inside. Had I known you were coming, I would have put you both in a family wagon." He runs a hand through his long, loose curls.

"Oh. Sorry." I step outside, looking back at the violet door with some amount of guilt. Maggie said something about the prohibition of men and women sleeping under the same roof, but I assumed it was because the characters we were playing weren't married. I didn't know the wagons had rules.

Eloise appears in the door, dressed and somehow looking as put together as if she'd had a lady's maid helping her. "I heard through the wall that we committed a faux pas," she says. "Allow me to add my apology to Damien's."

Jaqual sighs. "I'm sure, to you, the restriction seems arbitrary or even legalistic. But to us, the practice is spiritual. Wagons, in my culture, signify freedom and purity of spirit. We build each wagon by hand, infusing it with masculine, feminine, or duovine energy."

"Duovine?" Eloise asks.

Color stains Jaqual's cheeks. "Something else...like me." He places a hand on his chest. "Parents build wagons for their children during their teen years, and that wagon is as sacred as their soul. They're taught to keep it well tended, and we only consecrate a wagon for a family after marriage, at which point, the couple chooses one wagon to expand to a suitable larger size."

Eloise raises an eyebrow. "Your people don't, um, get

together before marriage?" She hooks her fingers together.

I had the same question, but I'm glad she asked it, because I'm sure I've embarrassed myself enough in front of Jaqual today.

But the Rivertoad king only laughs. "Oh no. Rivertoads celebrate pleasure in all its forms. They simply do it outside their wagons." He gestures toward the woods. "A maiden only invites a man *inside* her wagon if they are betrothed."

"But we are married and Eloise invited me inside, so we've not offended the wagon," I proclaim.

Jaqual closes his eyes and releases a pained breath. "You are not Rivertoads. This wagon belonged to the daughter of one of our families, a young girl named Elsabar. Elsabar died at the age of fourteen, making this forever a maiden's wagon. No one lives in it because we keep it as a remembrance in her honor. That is why it was available for Eloise."

I glance up at my mate, who now has a hand clasped over her mouth, no doubt remembering how we defiled the maiden's bed last night.

"I'll smudge the wagon myself," Eloise says. "I swear I will remove every trace of masculine energy, Jaqual, if I have to magic this sucker apart and put it back together myself. I'm so sorry."

Jaqual bows. "A simple smudge will do the trick. And perhaps, if anyone asks you at breakfast, do not mention your time of arrival, Damien."

In other words, don't let Elsabar's parents hear that I besmirched their daughter's bed and memory. I nod quickly, feeling like a rutting animal, and desperately change the subject. "I assume you've come this morning with an answer."

"The answer is yes." His shoulders sag, at odds with a stubbornly defiant tip of his chin. "You should know that the decision was not unanimous, but the majority ruled in favor of our bargain, and when it comes to Rivertoads and war, we act together or not at all."

"That's good," Eloise says, turning as serious as I've ever seen her. "This spell demands compliance, Jaqual, from all three of us. If your people don't participate, the spell will make them participate or die. Do you understand?"

"And the same goes for both of you?" The eye hanging around his neck winks.

I stare at Eloise. I hadn't realized the severity of the spell, but as I don't plan to break this agreement, I'm not concerned when she responds in the affirmative, and I know she's telling the truth. We will win this war, and Stygarde will have its first election, and if it doesn't go my way, I will have Eloise. A vision of us living in a tiny cabin we build ourselves fills my mind. That end would be no consolation prize. My mother and Karyl will be disappointed, but this is the only way we stand to win. And we must win. That is paramount.

"The same goes for both of us," Eloise says.

"Then make it so."

Eloise nods. "Wait here." She disappears into the wagon and returns with her satchel, then draws a canteen from its depths. "Follow me."

The canteen is thrust into my hands. "Drink," she orders.

I obey, and a hair-raising concoction of slime and fire

fills my mouth. I cough repeatedly but can't clear the taste. I thrust the canteen at Jaqual, and he has a similar reaction.

"What the hell is that?" he asks as Eloise drinks without incident.

"You don't want to know." She casts the empty canteen aside and leads us to the edge of the woods, where Phantom appears in all their white-scaled glory. I swear to the goddess, I will never get used to the thing's presence. I can feel the death coming off them, smell the flames brewing in their lungs. Phantom smells like the Darklands, like old souls and the forged metal of the gods. I keep my eyes fixed on Eloise as a deep rumble vibrates in their throat, and they lower their head over hers. The way they hover behind her, it's easy to see the dragon as an extension of her magic, of herself.

She may be my mate, but she is also the power of generations before her, the vessel of her family's witch-craft, the magic of ten thousand souls. It was much easier to underestimate her when the embodiment of that magic was a slight fox. Now, it is all I can do to keep my knees from quaking.

"Clasp hands," Eloise commands.

Jaqual's eyes swivel to lock on the dragon's enormous teeth, and I almost laugh at the drain of color from his face and the way his throat bobs with a nervous swallow. Even the eye of his amulet seems to widen. But Jaqual does as Eloise instructs. His hand in mine is cold and clammy. Eloise's is firm, competent. She slides her grip up both our arms so that we are holding each other's fore-arms rather than palm and fingers.

Only now do I feel how intimate this magical triangle

is. My mind wanders to Morpheus, to the power triune he used to bolster his power. This is not the same, but maybe not so different either. A tingle travels the length of my spine as purple ribbons of pure power wind around our arms and constrict like hungry snakes.

Eloise is chanting now. Some old Earthly language—Latin or Greek—the words fly too fast for me to register their meaning. Over us, the moonlit sky lightens, but not with a coming dawn. We are glowing. Our connection radiates like a small sun.

"Ah!" My inner forearms burn. Jaqual cries out too. The scent of burning flesh rises between us.

Eloise doesn't seem to notice. Her eyes have gone entirely white, as white as the scales of the dragon behind her. The purple ribbons constrict until I think the magic might break my bones. The light we're putting off turns red as blood.

"Ellllooooiiiissseee!" I howl.

She can't hear me. A storm is brewing around her, her hair floating in a sourceless wind, an icy coil of magic that cuts through the pain. She rises off the ground, floating like a mermaid in a sea of dark power. We are the only things tethering her to the earth.

The eye on Jaqual's necklace is gone, the stone simply white glass now. He's screaming into the wind, but I can't hear his voice over the roar.

My bones are breaking. I cannot shift. I cannot escape.

And then the ribbons cut through my skin, sink into my flesh, and disappear. The tightness, the pain, fades. Eloise lowers, feet touching the grass, eyes fluttering as her blank expression becomes hers again, her green irises returning, bright as ever. She releases her grasp on both of us, and her face eases into a smile. "It's done," she says, as if she's just finished the dishes. She hasn't even broken a sweat.

I, on the other hand, am trembling, as is Jaqual. I hold out my arms, palms facing upward, opening and closing my hands as the burning abates, and what I see etched into my skin makes my breath catch.

On the arm that clasped Eloise's, her key sigil, the one from her back that resembles a dragon, is etched into my flesh, the swirls and archaic symbols that make up its form seeming to pulse and spin as I study it. On my other arm, three lines signifying waves lap across my skin. The Rivertoad symbol. His sigil and hers.

Jaqual holds out trembling arms and stares at the dragon sigil on his arm. His other one is bare, likely because he already sports the river sigil somewhere else on his body. Eloise only has the river sigil, confirming my theory.

On his chest, I see the eye return, blinking sleepily.

"The war room is waiting, gentlemen," Eloise says. "We have a battle to wage."

29

THE TIES THAT BIND

ELOISE

All the way back to Aendor, Damien is silent. After performing the spell, I smudged the wagon as promised, while Jaqual retrieved his commander, Maximus, and assigned him to go with us to make plans for a coordinated attack. I suppose it's natural that there's some tension. After the energy we expended participating in the spell, I think nothing of it, chalking it up to extreme fatigue.

Until we reach the training grounds safely and introduce Max to Percy, who promises to give him a tour of the facilities and bring him up to speed with our plans. Damien grabs my arm and excuses us from evening exercises, citing my overuse of magic as justification. When I try to protest, he whispers, "We need to speak, alone."

I follow him to our apartment, where the bed beckons me. "You're right. I'm exhausted."

"You bound me," he says, the words coming out like a hiss.

I cast a confused glance at him. "What?"

"You bound me. Just like the Gowdies." He thrusts out both arms, showing me the tattoos.

Slowly, I register what he's referring to. "No, Damien. This is nothing like the Gowdies. I told you my spell would make it so that you and Jaqual must follow the terms of our agreement. We made an unbreakable vow tonight. The Gowdies enslaved you. I simply marked you with your promise. The mark will fade once you fulfill your side of the agreement."

"Oh? Because these sigils look a hell of a lot like the one the Gowdies burned into my chest."

"I don't understand why you're upset," I say. "You agreed to this. You wanted this. This agreement is our only option and our only chance to take back Stygarde."

The edges of his form flake away into shadow. His eyes turn diamond clear and hard as ice. "You sure as hell did not explain to me that this agreement would mark me with two binding sigils."

"I didn't know," I say honestly. "I asked Phantom for a spell to get the job done. I didn't ask about the… specifics."

He shakes his head. "I wouldn't have agreed to be bound like this." He holds out his arms. "You're the key. Break the bonds."

My mouth pops open. "No!"

"You can't do it?"

In fact, I can. But breaking his bond would also break Jaqual's. "We need their help."

His breath is coming in huffs, and he turns his head

away when I approach and lay my hand on his chest. His heart is pounding so fast I'm worried it will explode.

"Come lie down," I urge him.

He shakes his head.

"Why?" I ask. "I think you're having a panic attack."

"I prefer to exercise my free will, little dragon, or does my wearing your sigil take that away too?"

I draw my hand back as if he's burned me, and then I get it. "You're *afraid* to be bound again. The Gowdies enslaved you with a sigil, then Valeska enslaved you with sunlight, and now you think I've done the same. But this isn't a *binding* spell—it's a vow, Damien. It will disappear forever as soon as the election is over. You're still free. You simply have to keep your promise."

His eyes narrow, and he shows me the sigils again. "Where is my sigil, Eloise? Neither you nor Jaqual carries my mark, yet I carry both of yours."

Fuck. This part, I was hoping not to have to broach with him so soon. "You are a shade. You don't have magic, so you don't have your own sigil. Jaqual is part witch, and so am I. The bargain is only enforceable through me."

"What are you saying?"

"I'm saying that Jaqual must comply, or he dies. I must comply, or I die. If you don't comply…"

"You die," he says.

I nod. "If I die and you live, then my sigil will fade, but Jaqual's will not…until you hold the election. However, his magic isn't strong enough to enforce the agreement. If you defy him, his sigil will remain, but he will have no power over you."

He slides his lower jaw to one side. "But if you live, you'll enforce the agreement."

"My magic will. Why does that bother you? You knew that was the purpose of the spell!" I'm angry now. He agreed to this. He wanted this. We needed this.

"You should have warned me, Eloise. After everything, you should have known I would not want a sigil in my skin."

I can't stand the look in his eyes, like I've betrayed him. I try to close the space between us, but he holds up his hand. "No. You stay here. Rest. I need to think things through."

"Damien—"

He shakes his head. I hold open my arms, desperately hopeful he'll return to my embrace, but he siphons under the door before I can say another word. I can't recall Damien ever denying me physical contact, and I wonder if he left simply to prove he can, that he's still free, not beholden to me or anyone else.

Only after he's gone do I face what I've done in full measure. I freed Damien from the curse that kept him from his home world. I removed the skull and crossbones tattoo on his chest, which was the Gowdie sigil, with magic I didn't even understand yet. In doing so, I promised Damien, not in words but by actions, that he would be free. That my love was the equivalent of freedom. I enforced that promise when I freed him from Valeska.

It was an unspoken promise, a promise he returned when he freed me from King Entrydal. Placing those sigils on his skin would feel the same to him as him returning me to Entrydal's rack. Even if it were temporary, even if it meant we might win the war, if I were chained there, even if no one beat me, the act of being cuffed to that arch, the act of being in that room, it would break me. It would open a wound that might never fully close again.

Damien agreed to the bargain. He didn't agree to the sigil. And I have made a terrible mistake. Not only has my mate agreed to a magical vow with a group he never fully trusted, but he's made himself vulnerable to my magic for the good of his people. He trusts *me*, and I overstepped that trust. And although what I've done isn't permanent, and the damage I delivered wasn't intentional, those sigils, to him, are betrayal.

Heart heavy, I sink into a hot bath and then climb into the big, cozy bed, thinking only that I desperately miss being tangled with Damien in that tiny maiden's wagon.

THE MOON HAS SET, AND IT'S THE MIDDLE OF THE NIGHT when I hear Damien come in. One boot and then the other thumps on the floor as if from a great height. His sword rattles in its scabbard. He smells of sweat and an acrid, musky sweetness I can't put my finger on.

"I know you can't be drunk, so I assume you want to talk?" I ask, sitting up in bed.

"On the contrary, little bird," he slurs. "As I've explained to you before, I can't get drunk from your alcohol, but I can feel the effects of smoking feoral root."

"What's feoral root?"

He sighs. "Kind of mushroom." He sits down on the edge of the bed.

"Well, they reek. How about a bath?"

"Tired," he says.

"I'll do the work." I climb from the bed and take his

hand, leading him into the bathroom, where I start the water and add some soap powder to make bubbles. He won't look at me, but at least he's not fleeing the room. He leans heavily against the wall.

"I've been thinking about what you said."

"Oh?" He blinks slowly.

"You're right. You and I have both survived the most horrific traumas, Damien. I realized earlier tonight that those sigils on your arms are as heavy to you as the manacles would be if you returned me to Entrydal's rack."

He growls low and turns his face away. "I would never do such a thing."

"No, you wouldn't."

He says nothing, just stares at me, his expression impassive. I turn off the water and rise, reaching for him. But he pulls away. "I wasn't sure you'd survive that night." His stare turns vacant, and I wonder if it's the feoral root or the memory that distracts him from the now. "There was so much blood. You'd lost more than any human could and still survive, and although you were a vampire, you were just so fragile. I took you to Catarina. Dimhollow was the only place that was safe, and she the only one who could heal you.

"At first, she wouldn't let you in. Nevina had made you swallow that fucking tracker. Catarina gave you a potion to rid you of it. We had to give it to you, or you couldn't enter the village. But I could see it in the witch's eyes that she knew it might kill you. You drank it and then vomited more blood, blood you didn't have to lose. You did survive, but only barely. I would never put you through any of that again, Eloise. Never."

"Damien, I'm sorry. I should have dug deeper into the

spell and warned you of the effects. I should have known that this would be traumatic for you. That it would hurt you. I didn't mean to hurt you. I'm sorry." I reach out, and he almost falls over avoiding my touch. "I'm sorry," I squeak, my voice breaking this time and my eyes filling with tears. "I'll break the bond if you want me to. We will lose the alliance and Jaqual will never trust us again, but I'll do it if you ask me to."

His eyes are so cold. So impersonal. He's looking at me, but he might as well be staring at the wall. I have broken something between us. Unintentional as it may have been, the damage is done.

I fall on my knees and sob into my hands. "I'm sorry."

Minutes pass, me weeping in silence. Has he left the room? I'm afraid to look.

The relief is immediate when his warm, rough hand lands on my shoulder. His other one peels my hands from my face. For a long while, we just stare at each other, eye to eye, nose to nose. My tears fall, and I can't even wipe them away with his hold on my wrists.

He glances at my sigil in his skin and then at Jaqual's. Abruptly, he releases me and says simply, "I forgive you."

30
ABSENCE

DAMIEN

I wake to a throbbing temple and a cold bed. It's late. Eloise is gone. My obstinately greedy fingers search the other side of the bed for her, as if she might be hiding in the rumpled blankets, but come up empty. My body stiffens. Perhaps I was too hard on her. I'd consented to the spell after all.

I rise from the bed and dress for the day, ready to search the compound for her and do whatever I must to make things right between us. But I find a note in the bathroom and realize I needn't have worried.

Damien,

Went to meet Tempest for breakfast. I'll tell Thane you needed to sleep off the effects of the spell. Find me when you get a break from training. I love you.

Eloise

I lift the piece of paper to my nose and inhale her

scent. Not a hint of bitterness or anger lingers on the page. Only the soft, heady scent of her.

We are as we always have been.

I will never find it comfortable to fight with Eloise. My entire role as her mate is to please her. This isn't our first argument and likely won't be our last, but it's getting easier. Every disagreement is a lesson in her. After all this time, I am still learning how to function with half of my heart disconnected from my body, with another soul existing in the ripple of my own, staying in sync even when we disagree, like planets in rotation around the same sun. We are different; we are one. I would rather fight a thousand battles with her than enjoy a single peaceful day without her.

I find her in the war room, with Tempest at her side.

"Damien, how nice of you to join us," Tempest says. "I hope you've fully recovered from the side effects of your endeavors yesterday." The way she says *endeavors* gives me the impression that she knows that mine included smoking a field's worth of feoral root.

"Happy to say I'm as good as new."

I make my way to Eloise's side and lean down to whisper in her ear. "Are we okay?"

She smiles softly up at me. "I am, if you are."

"I am."

Her hand finds mine and squeezes. "Good, because Tempest and I have received some new information from our spies that could greatly improve our odds."

I examine the table in front of us. More pegs have been added to the typography in the Borderlands to represent our soldiers. Our troops now form an "H" with Blackspire and Entrydal's troops to the north and the silver coats of New Stygarde to the south.

I slant a smile in my mate's direction. "Don't keep me in suspense."

Tempest smooths her dark chestnut hair and gestures toward the troops that represent New Stygarde. "As we've discussed in the past, a major barrier to us winning this war is that New Stygarde's troops are augmented with Stygarde's own children. The young ones are drugged with Nevina's magic to fight to the death on her behalf. We've never been able to capture one of these children because the same magic that keeps them under her control can also be used to track them."

"It's the same reason that I can't develop a cure for the spell that controls them. In the time it would take me to study one of the children, the silver coats could find me five times over. Even using my magic, I can't guarantee I could conceal my work. Elven magic is foreign to me. A concealment charm might not be enough. It's very possible I'd be too busy running from advancing troops to actually find the antidote to Nevina's poison."

Tempest walks around the side of the table, to the portion of the map depicting Stygarde Castle. "Last night, our spies returned with some very interesting information, however. It seems that New Stygarde is keeping the children in a cluster of tents on the grounds."

"Tents?" I growl. "Why?"

"Simple," Tempest says. "As they've grown their army, they've run out of room inside the castle and the servants' quarters. The grounds are the only place they have space. And since the children are nothing but her pawns, they get the most meager accommodations. Our spies tell us they are fed only basic blood stew and water."

I shake my head. "Keeping them alive to die fighting," I say through my teeth.

"That's the general consensus," Tempest says. "But it does afford us an opportunity."

"If we could develop an antidote, we could efficiently administer it because they are all in the same place. We could break the spell over the children," Eloise says.

"You just said you couldn't develop an antidote because there's no way to study the children."

"Lucky for us, we don't need to develop our own. The witches of Dimhollow already have one," Eloise says.

"What do you mean?" I ask. How could they have the cure? They've been hiding at the top of their mountain for generations.

"It was you who reminded me of it," Eloise says. "When you told me about the night you rescued me from Entrydal, you reminded me that Catarina had detected Nevina's tracker in me. I was so out of it that night, I'd completely forgotten the incident. Catarina gave me a potion that caused me to expel the tracker."

"Yes. A potion that almost killed you."

"Almost, but it didn't. And I was a vampire then, much more fragile than I am now. If I can survive it, so can the shade children. All we have to do is get Catarina to share her potion with us."

I have to admit, it's a good idea. "So, have you sent a raven to Catarina, asking her for it?"

Tempest releases a heavy sigh. "I haven't been able to send a raven anywhere for months. Aendor is teeming with silver coats. They're like cockroaches around the

Palace of Dawn. Our aviary is in the top spire, but they watch it now around the clock. It will do us no good if they shoot our bird out of the air."

"Besides, I need to talk to Catarina to learn the nature of the antidote and how best to administer it to the victims. I have to go to Dimhollow. If I ride Phantom, I can get there in a fraction of the time it would take me to go by rabble beast or on foot, and I won't have to face the guardians." Eloise says. The two of them look almost smug about this idea, as if it's the solution to all our problems.

"This idea of yours has promise, but what evidence do you have that Dimhollow isn't protected from the sky as well as the ground, little bird? Do you remember the dome the mages cast over the village to protect it from New Stygarde?"

She waves her hand. "If I run into trouble, Phantom will help me navigate it. The moment Catarina sees it's me, she'll let me through."

"Maybe. *If* she sees it's you. But without a raven, she won't know you're coming."

She shakes her head. "We have to risk it."

My head throbs. What a conversation to have when I'm hungover and desperately in need of blood. Thoughts, like restless birds, cyclone in my head as I massage my temples. *Restless birds.* "Why don't you take the raven with you and release it before you reach Dimhollow?"

"Oh," Tempest says. "That's a wickedly good idea. Eloise, you can make yourself and Phantom invisible. Why not the raven?"

"Can we retrieve it from the aviary?" she asks.

"Absolutely. The problem is not reaching the bird in

the Palace of Dawn, it's in releasing it when the palace is under constant observation. But we can retrieve it through our system of tunnels."

Eloise takes a deep breath. "Then it's settled. I will carry the raven with me and release it over Wickham Wood, where it's safe. It's the perfect solution."

I cross my arms and groan at her maddening level of optimism. "Say you make it into Dimhollow and you are lucky enough to woo Catarina into helping you manufacture buckets of this antidote. How do you intend to get the children to drink it? We don't have an exact count, but it must be thousands."

Eloise glances at Tempest and back at me, her lashes blinking like anxious butterflies trying to escape a hurricane. "We thought one of us...most likely me because I can leverage Phantom...could sneak into the children's camp and add it to their drinking water."

Goddess, she has a death wish. "Little dragon, the likelihood of Nevina not having magical trip wires set up to capture you is zero. She is waiting for you to take that bait. There is no way you will successfully gain access to those children. Even before we left the castle, she was setting up a magical boundary for protection. No way will you slip past her guards and her magic. That's a suicide mission."

Tempest laughs. "I told her the same thing."

Eloise huffs and turns back to the map. "Then who? She can't have accounted for everyone. You turn into shadows. Her spell has to be specific, or every swaying branch would set it off. What we need is someone Nevina won't expect. Someone she won't be looking for."

"One of the Rivertoads?" Tempest suggests.

Eloise shakes her head. "Jaqual told me that he's gone rounds with Brahm. They can no longer pass as friends of the crown." We all groan in unison. "Maybe one of the vampires?"

"They can't shift into shadow. They would be at a distinct disadvantage sneaking into the camp and be more susceptible to capture."

"What we need is a ghost. Someone neither Brahm nor Nevina views as a threat," Eloise says.

"I know of no such person who would act on our behalf," I say. "It might be time to investigate Plan B."

We all stare at the map. This late in the game, all the pieces are on the table. I doubt there's a single person in Tenebris who wouldn't risk everything for this cause, but sacrificing a single player will only hurt us.

The door opens, and we all look up as Cassius slips silently into the room. "I was hoping to find you here. Damien, we need your help leading exercises."

Every eye locks on the former umbrae. Eloise darts a glance between Cassius and me. "I think we found our ghost."

3I

DIMHOLLOW

Disguised again as a peasant girl, I navigate the streets of Aendor toward Wickham Wood. Tempest wasn't exaggerating. The port city is lousy with silver coats. Too many. Most of them look bored, as if they've been asked to guard a single square foot of sand and now don't know what to do with themselves. I slip past them easily, the raven and its cage concealed in my rucksack.

When I'm far from the crowded streets, I cloak myself in invisibility and run for the border. Phantom meets me halfway, and I climb aboard their back, securing the cage to the saddle. The message that I'm coming is already attached to the raven's leg. We rise into the night, and I release the bird, then follow it toward Dimhollow.

When I last left the village, the witches were at a lower altitude, although the bitter cold told a different story. Mount Perilon is enchanted to always be winter, a determined frigidity that is the same at every elevation. As I close in on the new location of the village, snow stings my skin like a million needles, and I shiver violently in Phantom's saddle.

Even we are cold, they say into my head. *And we are dead.*

Do we have a warming spell to counteract the chill? I ask.

Won't work against this magic.

I drop our invisibility and pray to the goddess that Catarina received our message. She must have, because I see her run from her thatched-roof house and wave her arms frantically at me, holding out her hands in the universal stop signal. I pull back on Phantom and circle in place.

"What do you think she's trying to tell us?" I scream into the icy wind.

Phantom rumbles their discomfort. *I don't know, darling, but I'd prefer a warm fire to whatever this is we're doing.*

Catarina appears to be doing an interpretive dance, flapping her arms and spinning while her mouth moves in a rhythm as if she's singing a song I can't hear. Then she pulls back a hand and throws an invisible ball toward me. A violet ripple casts across the sky, and I gasp. Thousands of icicles point in an arch above the village, daggers promising to shred anything that attacks from the sky.

"How do I get in?" I cry, although there is no way Catarina can hear me over the roar of the wind. Still, she gestures to my left. A break in the icicles forms a perfect, unguarded circle.

Can we fit? I ask Phantom.

Lie flat against me, darling. One way or another, we're going in.

Phantom circles, tucks in their wings, and we dive. "Ahh!" I howl when an icicle clips their wing, a bloody slash appearing on my arm a second before the front of my calf slices open. Phantom roars. I can feel the witch's death magic squirming through my body like icy worms. We careen toward the space between the cottages, Phantom's injured wing refusing to properly hold their weight.

Until Catarina extends a hand and we slow to a stop, dropping the last foot or so to the frozen earth.

"All the gods and souls in the Darklands, what do you think you're doing, Eloise Hymir? You're lucky you didn't get yourself killed!"

"Need to talk to you," I whimper.

"So I gather!" Catarina yells. "I was attempting to tell you to wait until I could make the entry point bigger. What did you think I was doing down here?"

"Interpretive dance?" I give a pained smile, and my teeth chatter.

She gives me a confused and pointed look. "*What?* And when did you find the dragon? Oh, never mind. It can wait. If we don't get the antidote into you, I'll be feeding you by spoon for the next three days. Come to my cottage. Bring your—" she circles her hand toward Phantom, whose injured wing now appears skinless and skeletal "—familiar. I'll fix them too."

I limp after her toward the cottage that is quite obviously all hers, designed of twisted wood and tangled ivy, windows cloudy as baked sugar and perfumed by the scent of herbal tea that wafts from beneath the front door. Phantom disappears as I cross the threshold, still with me, but in their incorporeal state, and I rush to flop onto the sofa.

Catarina comes to me with a pot of tea and an herbal compress. "Next time, send the raven in advance! I barely had time to keep you from shredding yourself."

My brow furrows. I love Catarina, but hot, violent anger boils up in me, and I need to release some steam. "Why didn't you know I was coming? Why didn't you suspect we'd need your help at some point? Do you even know what's happening down there?" I point a hand in the direction I think is downhill. "People are dying, Catarina. Children have been drugged into slavery. The resistance is running out of time. Entire villages are being burned to the ground. You sit up here in your bubble of ice, and you think you are playing the role of some neutral good, some benevolent observer. When really, all you are is a community that did nothing, does nothing, but waits until fate catches up with you. And then, whatever happens, however many die and whatever atrocities occur, you'll blame the stars, even as your own witches burn. Why haven't you asked what your witches could do to help in this war? Why haven't you checked in on the health and well-being of people who are supposed to be your friends? Why haven't you provided us a key to enter your castle of ice when we need you? You offer your hand, Catarina, and then yank it away when we need it most. So don't chide me for bulldozing through your icicle dome. Take accountability for making it so that I had to!"

Catarina's eyebrows have lifted into her tangle of dark, graying hair. Her lips twitch, but she does not speak. She threads her fingers together in front of her hips. "This may be a good time to mention that the healing tea I've given you has a side effect of irritability and verity. I think we can assume it's working."

I glance down at the gash in my arm to find it fully healed, as is the one on my calf. "So it is," I say flatly.

She pours me another cup, and her voice is soft as she asks, "Should I also treat your dragon?"

I reach down my bond with Phantom and check on them. "No. They're healed. We are connected. When you healed me, you healed them."

She wipes her hands on her apron. "How convenient."

The heat from the fire finally seems to reach my skin, and I shift uneasily on her sofa. "About what I said before… Perhaps I was a bit harsh."

"No, you have a point, Eloise. The witches of Dimhollow have long been observers, but it is by necessity, not by intention. We are not warriors. Our magic is predominantly defensive by nature. We are small in number and limited in usefulness when it comes to war. However, we still protect and house the former queen and princess of Stygarde, and I assure you, after you've won this war, we will aid in healing those who survive."

I twirl a finger in my hair. "So…if there were a way you could help, you would? You just believe there's nothing you can do?"

"Exactly," she says with some measure of relief.

Check and mate. "I'm glad to hear that, because there is something you can do."

"I don't understand."

"The night Damien rescued me from Entrydal, you gave me an antidote that made me expel Nevina's tracker. I need that antidote. We need to use it to free Stygarde's children from Nevina's enchantment."

"Who said I gave you an antidote?" Catarina tilts her head inquisitively.

"Damien. He said you had a crystal that could detect the tracker inside me, a tracker I'd ingested weeks before, and that you'd given me a potion that made me expel it."

"Yes, I have a potion that will make the children expel what magic is in their bodies, but what if the spell she's given them isn't a gumdrop like she fed you, but a tea fully absorbed into their blood? What if the magic has fused to their bones?"

"Can elven magic do that?"

She scoffs. "That and worse. When I gave you that elixir, I wasn't sure you'd survive it. I risked it because none of us would have survived if I hadn't. Without knowing the nature of the spell on the children, we risk injuring or even killing a great number of them."

I cringe at the idea of intentionally hurting Stygarde's children, but my mind keeps turning over her story, considering how she relieved me of Nevina's tracker, the risk she took on me. "You gave me the antidote because you knew that even though there was a chance I might die, if you didn't give it to me, we would all die."

"Yes."

"If we don't cure those children, Catarina, they will all die, some of them at the hands of the people who love them most. Nevina will wield them as a weapon. The scenario is the same. It's dangerous but necessary."

She shakes her head. "I can't guarantee it will work if—"

"Life has no guarantees. All of us live in that knowledge every day. What we have now is hope. You and this potion are the best hope for saving these children and saving Tenebris."

Quiet brews between us in the warm, herbal-scented

air, her fingers tangling in her apron. "The herbs necessary for the potion are few and difficult to obtain. How many children are compromised?"

"Hundreds."

She scoffs and waves a hand in the air as if the mere idea she could make enough is ridiculous. "We believe they are being kept together in tents on Stygarde grounds. A brave shade has agreed to sneak it in and add it to the drinking water."

Her eyes narrow. "If that's the case, you'll need it to be concentrated to achieve the correct dosage."

I nod. "Enough for ten large barrels of drinking water. Teach me what I need to do. I'll help you make it."

Her eyes drift toward the ceiling. "It's possible in theory, but I'll have to check my stores."

"I'm not going anywhere." I release a deep sigh as she hustles out the door, leaving me to watch the crackling fire.

When the door opens again a second later, it's not Catarina standing there. Damien's sister, Karyl, lets herself in, a wide grin spreading across her face. "Eloise!"

32
SLUDGE

Karyl embraces me in a tight squeeze. "I heard you were here! Mother and I have been so worried. We haven't heard from you or Damien in ages. She's coming, by the way. Catarina needed her help carrying something up from the cellar."

"I've missed you too. Unfortunately, things are far worse than before, and I'm here on a very important mission." I fill her in on the highlights of everything that's happened, including why we haven't been able to send a raven.

"I knew we should have sent one to you. Catarina can see through her raven's eyes, and I kept asking her to send it to find you. She insisted that you were traveling and that she checked in on you in her dreams. She swore you were fine."

I shrug. "Honestly, she was right, until recently."

Karyl's shiny black braid swings over her shoulder.

"I've had enough of this hiding. If the rebels are on the brink of war, we need to join the fight."

"You are no warrior," Queen Nyxadora says from the door, the handle of a large basket of herbs slung over her elbow. When she sees me, she spreads her arms, and I accept her enveloping hug.

"I don't have to be a warrior to help, Mother! I'm sure there's plenty I can do."

Catarina walks in the door, breaking up the start of what could be a major squabble. "Do you have enough?" I ask her.

"I think so. Without knowing exactly how much water is in each barrel, there's no way to to be certain of the final concentration. I'll make as much elixir as I can with the ingredients I have on hand. The rest will be up to you. Although, I'll warn you again that this is expulsion magic, and if the spell can't be expelled, it could kill the children."

"Kill the children?" Nyx drops the basket in her hands and gives me an incredulous look.

"It's a risk we have to take. They are bound." I explain it all again for her to hear.

The former queen studies me for a long, hard moment. "How did you free my son from his bonds?"

I can follow what she's getting at. I am the key. In theory, I should be able to break the charm on the children. "I threw the object binding him into the fire. I don't know exactly how I did it, but I think it had to do with my house being possessed by my ancestors."

Catarina scratches a mole on her chin that's sprouted a gray hair. "It's a wise question, Nyxadora. She is the key."

"I am," I confirm. "But my ancestors say that it would take them days to develop a potion that would serve as an antidote. None of my ancestors understands elf magic. We'd need to capture and study an infected child, and there's no way to do that without putting the resistance at risk."

The witch lights up from within, her eyes sparkling. "I understand elf magic, Eloise. We don't need the child. We only need to augment my recipe with your blood."

I reach out to Phantom and have a quick conversation with Aunt Sara. "How do we know it will work without testing it on a child?"

Catarina takes a deep breath. "We don't, my dear. It's all theory. But I believe it will have a better chance of success than my expulsion elixir alone. Come, let's get started." She leads the way into the kitchen and doles out roots, branches, and berries to each of us, instructing us how to prepare the ingredients for the cauldron. I'm handed a thick branch and a knife to peel the bark. Katarina mashes berries with a mortar and pestle, and Nyx dices a hefty bunch of herbs with all the dexterity of a woman who has spent most of her life not having to cook for herself.

"Now that you're healed and we have a plan, tell me, when did you find the dragon, Eloise?" Catarina asks.

Nyx and Karyl stop what they're doing and stare at me.

"You have a dragon?" Karyl asks.

Catarina laughs. "She rode it here. Magnificent beast."

"I thought it was dead," Nyx says.

"I found her bones in the bowels of Mount Damocles. She is dead." I concentrate on my bark, finishing one branch and grabbing the next.

"You resurrected the dead?" Catarina says in a grave tone edged with accusation.

"No," I say, meeting her eyes. "The dragon's flesh is inhabited by my ancestors and is the anchor to my spirit magic. I did not raise a dead dragon. I possessed a dragon body with the anchor of my power."

The spoon in Catarina's hands slips from her fingers and clatters to the floor. She curses and tosses it into the sink, grabbing another one.

"Can we go back to the part where my sister-in-law rode a dragon here? Where is this dragon?" Karyl asks, eyes wide.

"Phantom comes when I beckon them."

Nyx is chopping again, slowly, methodically. "This is good news. The dragon is powerful. Surely, Stygarde will be ours again. We will avenge Malek's murder."

I wince. She has no idea the agreement we made with Jaqual. Am I to be the one to tell her? Hell no. Certainly, she should hear from her own son that their ruling line might end with this battle. "The only thing that will help us win this battle is more warriors," I say carefully. "We need every free citizen to fight as they've never fought before. We are outnumbered, and they have magic we don't have. They also have our children."

Caterina adds my bark to the pot and stirs. "When I interpreted Mother's prophecy, I thought you were the dragon. This changes everything."

"Funny thing about prophecies, everyone seems to have their own interpretation. Did you know that the king of the Rivertoads is half witch and has a gift for seeing the future?"

Her hand keeps stirring, but Catarina's expression

goes slack, her complexion paling by a few degrees until her lips turn ashen.

"Can I see the dragon?" Karyl asks, staring absently into her berries. "Alive or not, will it let me touch it? Does it obey you? Does it have to eat?"

I turn to her and smile my first genuine smile since arriving here. Karyl is the most unguarded person in this room, and right now, there is nothing I appreciate more than her authentic nature. "They think for themselves because my ancestors embody the flesh, and yes, they eat and drink. Physically, they are a living, breathing dragon, just with some magical qualities. They can even blow fire."

"The dragon breathes fire!" Karyl's eyes pop. "Holy gods above and below, Eloise, you are truly a powerful witch."

"When we're done here, I'll introduce you to Phantom," I promise.

"Oh well, you'll have to. I imagine we'll be riding together back to Aendor."

I stop what I'm doing. Did I hear her correctly?

Nyxadora's knife clangs against her cutting board. "What are you talking about?"

"I'm returning with Eloise to help the rebellion. You heard what she said. They need every citizen to fight. That includes us."

"You are no warrior, Karyl," Nyx snaps.

"I'm no witch either, but here we are." She holds up her mortar and pestle. "I am a royal, a princess of Stygarde. That title is a privilege but also a responsibility. My people count on me to fight for them, and I won't stay up here in this snow-covered tower while they get slaughtered on my behalf."

Nyxadora turns to me. "Eloise, tell her she will be of no help to you. She can't even hold a sword. She'll only be in the way."

"I'll tell her no such thing," I say. "This rebellion is composed of more than just warriors, and we can use all the help we can get. In fact..." *Here goes nothing.* "...even the Rivertoads have joined us."

"What?" Agitation heats Nyxadora's voice, and if I didn't know better, I'd guess she could breathe fire as well.

"We have formed an alliance with the Rivertoads. They will be fighting on our behalf."

"Including their king?" Catarina asks softly.

"Yes. Their king has committed the full force of his people to helping us take back Stygarde."

"You can't trust them, Eloise. They will turn on you as swiftly as they will take their next breath," Nyx warns.

I shake my head. "He won't. He can't. We are bound." I slide up my sleeve and show her the Rivertoad mark. But while Nyx simply sneers in disgust, Catarina actually gasps. She drops the spoon into the cauldron and races from the room.

"You will not join the rebellion," Nyx says to Karyl through her teeth as I chase Catarina from the kitchen. I find her in her bedroom, with one hand on her heart and the other gripping the edge of a chest of drawers.

"Why does my bond with the Rivertoad king upset you, Catarina?"

Her breathing is labored, and her eyes are closed. "What did he look like?"

"Who? Jaqual?"

"Jaqual? That's his name?"

"Yes. Uh, he's tall, ropy, tight curls of black hair, violet eyes, a constant smirk."

She laughs, her own lips tugging into a smile.

"Why? How do you know Jaqual, Catarina? Why are you so interested?"

She cups a hand over her mouth, her eyes filling with tears. "I had no idea he survived."

"What are you talking about?"

One quivering hand grabs the handle of one of the drawers and pulls it open. She retrieves a red box and places it on her bed. From inside, she pulls out a tiny blanket—a baby blanket—a lock of dark hair tied with a ribbon, and an amulet with a blinking eye. An amulet that is the exact twin of the one I saw on Jaqual.

"I am interested, Eloise, because I believe Jaqual is my son."

"Your son?"

"When I was a young woman, I met a handsome and charming Rivertoad who had wandered into our village. He had the heart of an explorer, you see. Wanted to meet the famous witches of Dimhollow. Of course, he was almost killed by the guardians. I nursed him back to health, and he lived with us for some time. We fell in love, and I became with child. I planned to return with him to live among his people. Impure relationships are not accepted in Dimhollow. Witches marry witches. Always, you understand. A non-magical child would never survive among our kind."

"I didn't know."

"Aurora was supportive of my leaving. I was young, but old enough to make my own decisions. But when we descended the mountain, we were attacked by elven hunters. They killed Wolfram and took every quill we had saved for our journey. In time, I learned the truth. Wolfram had come to Dimhollow not as an explorer, but to escape his debts.

"Devastated, I lived alone in Wickham Wood until the baby came. I left the infant with his people. Left him with the sister amulet to this one." She holds up the eye between her fingers. "Yes, I am interested to learn that my son has risen to be king of the Rivertoads, and I fear for his life now that he's helping you fight this war."

I release a huff of frustration. "Is that what you think? Do you think the Rivertoads are helping *me*?"

"Isn't that what you said? The bond you formed, he'll be fighting for the rebellion." She juts her chin in the direction of my arm.

"He's fighting for *his* people, Catarina. Haven't you been listening to me at all? King Entrydal wants all of it for the elves. All of it. Every wagon. Every home. Entire towns have been burned. Jaqual is a wise man. He saw New Stygarde coming for his people and decided to join us. He's not fighting *for* us. He's fighting *with* us. We are fighting together against a common foe. And make no mistake, if we lose, Entrydal and New Stygarde will come for you next. You are already at the peak of Mount Perilon. The only way to go is down. You and your people need to consider what you will do if we fail."

Lip curling, she shoves the blanket and the hair back into the box, along with the amulet. "How my mother got it wrong. The prophecy said you would defend us. We are not warriors. Our presence on the battlefield will end only in our deaths."

I lift my chin and say the words that have been

burning in my chest. I don't enjoy confronting her. I owe her my life. But leaving this unsaid could compromise her future. "You can make a difference," I say. "The vampires helping us are vulnerable to sunlight magic. They won't be as effective as shades against New Stygarde unless you help shield them. If all you have is defensive magic, then we will use those defenses. Your defense will become a key part of our defensive strategy. We can win this war with your help. But you have to decide to engage. You have to stop gazing at the stars and studying prophecy and start fighting. Because at some point, your decision not to stand against Entrydal and Nevina is a decision to be complicit in their rule."

Silence wages between us until Karyl appears in the doorway. "Mother and I have finished preparing the ingredients. What should we do next?"

Catarina straightens. "We add them to the cauldron and brew for twelve hours."

Karyl turns on her toes and strides for the kitchen. I move to follow her, but Catarina grabs my arm. "I will try. I will speak to the other elders, and I will recommend action."

A bloom of hope expands in my chest, and I pull her into my arms, my eyes stinging with unshed tears. "Thank you. It's the right thing to do."

Clumsily, Catarina moves past me toward the kitchen, supporting herself on the doorframe in an all too human way. "The problem with doing what is right, Eloise, is that the ones who give the most rarely have the opportunity to enjoy the outcome of their sacrifice."

33
ATTACK

DAMIEN

I wake in my room above Maiden's Voyage, shadows vibrating around me in a way that makes my hair stand on end. Quickly, I dress in my uniform, sheathing Dawnbreaker on my back. Some deep mating instinct has me calling for Eloise, but she's gone. As far as I know, she's still in Dimhollow. I rush into the hall to find a dark cloud coalescing there. Thane.

"Code red! We've been breached!" he yells. "Prepare for battle. Incursion in sector one."

I twist into shadow and surf across the darkness to the area where my men sleep. They're awake but in various states of readiness. "This is not a drill," I announce. "We're under attack. Operation Aendor is in motion!"

We've been planning this for weeks. The first step in waging this war is securing Aendor—and my men, as former umbrae, are responsible for leading that offensive.

Warbill takes up his sword. "Finally, we get to kill someone."

I chuckle. "Just make sure you stab the ones in the silver coats." As for us, we're all wearing black. A decision made of necessity rather than aesthetics. Black is the cheapest and most available color of material in Tenebris. I wait as my team arms themselves with Stygian blades of every length and type.

We may not have many advantages in this war, but thanks to Seamus, we have plenty of weapons.

In minutes, we are ready, and we surf to sector one, the long passageway that leads to the hidden door behind the Maiden's Voyage. Now, the wisdom of this compound's design shines through. As the silver coats charge us, arrows fly from the slits in the walls, the Stygian steel slicing through heart and head.

At the front of my men, I make eye contact with the shade leader attacking us. It's only a moment, but I see fear in his eyes. His lips move, and the shades among them shadoweave toward us as the elves in the group draw their sunlight swords.

We collide in a frenzy of tangling shadows.

The clash of steel-on-steel rings through the long room. With a grunt, I lop off the head one of our adversaries, then shift and stab, shift and slice. They do the same. It's a dance, in and out of existence, listening to the hum of the shadows and trying our best to foresee where our attackers will move next.

"Sunny-side up!" Warbill yells as he splits an elf down the middle, then dodges out of the way of the sunlight sword as it clatters to the ground and goes dim.

One of our men screams, but I don't have the privilege

of time or space to see who it is. I focus on the warrior in front of me. The elf behind him. The strain on my muscles under Dawnbreaker's weight. The hot, tacky grip of the hilt of my blood-drenched blade.

We are halfway to the exit and nowhere near halfway done with this battle.

Silver coats pour in through the narrow doorway at the end of the hall. Arrows fly. Bodies pile up.

"For Victus!" Warbill howls, slicing a man in half. He, at least, seems to be enjoying himself. But then, the man has decades of pent-up rage between his ears.

I signal to the men behind me, and they drop into formation, their shadows shooting across the room at ankle level. Blood spews as a dozen more soldiers topple off their feet. The shades will heal, but the elves are down. We behead one after another.

But we can't save Levitous, who falls to an elf's bright blade when he tries to form from shadow on the other end of the room. I channel my anger, driving through the next man and the next. Kick, slice, punch. Shadow out. Spin. Under. Stab.

The death goes on and on until we are finally through the door that opens to the Maiden's Voyage…and find another legion of silver coats waiting for us.

ELOISE

KARYL DOESN'T MAKE A SOUND AS WE SOAR DOWN THE SIDE of the mountain toward Aendor. I'm not even sure that she's breathing. She's strapped into Phantom's saddle, her arms hugging the large bag of vials full of elixir from Dimhollow. The tension of her fingers on the burlap is enough to turn her knuckles white. A rucksack of her belongings is sandwiched between us.

"We're almost there!" I assure her.

Strands of her hair whip against my face as she nods, eyes wide in the wind. Neither of us is wearing goggles, and I have to squint to see anything. Shades are not fragile like humans, but even they know the sandpaper feel of a wind-burned eyeball.

This is the first time I've had an adult ride with me. So far, I haven't felt my magic weaken under her weight, but I'm not taking any chances. I'm leveraging my dragon's wings for as long as possible, using physics rather than magic to carry us down the mountain.

Karyl's accompaniment was nonnegotiable. She told me in no uncertain terms that she was coming with me once we finished the potion, and even her queen mother could not hold her back. Karyl had her bag packed and was on Phantom before I could tell her no. I don't know where she found the bravery to do such a thing, but she was and is as determined as I have ever seen another woman. I hope that her example spurs Catarina and the other witches into action.

As for Nyx, she can stay in her ivory tower of snow, but she might soon find herself lonely there.

"Eloise!" Karyl cries, turning her head to look at me and pointing toward the red sand beach of Aendor that has just come into view. At first, all I notice is a blur of white and black, like an army of ants marching in the snow. Then I realize what I'm seeing. Silver coats!

"Hold on tight!" I scream into the wind, driving Phantom toward the clashing armies.

"What?" She makes a sound like a yip as my stomach drops out and Phantom banks over the water.

"You know what to do!" I say to Phantom.

"No! What do I do?" Karyl cries.

"Not you, Karyl! I'm talking to the dragon." Phantom's chest glows fiery orange, and we are enveloped in heat as we swoop in closer and closer. The silver coats don't see us coming until we're almost upon them, and by then, it's too late. Fire pours like a stream of molten magma from Phantom's mouth, incinerating dozens of silver coats into a pile of ash in seconds. Only when they run out of fire do we pull up and bank for another shot.

"*Dragon!*" The silver coats point at us and scream, their elf counterparts sheathing their swords and grabbing their bows and arrows off their backs.

"Oh hell!"

"What now?" Karyl asks.

"I wasn't worried about the swords, but those arrows can kill us. Hold on tight."

Phantom blows fire just as the elves release their arrows. We barrel-roll, maneuvering toward the ocean, dodging right and left until Karyl's face is as green as the seaweed in the water. Somehow, we make it through and take out another hundred or so silver coats. The rebels cheer.

Something hot and wet slithers over my lips, and I wipe my nose with the back of my hand. Blood. I'm overusing my magic. "I have to land!" I say to her.

"Land? Where?" All around us, waves crest. Nothing but water. And a tall ship, straight ahead. I land Phantom on deck, thanking the goddess when it appears the ship is abandoned. I help Karyl off.

"What are you doing?" She points at the men on the shore. "The battle is still raging. We need to help them."

I wipe my bleeding nose again as Phantom lies down and disappears. Karyl gasps.

"Phantom is an embodiment of my magic. We would have fallen out of the sky if we'd stayed engaged. There's nothing more I can do."

We both walk to the railing and stare at the battle happening on shore. "I think I see more black than white," Karyl says hopefully.

I hope she's right. From this distance, all I see is gray. We lean against the railing as we watch, we wait, and we pray.

34

BATTLE AT THE BORDERLANDS

DAMIEN

In every battle, there's a turning point, a moment in time when the tide shifts so abruptly that you feel swept forward, a cresting wave crashing down on your enemies. We may have started this war equally matched with the silver coats, but everything changes when Phantom roars down from the sky and divides their ranks. We waste no time taking advantage of the turn in our favor. Our unit quickly eradicates those separated from their brethren and distracted by the stream of fire. We charge through the flames in our shadow forms and attack, slicing through the enemy while they gawk at the sky.

Phantom's second pass weakens their forces even more. We push through to the other side of the port. As my team finishes off the enemy, Undaku orders his men to secure the border, and Prandle's unit scours every building, rounding up any prisoners for the stockade. There aren't many.

Cassius's team puts out the fires that the silver coats started. Most of the port city has been burned, and the Maiden's Voyage is a wreck of smashed tables and chairs. But there is nothing here that can't be rebuilt. The only thing we've truly lost are the warriors who have died, and we won't know how many until we sift through the bodies. Tempest arrives with a team of healers and starts methodically working through the fallen men, while others begin the process of burying the remains of our enemies.

Somewhere, I hear a trumpet blare. Thane lights the cressets in front of the Palace of Dawn. Window by window, the candelabras inside are flare to life, and then a raven flies from the aviary to share the news with our allies.

We have taken back Aendor.

But all I care about is Eloise. I search the skies but can't find Phantom. The last I saw her and the dragon, they were flying over the ocean. Did one of the sunlight arrows hit them? Did they crash into the sea? Is she out there somewhere, even now, struggling to take her next breath?

I race for the shore, my heart pounding and my eyes wild with the need to find her. But I needn't have worried. She is there, rowing a dingy to shore with my sister Karyl at the bow.

"What the actual fuck?" I mutter.

Eloise is covered in blood as if she's had a major nosebleed, and Karyl is carrying a rucksack and an enormous bag that clinks when she moves.

"Brother!" she says, dropping the bags on the red sand and running to me with her arms spread wide.

"What are you doing here?" I growl.

"I came to help." She releases me, and I turn to Eloise.

"Are you hurt?" I ask, alarmed at the blood.

"No. Just overused my magic. Phantom is resting." She eyes me up and down. "You?"

I look down at myself. There isn't a single inch of me that's not stained red. "Fine. I was cut a few times, but the wounds have already healed. We won Aendor. Undaku is securing the border."

She flies into my arms, and I swing her around.

"Prince Damien, Lord Thane would like to see you in the war room right away," a boy in a black uniform says.

I set Eloise down but don't break eye contact. "Tell them I'll be right there."

"You should go. I'll help Karyl find a room," she says.

"You brought my sister to the war zone," I say, unable to keep the accusation from my voice.

She raises her brows at me. "Your sister chose to help us fight, and she helped complete the potion we need."

Karyl reaches into the burlap bag and holds up a vial of black sludge.

"You convinced Catarina to make it for you?" I say, utterly amazed.

"I did." She flutters her eyelashes at me like she isn't the absolute badass who just busted through enemy troops.

I take her hand in mine. "Come. Bring the sludge."

"Where are you taking me?"

"To the war room. Your presence is just as important

as mine." I grab the boy's arm as I pass. "Find my sister a room." I point at Karyl.

"Yes, sir," the boy says and scurries to Karyl's side.

Hand in hand with my mate, I make my way through the bodies, through the smoke, into the compound and to the war room.

Eloise has her chin lifted, her eyes straight ahead. She's trying not to see the bodies.

"There are no children among the dead," I whisper. "Not that I can see anyway."

The revelation doesn't comfort her the way I'd hoped. "I remember Tempest telling me that Aendor sent them only young men, and few at that. I suspect Nevina thought this would be an easy win. She's keeping her secret weapon—the children—for another battle. Saving them for the Borderlands and Zephrine to shield their forces from any who oppose them."

"But you have the potion."

She nods. "Thank the goddess. We have time to free them."

Thane is shouting orders when we reach the war room. "Use the west wing for anyone recovering, and I want those prisoners guarded around the clock. Damien! Thank the goddess. What's our next move?"

I take my spot at the head of the table, feeling as if I'm standing in my father's shoes and not liking the fit at all. No matter that I was raised a prince and fought my share of battles. No matter that I learned military strategy at my father's knee. I am not my father, and leading this offensive is as foreign to me as Eloise's Earth once was. Nothing prepares you to lead your people toward possible death. Nothing prepares you to face a situation where your own death is not only probable but worth it.

I turn to one of the envoys waiting near the door. "Send word to Seamus through the shadow network. It's time. Deploy the mountain dweller forces to defend the northwest. Careful, though. New Stygarde will be listening. It will be enough to say the weather is turning. Understand?" The boy bows and leaves the room.

"Thane's and Percy's teams will stay here to hold Aendor and prepare to advance on New Stygarde when the time comes." I look toward Eloise. "Wait for the code 'the dragon roars.' Do not trust the shadows without that code."

"Yes, sir," Percy calls and races from the room. Thane bows and moves out after him.

"Cassius, deploy your vampires to the Borderlands."

"Is that wise, Damien? My vampires are the most susceptible to sunlight. You'll have them sandwiched between Entrydal's and New Stygarde's forces." I have to hand it to him. There is no accusation in Cassius's tone. His voice is a smooth, unemotional challenge to my logic, not my authority.

"Unfortunately, that vulnerability will occur anywhere. Maximus—" I turn to the Rivertoad general "— you will deploy your men across the Borderlands as well. Together, you're a sizable force. Try to use your numbers to your strategic advantage by shielding Cassius's men from elven magic. Vampires have no heartbeat. Even the hunters won't hear them coming."

Maximus bows and leaves the room. Cassius's eyes meet mine, and I send him a message down the shadows that we have the antidote and I will need his help delivering it. He places a hand over his heart and nods.

"All other teams, including mine, will deploy to Zephrine to take back the west villages." I look to Lord Prandle, and he gives me an affirming nod.

But Lord Undaku scowls. "You'd have shades from the Borderlands fight in the west?"

"Yes, Undaku. The west has suffered the ravages of starvation for far longer than the Borderlands. The troops from the region don't have the strength to hold it alone. I need you to help secure Zephrine the same way we did Aendor."

His scowl twists skeptically. "I think you foresee New Stygarde using our children against us and have sent the vampires to the Borderlands because they are from another world, and therefore are not related to anyone on the battlefield. The vampires have no bond with anyone the queen enchants to attack us. They will not hesitate to kill our babies to take back the castle."

Bile churns in my gut as I face him, knowing that every word is true. "Eloise has a plan to help the children using her magic. It's not foolproof, but we are going to try. However, you are right. If we fail, I wish to spare you that indignity." Our eyes meet and hold. The hatred in Undaku is not for me. It's for New Stygarde, for the loss they've endured. While the west starved, the Borderlands attempted to sacrifice the few to save the many. But there was no right answer. The west lost a few children to starvation. The Borderlands lost more to New Stygarde. "It is sound strategy," I say softly.

His throat bobs on a hard swallow, and then he bows, removing himself from the room.

"Tempest."

"Yes, Damien?" She is the last in the room, other than Eloise. "I am giving you charge to direct your healers. Send at least one medical unit to every region."

"A wise choice." She raises her fist in the air. "For Stygarde."

I echo the motion. "For Stygarde."

When the door swings shut, Eloise and I are the only ones left in the war room. I turn to her and grip her shoulders, knowing that my next command will be the most difficult to execute. But being a true leader requires sacrifice. The same sacrifice I've asked Undaku to make for Stygarde.

"Cassius is waiting for you," I tell her. "It will take two days for our troops to fully deploy as I've ordered. Weapons and tents will have to go by rabble beast. Food and medical, too. New Stygarde will be distracted with readying their response. You have an opening. Use Phantom. Are they strong enough?"

Her eyes go vacant for a moment, and then she nods. "Yes. They are recovered."

"Good. Take Cassius and the antidote. Be careful not to trip Nevina's wards. I will meet you in southern Zephrine as soon as I am able."

She searches my face, clutching the bag containing the potion vials to her chest. "I won't let you down."

"The only way you could ever let me down is if you leave me, Eloise. Promise me you will keep yourself safe and return to me. Use Cassius. He is the finest shade warrior I have ever known."

She nods enthusiastically. "I will return."

"Good. Because there is nowhere on Tenebris or Earth

or in the bowels of the underworld that I won't come for you, Eloise. If you are captured or die, I will let this world burn, drop all my responsibilities to my people and to my kingdom to come for you. Do you understand? It is all I can do to give you my blessing. You don't want the blood that will be shed on your hands if you don't return to me."

Her hand rises to cup my cheek, and I swear I see fire burning in her eyes. "I will return to you, Damien. If there is nothing but magic holding my bones together, I will return."

Our lips join in a deep, bruising kiss that is far too short, and then she is gone and I am left staring at the map, at the figures that represent my world and its people, as the room grows painfully, ominously quiet. I give myself time to draw one deep breath, and then I move.

35
HELL IS FOR CHILDREN

ELOISE

"There." Cassius points to a valley of thick forest freckled with towers of red, stony rock formations. From the air, it reminds me of Arizona, if the red rocks were surrounded by the redwoods of California. Nothing exactly like this exists on Earth, although somehow it feels familiar.

I land Phantom on one of the stone towers, and the dragon crawls us down to the forest floor. "Where are we?" I ask.

"They call this Souviette Valley, the place for remembering," Cassius says.

"What's to remember?"

He points at the side of the rock we just climbed down. The stone is carved in waves as if by the wind or water, although that seems impossible, considering the trees here are enormous and loaded with leafy branches.

Any wind or water strong enough to carve stone would also be strong enough to take down the trees.

"A long time ago, this valley flooded. A river to the north marks the edge of the valley. It overflowed, the force of it tearing the forest out by the root. The flood carved these rock formations."

"It would take thousands of years for water to carve this deep."

He nods. "Yes, it did. It was before my time. Before my father's time."

I look up at the stars through the dense branches, trying to wrap my mind around that.

"When the floods came and knocked down all those trees, the nuts, seeds, and pollen of the plants sank to the bottom, and the decomposing bits of all that greenery built up over time into a rich, wet mash. Eventually, the rains stopped and the water ebbed, and when the trees and shrubs sprouted again from the silt, they grew back stronger and faster than ever."

I try to picture the tree in front of me as a sapling and can't. It's as wide as I am tall.

"The people of the west considered rebuilding homes here. But the elders of the community found an orchid among these trees that they hadn't seen in a lifetime, one they'd thought was extinct. They use that orchid to make a tea that helps ailing mothers give birth. Few medicines can treat shades. To be sure, there are only a few occasions we need medicine, especially if we are well-fed. But childbirth is rare and dangerous for our kind."

"Oh. I didn't know."

"The orchid was viewed as a gift from the goddess. And it was decided that this forest, this ancient place of remembering, would be left intact, in case it held other memories, other gifts. Other than being used for recreation, it remains untouched and protected."

"It's beautiful," I say. "How does it help us get the children back?"

He takes the bag of vials from Phantom's saddle and slips his arms through the loops so that he's wearing it as a backpack. "This valley is the closest western point to the castle. Remote and difficult to navigate. Nevina wouldn't bother enchanting this area to detect your presence. Even if she tried, the flora here would likely break down her spell in a matter of days. But we're not far from the castle. I should be able to slip in without detection."

He gestures for me to follow him, and I do. But when he breaks into shadow, I'm left behind. He forms again at my side. "Why aren't you following?"

"I can't shift at will."

Cassius curls his lip. "Still?"

"I have shifted before when I'm upset or afraid, but I can't just do it willy-nilly. I've been practicing, but I've never been able to pull myself apart."

"That poses a challenge." He studies me for a beat. "Our plan, then, is this. You will walk in that direction—" he points east "—until you reach the edge of the forest. Wait there. I'll meet you when it's done."

I agree, and he twists into shadow and is gone. Technically, I could ride Phantom to the edge of the forest, but I opt to walk. This valley is the most peaceful place I've ever been. Even the cliffs beside Harcourt Manor harbored the sound of the rushing river below, but here, there is only the occasional skittering animal and the flutter of insect wings.

What will happen to the children once the curse is lifted, darling? Phantom asks in my grandmother's voice, the words sounding abnormally loud inside my head.

We don't know, I answer honestly. *Cassius is going to add the antidote to their water supply. We have no idea when the children will drink it. And once they do, they will likely be incapacitated for some time. The potion might make them ill. I slept for days after I took it. But this version is different. Catarina used my blood as a catalyst. We hope it will ease the transition. But if it doesn't, well...*

You want to cure them, but you also want to make sure they can't be used in battle.

If they're sick enough, they can't be infected again. Nevina will have to heal them before she can drug them, and she'll be too busy fighting the resistance to have time for that.

But what if the children don't survive?

I rub the sudden ache in my chest and fight back the tears that threaten to fall every time I think of this. *We have to have faith that they will. It's in Thanesia's hands. There's no other way.*

I reach the edge of the forest soon after and look out across the distance at the tents, which, according to our spies, have been set up to house the children. The conditions are deplorable. Even at a distance, I can smell the foul odor of unwashed bodies, fecal matter, and rotting food. My stomach clenches.

I can hear what you're thinking, Eloise, and it's a bad idea. You told Damien you wouldn't take unnecessary risks.

I try to push the thought out of my head, but no child deserves to live like this. *I can't stand the thought of them suffering there. I am the key. Perhaps I could break the ward without detection, draw the symbol inside the tent, and pass the children into the Borderlands where they could be reunited with their parents.*

While they suffer the effects of the detox? While their parents are under attack by the enemy?

I could pass them to Harcourt through the underworld. Ren is a nurse. She could care for them.

And then you'd be drained and unable to defend Damien when he needs you.

I could...

Wait for Cassius as planned. If you get yourself captured, darling, before the war has even begun, you will jeopardize more lives than your own.

But I can't just leave them there! They're only children. What kind of monster leaves children in a filthy tent to suffer? A hot tear cuts down my cheek.

You would allow your selfish need to relieve your guilt and sadness in this moment to ultimately damn every one of those children to death?

I turn to stare at Phantom, who has manifested beside me, their dragon head glistening white in the moonlight. *You are the queen of Tenebris, Eloise. All of Tenebris. Not just these children. If you are captured now, you will undercut all of Damien's hard-won plans. You will put the lives of every warrior you brought here from Earth, including Cassius, in more danger. And you will distract Damien from becoming the king he was meant to be. And for what?*

I scoff and gesture toward the tents. *To save the children.*

You won't save the children. You'll simply prolong their suffering.

The truth of Phantom's words lands like an arrow in

my heart. *What type of person knows what's going on in those tents and does nothing?*

No one is here to judge you, Eloise, but we believe a person who is strong enough to delay immediate gratification in order to achieve a greater reward is a conscientious adult.

That's not—

You said it yourself. Curing the children but leaving them is the logical thing to do, the thing that will save the most lives. They are shades. They will most likely survive. But it is just as important that you survive to fight another day. Choose the battles that are most worth winning, my dear. Fight not only to save these children today but to change this world so they will grow up in a place where they will never have to face this again.

I hate it when you're right. I swipe my tears from my cheeks.

Oh darling, if you only knew how much we don't want to be right. We—generations of your ancestors—only want you to see that the darkness inside you is neither good nor bad. Your heart, now made of shadows, wants to do what's right. You want to bring goodness to this place where light kills, where innocence is weaponized, where beauty masks a venomous poison. This is not Earth, and you are no longer human. We only wish for you to see that the shadow in you is your power. Your ability to wait can change this world. Like a spider in her web, wait and strike when it matters most. We wish not to be right but to help you understand that the only way to do good in this world is to lead and to rule, and that means putting your faith in the people who fight for you.

Phantom fades from existence beside me. How I ruminate on their words, so similar to George's. My shadow heart. I am a product of everything I've experienced, my parents' deaths, my grandmother's illness, Tony's hands choking the life out of me, Damien's love, Maeve's friend-ship, facing the goddess, becoming a shade. Through all of it, I've made choices. Not always the right ones. Not always the smart ones. What's important is that I've learned. I've become stronger.

What's important is making peace with the darkness. But Phantom is wrong about one thing. I am no spider. I am a dragon. And I wait not in a web, but in the skies. And when I choose to unleash my fire, even the gods will fear me.

I turn my attention back to the tent and wait for Cassius. Hours pass. I try to reach out to him down the web of shadows. But I still can't do it. So I do the only thing I can do—I wait and have faith.

Finally, shadows bleed from under the canvas and twist like a dark mist toward the forest. He forms with nimble grace and hands me the empty bag.

"What took you so long?" I whisper.

Cassius begins walking away from the camp, gesturing for me to follow, putting distance between us and our enemies. "At first, I did as you suggested. I added the vials to their water sources. It took some time. Hundreds of children are piled up in those tents, Eloise. The youngest are hardly old enough to shift. And Brahm and Nevina have barely fed or cared for them. It is a horrific sight."

I stop walking. Was I wrong before? Should I have done more?

"But then I saw Gregoris," he continues.

"Gregoris?"

"Lady Odette's nephew."

I remember the boy now. He'd been cleaning my room, his eyes glazed from whatever drug Nevina used to control him. Lady Odette used the planning of the Harvest Festival as an excuse to visit him.

"He appears young," Cassius says. "I am sure that is why Odette handed him over as a sacrifice—but the man is a trained warrior, an adult. I decided to give him the antidote directly."

"What? But the concentration—"

"I diluted it first, as you instructed, but I poured it into Gregoris's mouth, and then I prayed." He brings his fists together under his chin and grins at me, a smile that beams like its own star. "It worked, Eloise! And not violently, as you were expecting. His eyes cleared, and there he was, once a ghost of a man, and now, restored. I covered his mouth because when he saw where he was, he almost screamed. A natural reaction to the horror. But I used the shadows to explain to him what was happening. That's what took me so long. He is going to help the others. He is going to lead them."

"Lead them where?" I look back toward the tent. "Should we guide them out?"

He grabs my elbow and pulls me deeper into the woods. "No. Lead them into battle. They will pretend to be fighting for Nevina and Brahm. They will follow New Stygarde into battle and then turn on them when the time is right."

A prickly weight expands in my stomach. "No. It's too dangerous, Cassius. We have to get them to safety. We can't have children fighting on our behalf."

We've reached the stone we landed on, and he stops to turn to me. "You've always had such a good heart, and your worry for those children is in keeping with your character. Trust me when I say to you that Gregoris and every child in those tents will benefit from being part of the fight."

"How can you—"

"Every child in those tents needs to feel they've had their revenge. After everything, they will never heal if they're left feeling helpless. This way, they are part of the rebellion. They have agency in their own salvation. Don't take that from them."

Phantom appears beside us, and Cassius climbs on first. I draw a deep breath into my lungs, hating this. It goes against my every instinct to leave the children. But they are shades, and Cassius knows his kind. What he says makes sense. And most importantly, there is no other choice that won't endanger the rebellion.

I climb behind Cassius, and we take to the skies, mission accomplished.

36

THE DARKNESS WE UNLEASH

DAMIEN

We attack at dawn. The moment the silver light breaks the horizon, we execute the plan to take back Zephrine. This war, this battle, is not like those in Eloise's Earth history where armies line up and face off against each other, head-to-head. We arrive quietly, infiltrate the cities that have already been burned and pillaged by silver coats, and attack.

It's easy at first. The New Stygarde soldiers occupying what remains of these villages have become fat and lazy, feasting like kings while villagers starve at their mercy. We are an unwanted morning surprise. I order my men to end them in their beds.

But the ones we miss, the soldiers who wake before they meet our swords, have a surprise for us as well.

"Sunlight weapons!" Warbill screams as he takes out a shade at my side. "All of them! Not just the elves."

I dodge an ax that sizzles as it grazes my skin. With a

whirl and slice, I send the soldier's head rolling. Warbill and I are back-to-back, surrounded by silver coats, the shine from their weapons heating our faces. "Could be worse," I say to Warbill. "Could be arrows."

"Hilarious, my king. Any idea how we get out of this?" he grunts as he meets our attackers, blade against blade.

"I have a theory." I coax the shadows to lasso a soldier's ankle and yank them off-balance. He shifts into shadow to avoid the fall, and his sunlight weapon clatters to the ground. When he forms again, I slice him in half. "They can't maintain their hold on their sunlight weapon when they shift!" I yell to him. "Elven magic is incompatible with the shadow network."

"Bravo, my king."

Warbill catches on right away with no further explanation. Working together, we force each soldier into their shadow form. These shades have spent their entire lives using the shadows and have only recently been handed sunlight weapons. It's child's play to trigger their instincts to shift. Once they're disarmed, we end them. We do it again and again and again.

But just as I begin to think we have the upper hand, the archers arrive—this time, a unit of elves from the north. Our new strategy won't work on this set.

"Take cover," I call to my unit. We break into shadow and hide behind or under anything we can find when a deluge of arrows carves bright as lightning through the dark sky, a cascade of deadly shooting stars. One of our men has nowhere to hide. There's no place left. Too many of us. Not enough cover. He stares at the incoming arrows, face going impassive as if he's accepted the inevitable.

I want to scream. But then I see something on the horizon.

Eloise is there.

With a roar that rattles my bones, her dragon sends a stream of fire that engulfs the arching arrows. When the dragon fire stops, the arrows keep coming, but our man is showered by nothing but ash.

"Huzzah, dragon!" Warbill cheers as he surfs the darkness across the space between us and our enemies, a sword in each hand. He lops the heads off two elves before I've even reached the battle.

My muscles ache, but I keep going. Bodies fall to my right, to my left. I crawl over them, shake the blood from my hands. By the time we can say with certainty that we've secured the area, I'm panting hard and splattered with the blood of my enemies. Eloise circles the sky above me twice, then swoops down to land in the center of the village.

Voices ring out, my men crowding around her, slapping her hands, and crying out their thanks. I have to push through them to get to my mate.

"Please tell me that most of that isn't yours," she says to me. I look down at my bloodstained skin.

"Not enough of it to matter," I confirm.

"Good, because I'm afraid the fight isn't over."

My brow sinks. "Where?"

"The mountain dwellers are struggling to take back the area around Bolvet. Their units aren't as strong. Many have fallen."

"Is the way to Bolvet clear?" I have to look over Phantom's head to see her sitting on the beast's back, her spine as straight as a queen on her throne. One of our men staggers backward when Phantom's head comes around. My mate is intimidating, a force of nature if ever there was one. The corner of my mouth tugs up in pride,

"It's clear. Undaku's team has it secured."

"I'm on my way." I send word down the shadows, and my men return to me one by one, columns of darkness coalescing into a band of umbrae.

"Do you have a report from the Borderlands?"

"Going now," she says. She turns the dragon between us and, with a flap of Phantom's wings, she's gone.

"Bolvet," Warbill says, sounding exhausted.

"Can you make it, old man?"

"For my village? If they succeed in killing me, they will have to grind my bones to keep my corpse from fighting."

We both share a dark laugh and then shadoweave north, praying we reach the mountain dwellers in time.

ELOISE

"This doesn't make sense. Where are all the elves?" I ask Phantom. We're soaring above the northwestern Borderlands. Fields of stubble where red wheat once grew before the harvest stretch out like scattered hay beneath us.

We saw plenty of elves, darling. Fried their arrows to ash.

"Not enough, though. Entrydal has a vast army of soldiers and hunters. I don't think we ever got a proper count, but most of the bodies today were shades. Why are they holding back?"

Phantom doesn't answer. My ancestors are powerful practitioners of magic, but they aren't warriors. In fact, my great-grandfather, Henry Harcourt, was a photographer, well-known for his pacifism. When Henry went on safari to shoot animals, it was with his camera. The only things that came home with him were photographs. He was a spiritualist and obsessed with the occult, but he was no killer. Phantom will fight for me. They will protect me. But they can't advise me on military strategy.

But I am the dragon.

I am the first generation with dragon blood in my veins. A dragon has sharp teeth and claws for a reason. They know how to kill. My magic may be powered by the past, but I am forging my own future. And today, I have to trust myself. My gut tells me something is off.

My intuition proves accurate when the battle for the Borderlands comes into view. The elves are here. Thousands of soldiers with sunlight weapons are lined up at the border with Willowgulch, and our forces are losing. A hard lump forms in my throat when I see piles of ash that I know were once vampires. Cassius? No. He is there, fighting side by side with the Rivertoads, covered in blood.

Where should we start, my darling? Phantom asks me.

There. I point to the place where a line of elves behind the battling throng raises their arrows. *We cut them off. Cut their forces in half. Take out their archers and distract the others to give our forces a foothold. Are you strong enough?*

Never stronger, they say as their chest fills with fire. We swoop down. I concentrate my magic and intention, focus, take aim, and then release our fire. Heat singes my cheeks as the stream incinerates the entire line of archers as if they were ants under a magnifying glass. The other soldiers scatter, some running right into enemy hands.

Vampires rush them and tear out their throats. A River-toad squadron cheers as they lop off pale heads and use their shadows to stab the elves through their hearts.

Phantom gains elevation and banks hard, turning for another pass. *You're tired,* I say to them. *We should find a place to rest.*

We have one more in us, darling. Shall we go again?

One more, then, I say. Quickly, I scan the battlefield. The elves have a section of carts near the back. It's hard to see what they're filled with from this height, but they might be cages for prisoners or supplies of weapons. Yes, I see the glow of something inside. Sunlight. *There. The cages. We take those out.*

The dragon rumbles with laughter. *Brilliant. Hold on tight. We're going in hot.*

Their chest fills again with lethal fire, and we swoop down to release it. The elves who aren't caught in the blast scatter, wide-eyed and screaming. We power through their supplies. Carts of weapons go up in flames. Cages incinerate. We drive toward an odd-looking contraption. A weapon of some kind. What is that?

Phantom's fire reaches our target just as a bowling-ball-sized star flies into their side. I have only a millisecond to register that we've been hit. Less time to feel myself fall. I fall through fire and smoke and bones.

Everything becomes nothing.

37

THE MONSTER IN ME

ELOISE

I wake in all too familiar chains, bound to an all too familiar arch, in an all too familiar room. I've been hanging a long time by the look of my wrists and the low burn of the candles in the candelabra. I reach out for Phantom and sense my power a long, long way away. The Darklands. My stomach drops when I realize what this means.

My dragon, my anchor, is dead.

"At last. She wakes." Adril Entrydal steps into the room, his heavy footsteps thumping on the stone floor. When he comes into view, he is dressed entirely in silver velvet, a crown atop his head, smooth gold with pointed sections as if the molten metal were dripped into shape. "You should know we killed your dragon, and my troops are even now slaughtering your meager rebellion." He presses one finger into the underside of my chin and lifts my head. "I'd tell you that I was going to torture you for military secrets, but what would be the point? I don't need them, and I've never liked playing pretend. I am going to torture you for the fun of it, Eloise Hymir. I am going to break you." He leans forward until his thin red lips and pale blue eyes are too close to my face. I hold my breath to keep from breathing the same air as him. "I am going to make you my pet. And when I own this world, you will lap milk from my boots and thank me for it."

As before, I don't react. I don't give him the satisfaction of seeing me panic, although inside, my heart is pounding in my chest, a wild animal thrashing the bars of its cage. My blood is ice.

He scoffs and backs away, strides to the back of the room, those stupid boots clapping the floor as he goes, making me aware of every place he walks in the room. I hear chains, the rattle of bamboo rods. What will he choose? What will he torture me with?

I squeeze my eyes closed, instinctively seeking the safety of the darkness, but my mind won't quiet. Memories of the last time I was in this rack come back to me with jagged, painful clarity. For now, I'm fully dressed in the black uniform of the resistance. Last time, he unzipped my dress so that he could watch my skin break under the force of his blows. I wonder if he'll cut the shirt off me this time. I wonder if my blood will splatter the walls again along with that silver coat of his. I wonder—

I open my eyes and remember Nathanial stepping into the room from Paragon, remember him feeding me his blood, blood that runs through my veins.

Remember that *I* am the dragon.

Phantom isn't *dead*; they are simply waiting for me to pull them back from the underworld into whatever pile of bones I choose. I have nothing to grieve. Not yet. Slowly, I remember who I am.

I am Eloise Hymir, Queen of Stygarde.

My heart is made of darkness.

Entrydal will never own me.

No one can cage a shadow.

I was chosen by the goddess herself, and I will save my people.

I glance at my wrists, noting he didn't use sunlight cuffs. Why would he? He believes I'm a vampire. Nothing more. My mouth curls into a smile, and I feel it, that cool chaos in my veins. Not my blood—my inner shadows. They coil and stretch with my fear, just as they did the night I visited Bad Witches' Club and Grog dangled me by my collar. Only this time, I whisper to them, coax them. I am the pied piper of shadows, thrumming a soundless string, vibrating at a frequency that calls them to me.

His heavy footsteps round me again, and he sets down the rod he's chosen to remove his velvet jacket, leaving him bare-chested in nothing but breeches and boots. And still, he wears that fucking crown.

"You're giggling, pet. Could it be that you're going to enjoy this as much as I will?"

He lifts the rod to taunt me with it, then licks it with the flat of his tongue. Gross.

"I'm laughing because I can hear your heart."

His brow furrows. "Why would that make you laugh?"

My mouth spreads into a wide, Mad Hatter grin. "Because it reminds me I have one too."

He tips his head, and I know the second he hears my heartbeat, knows I am a shade, knows that the cuffs won't hold me. His eyes pop, and he raises the rod. But he's too late. I break into shadow and jet across the room. Jet right through the center of his chest.

When I form again, I'm holding his heart in a monstrous, beastly hand. My hand, complete with razor-sharp talons and skin as black as leather. The weight on my back shifts, and I see a wing arch over my shoulder. The swish of something behind me is a tail like Damien's. My tail. I stare down at Entrydal's dead body from an advantaged height and know that I've assumed my battle form for the first time.

The heart in my palm is a repulsive, oily shade of dark blue. It gives one last beat in my palm, releasing a spout of blood that splats across the floor. I removed it fast enough, it still believes it's alive. The notion makes me laugh.

Once I would have hesitated, held fast to an ideal of what was morally right or wrong. Once I chose to save an evil man's life to preserve my virtue. And in the end, it changed nothing. In the end, it was him or me.

Never again.

I crush the heart in my fist.

"I am no pet," I growl at Entrydal's corpse. I hurl the goop that remains in my hand at the wall. On my way out, I sweep his crown off his head and place the bloody ring of gold on my own. "And now, this is mine."

I consider taking his entire head with me, but when I bust through the door and into the hall, I see that the crown will send the message. A servant spots it and runs like a rabbit.

I run too. Straight toward the battlefield. I only hope I'm not too late.

DAMIEN

Eloise isn't here. I slice and kick and use my wings to claw at my enemy, my body a tower of pain and fatigue. I was told she fell. Before we ever reached the battle in the Borderlands, before we ever saw how bad the tide of this war had turned, we saw the bones. Phantom's bones. Strewn across the battlefield along with the bones of so many others. The grass is wet with blood. Our forces have been pushed back from New Stygarde into Willowgulch territory, where we are sandwiched between sunlight weapons and fresh shade forces that, unlike us, are not weary from battle.

Eloise isn't here, and I fear she is dead or worse.

We are at the end of this war, and I face the stark possibility that we will not stand the victor.

"Remember your promise!" Jaqual yells to me, his blades swinging furiously in the taloned hands of his battle form. "If I die, you are still bound."

I snort. "What makes you think that I will live?" We are surrounded by the enemy, six deep on either side.

"You Hymirs are like wagon bugs. You can survive anything." His head sinks below a throng of silver coats, and I lose sight of him.

"Wagon bug. Can survive anything but the bottom of a shoe." I grunt, shadoweave, and stab the elf ahead of me, but I take a sunlight blow across the stomach from his brethren. I collapse, where my blood mixes with that of my enemies and soaks into the ground. Opening the shadow channels, I send a message to our troops in Aendor—*the dragon roars.*

We can't wait any longer. We need all the help we can get.

As soldiers march over me, assuming I'm dead, I stare into the star-filled sky and see a raven staring down at me. Hovering. Watching. Somewhere in the distance, a horn blows. And then I truly believe I have died because I see something I never thought I would see.

Brooms.

Robes flowing behind them.

The glow of magic.

Witches.

Catarina. At least a dozen others.

No one sees them but me. They float in silently, their brooms connecting to form a pentagram. Their wands circling in complex patterns. At first, I can't glean what they're doing. I lose sight of them on occasion as warriors step on top of and over me in battle.

Then I feel it.

Wind.

It drives straight down and blows out, sending a plume of grit gusting over me.

Screams. Shouts. A flash of silver as an elf flies over me like an oversized kite. I have to squint and turn my head to breathe. When I do, I find two violet eyes squinting back at me. Jaqual is still alive, flattened to the blood-stained earth, clinging to it to keep from blowing away.

It goes on and on until all the silver is gone and I see nothing but red and black around me.

At once, the wind stops. Boots land between us. Catarina reaches down and lifts Jaqual's head, offering him her canteen. Their eyes meet, and something passes between them, wordless but palpable. Jaqual's eyes widen.

Catarina releases him and moves to my side, lifting my head and bringing the same canteen to my lips. I cough at the putrid flavor but manage to keep it down. She releases my head.

"Hurry up and heal," she says through her teeth. "We won't be able to hold them for long."

38
UNEXPECTED GUEST

ELOISE

My transition from my battle form to my corps or human-like form is quick but effortless. I don't even notice I'm changing at first, not until the crown on my head suddenly feels heavy and cumbersome. I make my way through the halls of Blackspire with my daggers in my hands, ready to kill. Only, I never have to use them. Anyone who sees me, runs.

Good. I will need all my energy to pull Phantom's bones together and return my ancestors to the dragon's flesh. The faster my anchor is in place again, the faster I can rejoin the battle. I turn the corner into the grand foyer.

Rays of purple light rise up in front of me, blocking my path. Instinctively, I lift an arm to shield my eyes. What is this magic? An elf trap?

"Eloise?"

I blink rapidly, allowing my vision to adjust. My best

friend stands in the center of the key symbol, looking wildly determined as she takes in the details of the room. Dressed in black pants and a long-sleeved black shirt, she could easily fit in with the rebels. "Maeve!" I sheathe my daggers and rush into her arms.

"I came to help. I told you I would. Why didn't you call me?"

"Been busy," I say, gesturing at the blood on my clothes and the crown on my head. "How did you know to come?"

"The clock in the parlor started ticking again. When you didn't show up in the attic, I suspected it was time. The vial of blood you left me worked like a charm, by the way. Brought me straight to you."

"Thanks for using it." I try to hand her one of my daggers, but she doesn't take it. "Beyond that door is a war zone. It's a mess out there. Goddess, I need to find Damien." A pang of worry zings through me, and I pray he's okay.

"Dead bodies?" Maeve wrinkles her nose.

I nod solemnly. "Fields soaked with blood. And I have no magic. I'm going to have to pull my dragon back together before I can anchor." I hold out the dagger again. "Take this. For protection."

She sniffs. "I don't need that, Eloise. You keep it. I wouldn't know what to do with it."

I shake my head. "You don't understand. It's not safe." I can hear the battle raging beyond the entrance to the castle. "At least stay behind me."

She pushes her thick, dark glasses up the bridge of her nose. "I love you, Eloise, but sometimes you're a real ditz."

"Huh?"

"I was a witch before you even knew magic existed."

Her bright-red lips spread wide. "There are limits to what I can do on my own, but I'm certainly not helpless."

I raise my eyebrows, letting that sink in for a moment. Maeve is a Gowdie witch. I'm not sure if she knows what she's getting herself into, but I'll take any help she can give me. "Okay. In that case, let's fight our way out of this kingdom and go find Damien."

"Sounds good to me."

Working together, we shove through the doors and my stomach pitches at what is on the other side. We vastly underestimated the size of the elf army. Rows and rows of them, as far as I can see, are showering golden arrows toward the rebel troops. Only, those arrows are useless, because a dome of red magic shields our forces from impact.

"They came!" I pump my fist toward the sky.

Maeve is squinting. "What do you see? I see a bunch of archers with arrows. Are those the good guys?"

"Oh. Sorry. I forgot you have human vision. No, all these dudes in silver are the enemy. Up there, the witches of Dimhollow are protecting our forces from their arrows. I didn't think they'd help us, but they did. I just hope I can reanimate Phantom and destroy this army before the witches' shield gives way."

"Can you get me near the bones?" she asks. "You're going to have to lead me. I can't see in this dark."

"Good idea." If Maeve pulls Phantom together, I'll have my dragon back in no time. I sweep her into my arms and run toward the battle, stopping about a hundred yards behind the elven forces. This is as close as we can safely get to where Phantom and I were knocked out of the sky. Thank the goddess, the soldiers are all too busy trying to take down the shield to notice us.

Maeve turns to me, her eyes vacant as if she can't actually see me in the dark, and brings her finger to her lips. Then she raises her hand to the sky, forms a fist, and punches the battlefield.

I hear her magic ripple through the ground like an earthquake opening a fault line. It's as loud as a crack of thunder. Loud enough that the elves stop and look down at their feet.

The entire battlefield seems to draw a collective breath.

A scream rings out and an elf's arms flail as he is pulled straight down, into the earth.

Another scream, this time across the battlefield. All I see is a spray of red and then a cascade of wet bones arcing over an archer's head.

One by one, the elves start to fall.

A shriek to my left. A howl to my right. The snap of bones breaking. Arrows fly, not at the rebels but into the crowd of archers, at the ground, toward each other. My mouth drops open when I see why. Warriors rise from the dirt at their feet. Dead warriors. Some with half-missing skulls and bloodstained uniforms. Others, nothing more than animated skeletons. One of the zombies takes a sunlight arrow to the abdomen without reaction, then grabs the archer's throat and tears it out with blunt, bony fingers.

None of this should be a surprise to me. I knew that Maeve was an animator and that her sigil, a skull and crossbones, meant that her Gowdie family strength was animating the dead. I knew that vampires feared her family because they were powerful enough to take control of certain vampires, who, after all, are dead. But it's easy to forget that your best friend is capable of raising zombies when you don't see her do it on the regular.

She giggles beside me. "I've always wanted to do this, but it's not as if there's much reason to pull out the big guns at home," she says breathlessly. "How are they doing? I can't see them well enough to give specific direction. I'm sending a general order to kill anyone between us and the dome."

"It's working!" I say. "Keep going."

In fact, her spell is even more effective than what the resurrected army can accomplish on its own. The elves are panicking, shooting each other in their quest to stop the advancing dead. I am mesmerized. Maeve has...*saved* us. She's single-handedly changed the course of this war.

The screams grow louder at first, but soon, they die out altogether.

Maeve wipes blood from her nose.

"Stop," I say, my hand on her back. "The dead have reached the dome. You've done it! All the archers are dead."

She yanks her fist from the dirt and shakes her fingers like her hand is cramped. The clattering of bones marks the end of the zombie army.

She lists on her feet, and I draw her into my side. "I've got you."

We start walking toward the dome, but it is soon evident that her human strength is drained. I fling her easily into my arms and carry her the rest of the way.

"Goddess, you're strong now, El," she says.

"I guess I am," I say. "Not stronger than most here, but surviving has given me a hard outer shell."

"You're a walnut, now?" she says with a laugh.

"Or maybe tuberculosis bacterium. I'm guessing Brahm and Nevina think of me like a disease."

"If you're a disease, any population would be lucky to catch you," she mumbles.

"You know just what to say."

We reach the dome, and I stare through the spell at the rebels lined up inside. Flabbergasted doesn't begin to describe the expression on their faces. Damien forces his way toward me, his relief shining through the fatigue, blood, and sweat that cover him. He holds up a hand to me and then speaks quickly to Catarina. I can't hear what they're saying to each other, but one side of the dome lifts, and I'm able to carry Maeve inside. I set her on her feet and face Damien, his eyes drifting over me.

"We worried you were dead."

"Not quite. Phantom is a pile of bones, though."

His gaze focuses on my head. "You've been busy."

I remember what he's looking at and pull Entrydal's crown off my head and hand it to him. "We've taken Blackspire. The dark elf king is dead."

We're surrounded now by black uniforms, vampires, Rivertoads, and shades from every territory in Tenebris. Damien rotates the crown between his fingers, and the way he looks at me is nothing short of reverent. His mouth spreads into a smile, and he thrusts the crown into the air.

"The elf king has fallen! Willowgulch is ours!" he howls.

The cheers that echo his words are deafening. Our

friends and allies rush in, patting my back and shoulders and taking turns embracing us and each other. Cassius kisses the side of my head, Tempest hugs me as if she's my own proud mother, Thane, Undaku, and Prandle bow with hands over their hearts. Jaqual meets my eyes, kisses his fingertips, and blows the kiss toward me.

Catarina gives me a proud nod, then goes straight to Maeve, who has found a boulder to sit on, and offers her canteen.

Everyone is still celebrating when Percy shoves his way through the crowd to reach Damien. Damien raises a hand to silence the crowd.

"We've isolated New Stygarde," Percy says. "What are your orders?"

39

MY BROTHER'S KEEPER

DAMIEN

Ultimately, it's my decision. Our warriors are exhausted. Everyone needs food and rest.

But there can be no rest.

Catarina informs me that the shield holding off New Stygarde's troops won't last more than an hour. If we rest, we die. If we rest, we give the enemy time to regroup. In this war, there is no time for rest until it is done.

I turn to Jaqual. "It's now or never."

"I agree. We end this today." The Rivertoad king looks to Maeve. "I don't suppose you can manage another army on our behalf?"

Maeve shakes her head sleepily. "Not a chance. The only bones I'll be animating tonight are my own."

We both focus on Eloise. "Phantom?"

"I can reanimate the dragon, but it will take time and energy. Time I'm afraid we don't have. For this fight, you can't count on my magic, only my blades."

I kiss her soundly on the lips. A hard, fast kiss. It's all we can afford. "It's enough," I whisper.

I stride to the center of the crowd and climb atop one of the large rocks that peppers this part of the battlefield. The men and women around me are ready to fight, even though they can barely stand. I hold up Entrydal's crown. "Tonight, we take back what is rightfully ours. We end the nightmare that has held all of us in its grasp for far too long, and we restore the kingdom—for each of you and each of your children. I know you want to stop. You need rest. But I must ask you to keep going until we reach the castle. There are two more crowns that must be collected tonight. Crowns that belong to you." I swallow hard, and it's so quiet, I can hear it. "And once we have those crowns, everything changes. For I will not be your king by blood any longer." A murmur rises in the crowd. "The one who wears the next crown of Stygarde will be elected by you and will serve your will. We will create a government, not for the benefit of the kingdom, but for the benefit of the people!"

A cheer rises up around me, so loud and clear that it rings in my ears. Fists and swords and voices crescendo to a chorus of shouts. Somewhere, a horn blows. All around me, shades shift into their battle form, ready to fight.

I raise my own fist into the air. *"For Stygarde!"*

I nod at Catarina. She signals to the other witches to drop their shield.

And we fight.

I'm a warrior, but I don't love war. No one does. Still, there's a rhythm to it. A dance. A chorus of clashing swords. The flap of beastly wings. The slash of barbed tails. Shadows twisting in and out of existence as the moon rises, light pouring like spilled milk over trampled red wheat. The squish of boots in blood-soaked earth. The gnashing of teeth.

Nothing prepares me for the moment the soldier I'm fighting shadoweaves away and I'm left staring at a child. No, a wall of children, their swords held loosely in their hands. This is Nevina's final shield. To get to the queen, we must sacrifice the pawns. And there are so many pawns. Despite my promise to do the opposite, I hesitate. The young girl in front of me trembles, meets my gaze. Her eyes are clear.

She drops her sword. They all do. And then I see Undaku hugging a young man across the battlefield. Our teams part, and we let the children through. Along the shadow network, I hear Tempest ordering her healers to take them to the medical tents. I feel the collective exhale of held breath. Eloise's plan worked! The children are ours. The children are free. The young ones clear the way, and then it is just us, the warriors of the resistance, against a small unit of silver coats that stands between us and the doors of Stygarde Castle.

My team engages with the remaining troops.

I shove through the doors.

It has to be me. The resurrected prince returns. The risen dead come to reclaim his stolen life. I charge into the castle foyer and pass under the crest that is not mine. Brahm once told me that the depiction of the red and white stags, their horns entwined, represented how the prosperity of Stygarde and Willowgulch were dependent on each other. Nevina and her father promised peace but inflicted servitude. Today, I am the red stag come to lock horns with the white, not for peace but for vengeance.

The foyer is a blank canvas, draped in the colors of Willowgulch. The silver easily stains with the blood and filth that drip off me.

With every step, I leave my mark.

Banias waits for me at the end of the hall, guarding the stairs, dressed in his finery, his sword raised.

"Alone?" I ask. His grip trembles. "I did notice a few of your closest friends sinking into the mud on my way in—*parts* of your friends." His throat bobs. "Now, it's just you and me. Well, until the rest of my army comes through those doors and my mate with her dragon, flanked by the witches of Dimhollow and the parents of all the children you stole."

The tip of his sword wavers violently.

"I'm tempted to let them have you."

Banias pales.

I haven't even reached the man. Our swords have yet to touch. But I see the moment he gives up. Men like him feast on scraps of power and are never brave enough to go without it. He doesn't beg me for his life or give himself up. He simply swings his sword in the wrong direction and slices through his own neck.

It's a grisly wound, incomplete in its execution but effective. His blood paints the silver carpet red. The light bleeds from his eyes. He makes no effort to fight the darkness that comes for him.

Thanesia can deal with him now.

My boots splash through the pooling crimson as I step over his corpse, and I trail blood up the white steps to the second level. A servant in the hall points toward my brother's office. She looks painfully thin and relieved to see me, despite everything. I halt my steps when I notice a sunlight cuff around her neck. Rage fills me at the blisters that form along the edge—at the torture this woman has endured. With the tip of Dawnbreaker, I carefully break it off her. Before it even clatters to the ground, she's shifted. *Thank you*, I hear along the network of shadows, and then she's gone.

I continue to my brother's office. Locked. I break it open with a firm kick, the wood splintering from the force and the door dangling off the frame.

My brother stands alone behind his desk, his crown on his head and a dagger in his hand.

"It was Nevina, brother. She had me under her spell! I had no choice in any of this," he whines.

"I don't believe you."

"Arrest me, then. Let the people have a trial. I will explain everything."

I take a step toward him. "You want me to take you to the stockade? You want the people to decide what to do with you?"

"Yes, yes, brother." He points a knuckle at me. "You know I've always been a fuckup, prone to the seduction of women and drink. I can't be held responsible for my actions. I was conned by the dark elves. I'm as much a victim here as you. And the children. I had nothing to do with that. It was all her doing. I was in no position to stop her, Damien. I had no real power."

"No power as king? That's an interesting take." I move another heavy step toward him. "No money in the coffers. No access to soldiers to carry out your will. No ability to walk out the door."

He scoffs. "Not without losing everything. I had to maintain our family's power here. It was a long game."

"Maintain the throne by killing our father."

He grows more flustered. I slide another step toward him.

"You don't understand. I had no other choice in the matter. I'm not like you, Damien. I can't survive outside these walls. I did what I had to do. If Mother were alive, she'd tell you. I've always been sickly. I've always been easily swayed. I was entrapped, Damien. You must believe me!"

His eyes are wide and watery, his nose and cheeks red with his airless babbling. The crown on his head has slipped to the side, resting askew like the crown of a jester. Stubble fills the grooves of his cheeks. It occurs to me that I have only seen a single servant, and she looked tortured. I suspect that once the children were freed, the young ones used what remained of Eloise's potion to break the enchantment on the help, and any servants who could leave did. I wonder if this older, frail Brahm is the result of missing a meal or two in these final days. The thought gives me a measure of happiness.

"Good news, Brahm."

His lips spread into a wobbly smile. "You'll take me alive, then?"

I raise an eyebrow. "Mother and Karyl survived. They've been living among the witches this entire time. And, thanks to some brilliant magic, they saw what you did to Father. Saw what you did with your own two hands when Nevina was nowhere near you."

The corners of Brahm's eyes tighten, and his expression morphs from a sniveling idiot to a caged animal in a heartbeat. His lips peel off his teeth, and he raises his dagger, his sneer an ugly mask of narcissistic rage. "Father deserved what he got, and so do you!" He slashes toward me.

I'm physically exhausted, but his movements are so slow and unpracticed, I easily step out of the way. The tip of his dagger sinks into the opposite edge of the desk, the weight of his blow carrying his body over it, and my sword comes down. Dawnbreaker's Stygian steel easily severs his thin neck. His head drops, and his crown rolls like a coin on its edge. It clinks and clanks on its journey through the open door, where it hits the far wall and topples over onto its side.

I wipe my sword clean on the back of Brahm's velvet tunic.

Voices and commotion come from below. My men have entered the castle and are searching every abandoned room, securing what is left of this crumbling stronghold. I hear them call my name, but I don't answer. I have one more crown to collect, and I know just where to find it.

40

THE QUEEN

DAMIEN

I throw open the doors of the throne room to find Nevina at the end of the long royal hall, dressed in a pristine silver ball gown and sitting on my mother's throne. My mother's crown rests upon her head, gold spikes encrusted with dark stones.

If I'd never been to Earth, I wouldn't notice how much this place resembles a medieval church, the ceiling pointed at the center, arched stained glass letting in moonlight that casts the hall in geometric colors. In human lexicon, she might be mistaken for an angel, the way she glows on high. But after everything, I expect that slight, stick-insect body of hers to breathe flies and locusts.

"Stop where you are," she commands, tapping the base of her scepter on the stone floor. "Be aware, shade, the light around me will burn you. If you come any closer, I will strike you down with my magic."

I unhook Brahm's crown from my belt and throw it down the long aisle. "I have your father's too, although I left it with my men. I suspect it's in the latrine by now, covered in their shit."

The bubble of light around her expands but doesn't come close to reaching me. If she could strike me down where I stand, I'm sure she would. But she has to conserve her energy. Her red lips sneer, rippling speechless with her anger. "You filthy scum. You bastard smudge. Come closer and taste the sun."

"Nah. I think I'll wait here and watch you slowly starve to death. You can't stay in that bubble forever, and there's nowhere left for you to go."

"You ignorant fool. A dark elf queen can sustain herself for a very long time. My people will come for me."

"Your people are dead."

She rolls her eyes incredulously.

"Not all of them, I grant you. Only the ones who tried to fight. Unlike you, we didn't slaughter people in their homes or steal their children."

"Oh, how noble of you. As if you don't wear the blood of your enemies on your skin. Everything you've done since you returned to this world has been to win back what you lost. Every action taken in your own zest for power. You Hymirs are such hypocrites. Just like me, all you care about is this throne. You would kill your own brother to get it. You act all high-and-mighty, self-righteous, but you are just as bad as Brahm and me. We are the same."

I chuckle. "I am nothing like you, Nevina."

"No? How many citizens did you slaughter to stand before me now? And the next time there's an uprising?

How many more will you slay? You care nothing about life or about children. You care nothing for the will of the people. You think you're a hero, but you are a tyrant, just like your father. You tell yourself a story about being different, about doing right by the people, but all kings cling to power, Damien. You are no exception."

I nod. "You're right."

Her nostrils flare, and her lip curls in disgust.

"The Rivertoad king taught me the same lesson. It's why I'll be eliminating the monarchy and leading the kingdom toward a democracy."

She laughs wickedly. "You must be joking. I've heard some wild ideas in my lifetime, but we both know the people *need* a king and queen. They don't know what's best for them. If left to their own devices, they will all act in their own best interests and never agree on anything. The kingdom will fall into disrepair. The people need someone to tell them what to do."

I shrug. "I guess we're going to find out."

She shakes her head, the idea clearly disgusting her.

I take a step toward her.

"Stay where you are! I'm warning you."

A shadow moves behind her, the glint of a Stygian blade in her hand. I recognize that blade. It once belonged to Cassius. I smile when I see her, so happy that she's made it. It is poetic justice that she should be the one to kill Nevina. I don't look directly at her, just take another step forward.

"You are all rats. You shades are a filthy disease on Tenebris," Nevina says. "Father and I tried to reform you, but you never understood how good you had it under our rule."

"For the goddess's sake, shut the fuck up," my mother says, a second before she walks through the light and sinks Cassius's dagger into Nevina's heart.

"Nyxadora," Nevina sputters, blood staining her bottom lip and dripping onto her silver dress.

"You took something that is mine," my mother hisses. "And today, I take it back." Her skin blisters and burns in the dark elf's light, but she doesn't cry out. She is mortal and she is hurting, but it will pass. What she needs in this moment, she intends to take, and I will not interrupt the taking.

Mother yanks the blade up and out of Nevina's chest, and I watch the life drain from the false queen's eyes. Slowly, the light of her magic dies with her. With blackened fingers, Mother reaches out and drags her crown off Nevina's head. Nevina's body drops, lifeless, from the throne.

"You know, son," Nyx says, her voice as charred as her flesh. "It is a remarkable feeling to have birthed a child who is far wiser and more noble than either of his parents. And to know you have chosen a bride who is just as wise and just as noble makes me the proudest I have ever been." She hobbles toward me and passes me the blade, still thick with Nevina's blood. "Thank Eloise for lending me this."

I look at it and then at her, relieved to see the blisters on her skin are already healing. "I will."

Then she releases her grip on the crown, which rolls and clanks to a stop near my feet. "It's your kingdom now. Do with it what you will."

41

THE PEOPLE

ELOISE

Everyone sleeps in Stygarde Castle that night. Everyone who can fit. Damien insists. His only caveat is that we get the bed in his old chambers. No one denies us. The room has been locked off and is exactly as we left it. Our warriors fill every room, every spot on the floor, most of them so tired they simply lie down wherever they stop moving.

Maeve has no choice but to stay with us. Until I resurrect Phantom, I can't draw the sigil to send her home. I'm much too drained to do either tonight. Besides, she can barely keep her eyes open from her overuse of power, and she falls asleep on the settee in Damien's seating area.

Damien and I do manage a fast and very unsexy bath to remove the layers of blood and sweat that cake our bodies and hair. I clean out the wounds that are slow to heal on his side and forehead, the burn along the outside of one elbow and one leg. It's a short, efficient affair that results in a true heaven—climbing between clean sheets in clean pajamas. We are asleep in seconds, the snores of the other soldiers on the floor of our room a gentle lullaby.

We do not wake until the moon has set and risen again. I open my eyes to Maeve leaning over me, dressed in clean clothing that I recognize as my old riding gear, and adjusting her glasses on her nose. "I hope this is okay." She gestures to the breeches and tunic that once were Damien's. "I needed a bath, and it was all I could find.

"Of course. Goddess, anything, Maeve. I owe you my life."

"How about a cup of coffee and a Danish?" She places her hand on her stomach.

I smile up at her. "I think I can find a suitable equivalent." I glance over my shoulder and see that Damien is still sleeping. At least it looks as if the cuts and abrasions I noticed before seem to have healed. I crawl out of bed and step around the soldiers still sleeping on the floor to get to my wardrobe. I dress quickly in one of Ariadne's originals. Instinctively, I move for my daggers, then remember I don't need them anymore and come out from behind my dressing screen without them.

"Wow," Maeve says, taking in my emerald outfit.

"It's the style. I can dig out a dress for you if you'd like."

She laughs. "Unless you have something in that wardrobe in black with skulls, no thank you."

I shake my head. "Come on. Let's find the kitchen. You aren't the only one who's going to be hungry."

For once, I'm thankful for Nevina and Brahm's greed because I find their stores perfectly adequate to feed an army. I prepare a hot beverage for Maeve that is as close to coffee as we have on Tenebris and feed her red wheat rolls with plenty of butter and jam, alongside strips of cooked stag. I drink my fill of stag's blood, which grosses her out but invigorates me.

And then I get to work. I push the table in the dining room against one wall, and one of the previous servants, Roslyn, volunteers to help set up another table in an L shape. As we work, she tells me of how Damien freed her in the last moments of the war and explains how most had escaped after their enchantment was broken. I make sure she's eaten her fill, and then, together, we set out a buffet of simply prepared blood, meat, bread, cheese, and fruit.

As the soldiers wake, we serve them. It's an honor to feed the men and women who fought for Stygarde. An honor to be in their company. I learn each of their names and listen to their stories. I thank them for their service.

At some point, Nyxadora sees what we are doing and edges behind the table to help. Not to be outdone, Jaqual crowds in, following my example and thanking each man, woman, and child for their help.

"Already campaigning, I see," he whispers to me between dishing plates.

I snort. "I'm just feeding the men Damien and I are responsible for. I don't have ulterior motives."

"Goddess, you are annoyingly trustworthy, Eloise. When I'm voted in as leader of Stygarde, I'd love to hire you as my chief adviser."

"What advice could I possibly give the Rivertoad king? You already know everything."

"True," he says with haughty swagger. "But it's boring always being right. I enjoy the occasional challenge."

Laughing, I turn away from him when Nyxadora's hand lands on my arm. "Have you seen Karyl?"

"As far as I know, she never left Aendor. Tempest put her to work in the infirmary after we'd secured the area." Nyx releases a deep breath and nods as if relieved.

"You were right. About everything, Eloise. And thank you for lending me your dagger. It came in quite useful."

"So Damien told me."

I attempt to scoop some meat onto a plate and am confused when the plate is jerked away so fast I almost dump the food on the table. I look up to give the soldier a piece of my mind and see Warbill. Quickly, I return the serving back to the pan and round the table to pull him into a tight, tear-filled embrace. I don't know what to say to him. Thank you doesn't seem enough.

"Come, my queen. If Damien sees the way you are hugging me, he might have my head," he whispers tearfully into my ear.

Reluctantly, I let him go, only to be pulled into another hug when Cassius enters the room. This time, my happy tears fall like rain. "Thank the goddess!"

"It does feel like a blessing to see the moon rise today."

"I'm so sorry for the loss of your men... And George's." I place a hand over my heart. "How many?" My voice cracks, but I need to know the truth.

"We lost about a quarter," he says gravely.

I wipe a stray tear from my eye. His hand comes to rest on my arm with a steadying grip. "Eloise, everyone knew what they were in for. Every one of those vampires consented to come and fight, and Sabrina and Tobias understood I would not be returning with the same number of men I brought through the portal. The vampires who fought for you were warriors who died with honor. Their families will be well compensated. Do not take this guilt upon yourself. All is forgiven."

A familiar-looking couple chooses that moment to arrive behind him. "Allow me to introduce you to my parents, Jozius and Faurine."

"We joined the fight after the shield dropped in the Borderlands," Jozius says. "It's a gift to have this time with Cassius before he must return to Earth."

When I see the pure joy on the family's faces, I focus on that and not on our losses. No matter what happens next, the survivors here can go home. They can rebuild. And their children are safe now.

I'm still chatting with Cassius when warm arms wrap around my shoulders. Damien. He kisses me on the side of the head, his eyes roving to the banquet table, saying everything without saying a word. He pours himself a pint of stag's blood and drinks it down before motioning to Jaqual.

They exchange a quick conversation. With the River-toad king at his side, Damien steps up to stand on the table. A hush comes over the packed room.

"Spread the word among your people. An election is in progress in the throne room, and a decision regarding who will lead this kingdom will occur in three days' time, based on your vote. You may cast your vote for any citizen of Tenebris who you believe should lead it into the future," Damien announces.

"Male or female?" someone shouts from the gathering crowd.

Damien glances toward his mother. "Yes," he answers. "You should know that my father chose my sister Karyl as his successor when he believed me to be dead."

Whispers ripple through the crowd. Roslyn clears her throat, wiping her hands on her servant's uniform before stepping forward. "From any class, sir?"

"From any class, Roslyn."

She blushes when he uses her name.

Jaqual stands up straighter. "Any class, any region, any people," he clarifies.

Now the murmurs grow deafening.

"I have set up a locked box in the throne room. It will be guarded around the clock. Write a name on the parchment provided and drop it in the box. Everyone gets one vote. Use it wisely, for the future of Stygarde and all the regions within its borders is now in your hands."

Damien leaps down from the table, and I take his hands in mine. The tattoos on his forearms fade and then disappear. I roll up my sleeve, and mine is gone too. "So, we'll know in three days," I whisper.

"Three days."

"You have my vote."

He smiles down at me. "I'm not against the cabin on Mount Perilon."

I shrug. "Neither am I."

Maeve appears beside us with a raised hand. "I hate to interrupt, but if we are going to resurrect Phantom so you can send me home today…or tonight…whatever you call this time when the moon is up, we need to get started."

Damien reaches out and pulls Maeve into a hug, which leaves her bug-eyed and clearly weirded out. "Thank you, Ms. Gowdie, for helping us."

"Yeah, yeah." She pulls away and dusts herself off like

he's given her the cooties. "I guess it's the least I could do after my family held you prisoner for a few hundred years. Can we call it even?"

He nods and offers her a half smile, his eyes drifting to me. I know what he's thinking. If not for the Gowdies, we would have never met, and neither of us would be standing here right now. "Even," he declares.

"Now that that's settled, let's go. I'm sure Ren is worried sick." And I need a break. I walk with her through the crowds toward the front of the castle, through the chattering voices. "We can take a rabble beast to where Phantom fell."

"A rabble what?"

"Trust me," I say, heading for the stable.

"So, after all that, he's really going to let someone else lead Stygarde?" Maeve asks.

I nod. "It was never about being king for Damien. If his brother had been a just ruler, he would have happily supported him. All he wanted was justice."

"And you? What do you want?"

I snort. "I want us to wake up in that castle a week from now, knowing we're the reason this world is a better place. Damien is the only one with the vision to lead Stygarde into the future—and the kindness and empathy to do it with a gentle hand. I think the people can see that, and I think he'll win."

She gives me a reassuring nod, and we go about the business of sending her home.

42
ELECTION

ELOISE

Resurrecting Phantom is easier than I expect. We find the dragon's spine in the Borderlands where I remember falling, and Maeve uses her magic to call to the dragon's other bones. It's a bit eerie to see parts of the skeleton walk themselves back into place, but I'm thankful for the help. Once the beast is reassembled, I reach for my grandmother's hand. She must be waiting for me in the Darklands because I feel her essence immediately and the swing of the pendulum to return her and the others to Phantom's body feels almost effortless. Or maybe it's just because I've done this twice before. My heart swells with pure joy as my ancestors fill out the body of the dragon and roar back into existence.

Afterward, we return to the castle, and I gather Cassius and the vampires, thanking each of them profusely for their help. I draw the key symbol on the floor of the library and send them all home after promise after promise to Maeve that I will visit more regularly. As I watch her and the others pass through the purple light, I'm determined to keep that promise. Friends like Maeve come along once in a lifetime if we're lucky. We may not be related, but she is family. I don't take that for granted.

You're the key, darling. You can visit her whenever you'd like, Phantom says. I wipe my tears and hold on to that truth.

When it's done, I wash the key symbol from the floor and then make my way to the throne room. There's a line to reach the ballot box. At the front, I'm handed a quill and parchment, and my name is stricken from a list in an enormous book. I scrawl "Damien Hymir" and then drop it into the box, praying that it falls on a pile of similar ballots.

The days drip by like cool honey. Damien and I eat and drink and rest and make love as if we have no idea that the results of this election could change our lives forever. It's a happy time, with people coming and going peacefully to place their votes, stopping only to talk to us about what efforts are happening to revitalize their communities. Nyxadora and Karyl take up residence in their old rooms, knowing that their stay might be short-lived but relishing their last chance to experience what was once home.

Jaqual moves in as well, to oversee the process. He still doesn't trust Damien not to cheat, although Percy, Thane, Undaku, and Prandle take turns guarding the box.

On the day the votes are to be counted, Jaqual funnels to my side as I wait impatiently on the veranda, watching Phantom hunt in the distance.

"You can stay, you know," he says out of the blue.

I glance over at his bright-purple eyes to find his lips curled in a ghost of a smile. "Stay where?"

"Here, in the castle, if I win," he says. "I don't plan to live here. It's too big. I miss my wagon." He rests his hands on the banister and stares up at the swell of the moon.

At first, I think he's joking, but when he doesn't laugh, I say, "Thank you. I'm not from here, but I know for Nyx, Karyl, and Damien, this is the place that feels like home."

"Everyone should know a place like that," he says. "A place they feel loved. A place they belong."

"I agree. And I'm sure if Damien were here, he'd tell you that, if he wins, the Rivertoads will be free to travel your ancestral route. He understands now the importance of the caravan to you and your people."

"Kind of him. Although I doubt such a farfetched scenario as my not winning is likely."

I roll my eyes. "Do you ever get sick of fluffing up that ego of yours?

"Never."

"Shouldn't you be downstairs overseeing the final tally?" I ask.

"Shouldn't you be at your mate's side to comfort him when he loses?"

We both stare at each other for a beat.

"I saw you speaking with Catarina before she returned to Dimhollow," I say, wondering if he wants to talk about it. I am one of only a handful of people who knows the truth.

He releases a heavy sigh. "She's my mother." He runs a hand over the top of his head. "Explains some things, honestly."

"Will you see her again?"

He nods. "We've agreed to meet. It feels…odd. I've spent so long thinking of the Rivertoads as my only family."

"The Rivertoads are your family, but having more people in this world who love us is a good problem to have."

His answering smile is wistful.

From the hall, voices call to us. "It's time!"

We shadoweave to the throne room, where a group of shades is counting and recounting the votes, their tallies documented on a large roll of parchment spread on a table at the center of the room. Damien, along with the lords and ladies of the realm, hover over their work. Jaqual steps forward to join them.

I remain at the end of the aisle, waiting for the outcome that will frame my future, and knowing, whatever fate befalls us, anywhere Damien is will be home for me. Whatever happens, it will be okay.

"We have a clear winner." The head accountant hands what I assume is the final tally to Damien and Jaqual, who each hold a side and read the results.

"Did you—"

"Are you—"

"Certain—"

They blubber back and forth, looking at each other and then at the accountants. Tempest, Thane, Odette, Undaku, Eudora, Prandle, Nyx, and Karyl all read the results, their mouths dropping open a little. I walk forward, now acutely curious about who our new king is. Is it a tie? Someone unexpected, like Karyl or Roslyn?

Damien turns to meet my gaze, his expression unreadable. "We will *not* need to move, little dragon."

I step onto the dais. "You've been elected?" I say excitedly, but he shakes his head.

Jaqual steps aside so that I can see the results. Both Damien and Jaqual received a sizable number of votes, as did Nyx and Karyl, but my jaw drops when I see the winner.

My name is scrawled at the top, victor by more than double.

The people have elected *me*.

"She who tames the dragon rules the world," Jaqual says, a lazy smile breaking across his face.

I'm too flabbergasted to speak. Or move. My arms hang at my sides like dead weights.

Damien and Jaqual exchange glances under raised brows. "Shall I call Catarina back to restore you with a curative tea?" Damien asks. "By the goddess, breathe, woman!"

I try, but my breath rattles in my throat. It takes all my will to fill my lungs. "Are we sure about this? Is there any room for error?" I eventually manage to ask.

But everyone shakes their heads. "They were counted three separate times by separate employees, my queen," the head accountant says, then catches himself. "You will keep the moniker queen, I assume. We can change it, if you dislike the traditional title, but some habits are hard for people to break."

I turn to Damien, wanting to ask him if this is okay. He has the second-highest number of votes. If I step down...

"Don't even think about it," he whispers. "It's you. It was always meant to be you."

I swallow the lump in my throat, lick my lips, and search the faces around me. Everyone seems pleased, even Jaqual. No one but me is questioning this outcome.

Hand on my stomach to settle myself, I simply say, "Queen will do."

EPILOGUE: A PROMISE IS A PROMISE

DAMIEN

"You promised me a wedding, and by the goddess, you will give me the wedding of my dreams," Ariadne says.

I adjust the gold-embellished sash on the red velvet tunic she's dressed me in, feeling like it's far too pretentious, considering Eloise and I are now elected officials and not royals. "May I remind you, only a few weeks ago, you said that designing Eloise's gown for her coronation was your life's greatest achievement. She didn't have to have one, you know, considering she was elected."

She tosses up her hands. "The people want what the people want!"

"And they—you—got it. Didn't that settle any debt between us?"

She smooths her blond hair, glossy now that she is well-fed. Although her features are as sharp as ever, they are softened by rounder cheeks and a teasing smile. "A coronation is a coronation. A wedding is a wedding. You promised me a wedding."

"We are already married."

"That wedding in Dimhollow was a rushed tragedy of unfashionable and coerced vows. They barely count."

"They count. There was nothing coerced about them."

"Other than you thought you might die."

I purse my lips. "No sash." I move to remove it.

"You must wear the sash!" she protests. "It coordinates with Eloise's gown perfectly!"

I rub my forehead and groan as she physically adjusts the sash back into place and smooths it with her hands. "Can I ask you something, Damien?"

"Why do I feel you are only asking to distract me from all the glittery bits hanging off my chest?"

She folds her arms. "Was any part of you jealous when she won? Did you feel like your legacy had been stolen from you? Did part of you want to snatch it back, out of her hands?"

I rub my jaw. Ariadne hasn't kept a secret her entire life. If I tell her the truth, it will definitely get back to Eloise and circulate across Tenebris by the end of the week. Fuck it all. Do I really care who knows?

"I voted for her," I say truthfully.

Ariadne's eyes narrow. "*What?*"

"The morning of the vote, I woke up to find her feeding our people, sandwiched between my mother and the king of the Rivertoads, and it all became clear to me. Eloise was the catalyst for everything that occurred to save Tenebris. She recognized my brother's treachery before I did. She saved me from assassination. She befriended the witches and convinced them to help when they did. She was the reason the Rivertoads engaged with us and the vampires who fought for us were here at all. She killed King Entrydal, and her best friend used her powers as a witch to defeat the dark elf army. Eloise is the reason we are all here today. And so, I. Voted. For. Her. I was relieved when she won. The people love her. She is the best choice to rule."

She snorts. "But doesn't it make you feel like less of a—"

"Man? Shade? Warrior?" I laugh. "No, Ariadne. Serving this kingdom at her side is everything I wanted. It isn't easy loving a dragon, you know. Keeping her alive has been a hobby of mine for some time now. That day we died together, the day we were married, I would have given away the kingdom a hundred times over to save her." I spare Ariadne the memory I hold of the Darklands, of my father whispering to Eloise that the kingdom needed her. "Believe me when I say to you, it takes being a man—a strong one—to love Eloise the way she needs to be loved. I don't need to dominate her to possess her. I don't need to be a king to tolerate her being my queen. I am not so weak as that."

Ariadne wipes a stray tear from under her eye. "You are a rare male, indeed, and will always be a king to me." She smiles. "That's why I voted for *you*, and I would do it again."

"You'll have another chance in ten years. Eloise was adamant about term limits."

She shakes her head. "I do have to hand it to her. She's very open-minded and creative when it comes to this new form of government."

"I must agree."

Trumpets blare, and Ariadne shoves me toward the door. "It's time!"

I hurry out of the dressing room and advance to the dais, where the officiant stands ready to marry us. Hands folded in front of my hips, I lift my gaze to the head of the aisle. Eloise appears, and I'm glad I wore the sash. She's dressed in a sleeveless ball gown the color of blood, so dark it's almost black. Her bright-red hair is curled and woven through her crown. Her lips match the fabric. Her skin is the color of poured cream.

The day I met Eloise, I compared her to a tree that'd lost all its branches, all its leaves, everything but its will to live. But from the beginning, she looked at me as if I were the sun and all she needed to grow. How could I have known then what she would grow into? What we both would.

I think back to the last vision served to me as I left the passage out of Mount Perilon, the one I never told Eloise about. I saw a vision of Stygarde Castle falling around her. I thought she was being crushed by the stones. But I was wrong. She wasn't being crushed. She was tearing it all down.

Not to destroy it. No. My little dragon would rebuild it.

ELOISE

The throne room is overflowing with guests as Damien and I say our vows, which are remarkably similar to the ones we made in Dimhollow. I wonder what Catarina thinks of it. She's here today, as are all the lords and ladies of the regions and the friends we made along the way. Seamus and Amala are beaming at us from the second row. Ariadne and Warbill both look like they will burst with pride. Children and servants and warriors and farmers all smile at us from their seats.

My crown feels heavy, but my heart is light.

Last night, after we made love, Damien asked me what I thought of everything that had happened, if I'd expected the outcome in some deeply hidden region of my mind. I hadn't, of course. What human woman could have predicted the twists and turns in the road that I have walked. But, I told him, I had learned a few lessons along the way.

After everything, I know one thing for sure.

The day you decide you're worth more, and you step out from under the abuse you always took for granted and into your confidence, into your power, you have to be prepared to say yes to how the universe rewards you. The shadows we call to help us with our problems aren't half as important as the shadows we cast. The shadows we grow into. The shadows inside ourselves that we come to love.

I crawled away from Tony, bruised and broken, weak and powerless. But there was always a shadow in me, deep within the walls of my heart. The shadow of a queen. All I had to do was love her. All I had to do was meet another shadow who would teach me how.

As Damien kisses me and the crowd roars with applause, I am grateful to every god above or below us that our fates are entwined. Grateful to my ancestors for helping me along the way. And yes, grateful even to Tony, without whose cruelty I would never know true kindness, and without whose abuse, I would never have called upon the monster who awoke the monster in me.

A monster who would love.

A monster who would save a kingdom.

A monster who would rule.

Thank you readers for joining me on Damien and Eloise's journey. If you've enjoyed this novel, please leave a review on your favorite reading app or wherever you buy books.

You may have noticed this series contains short references to Paragon and dragon royalty. Eloise gains her powers from Nathaniel's blood and the Order of the Dragon. The Shadow's Bargain series takes place in the same universe as the Treasure of Paragon series. If you are interested in learning more about the dragons who started it all, turn the page to read an excerpt from book 1, The Dragon of New Orleans.

THE DRAGON OF NEW ORLEANS

I

Gabriel Blakemore was running out of time, which was laughable considering time had never meant anything to him in the past. As an immortal dragon, his life thus far had flowed like an endless river, each new day guaranteed by the last. Not anymore. He thumbed the emerald ring on his finger. Already the curse at its center gave the jewel the appearance of a cat's eye in bright light, a thin black pupil visible at the center of the green. His affliction was spreading.

Hunched over the seventeenth-century Spanish baroque desk in his office at Blakemore's Antiques, he sifted through the stack of papers in front of him, praying for a savior, anyone who had the slightest potential for breaking the curse. None of the candidates seemed powerful enough. He needed more options.

Anxiously, he tugged at the bond connecting him to his manservant. Richard appeared at the door to his office almost immediately, carrying a stack of papers that he squared on the desk in front of Gabriel. "More for you."

Gabriel nodded at the man. Impeccably dressed, as always, in a pinstripe three-piece suit, Richard had proved a crucial asset these days, researching magical options when Gabriel could not. Gabriel had bought the former slave's freedom in 1799, a wise choice. Not only had Richard become a close friend over the centuries, he'd retained a sharp wit and an eye for detail.

The man dusted off his hands before rubbing his sternum. "You don't need to scream down the bond, you know. I'm in the next room. I want to find a cure as much as you do."

Gabriel grunted.

"Are all dragons as friendly and chipper as you, or was I just lucky to be bonded to the best of them?" Richard folded into the chair across the desk, throwing a lanky arm across its back.

"How are sales today?" Gabriel asked, ignoring the man's gibe. He hadn't meant to cause Richard discomfort, but he didn't plan to apologize for it either. Not when the situation was so dire.

"Strong enough that if we all live another year, we can throw one hell of a party," Richard said. "How's that plan coming along? You find a way for us to do that? Live another year? There must be something here. For God's sake, we live in the voodoo capital of America, the home and burial place of Marie Laveau herself."

A whiff of cinnamon and molasses curled off Gabriel's coffee, and he took a long, steadying drink. "Marie would roll over in her tomb if she knew who was running this city now." New Orleans was brimming with humans claiming to have supernatural abilities. Liars, most of them. Unfortunately, the voodoo priestess who'd cast the curse on his ring was the real thing, and she did not take prisoners. Anyone left with true power in the city was either on her side or too afraid to oppose her.

Gabriel snorted. Three hundred years in this realm, only to be turned to stone by the jealous rage of a woman who couldn't take no for an answer.

The thought made his fingers drum against the desk. Tap-tap-tap. Always in threes. The compulsion to tap was so strong when it hit him, not doing so resulted in pain. Muscle tremors ran the length of his arms and hands. He flipped his thumb against the corner of the paper nearest him, hoping it would curb the impulse.

Richard frowned at his fidgeting. "You should rest, Gabriel. It's getting worse. This is the third time this morning."

"Soon."

"That's what you said an hour ago."

Gabriel pulled the pile of papers toward him. His hands cramped with the effort, and the stack spilled across the walnut desk. He cursed, but the word caught in his throat. A woman's picture had been revealed in the collapse, instantly catching his eye. He lifted the folded newspaper to get a better look.

Enchanting. That was the only way to describe her. He couldn't look away. The woman had eyes the color of deep water and curly black hair as wild as the hint of trouble she carried in her smile. He had the sudden intense desire to kiss away that lopsided grin and further tangle that hair. Where had such an urge come from? A dragon like Gabriel didn't often find himself drawn to human women. He closed his eyes and gave his head a well-deserved shake.

"Who is this?" he demanded.

Richard leaned over the desk in order to get a better look, and Gabriel turned the article in his direction. Richard groaned. "That, my friend, is a long shot."

RAVENNA TANGLEWOOD OPENED HER EYES TO DARKNESS. She blinked and blinked again, but the eyelid flutter didn't seem to help. This was new. While she'd slept, an irregular blotch had formed in her vision, partially obstructing her view. Now it painted itself like black ink against the sterile white walls of her hospital room.

A Rorschach test, she thought. What did she see in it? An oil slick. A dark cumulus cloud. A rough joke told by her brain cancer.

Cancer. That fucking bitch.

The aroma of this morning's half-eaten eggs and the tang of antiseptic brought her fully awake. She was in the exact same place she'd been every day for the past three months: the hospice at Ochsner Medical Center in New Orleans. Only the last time she'd drifted off, there wasn't a stain obstructing half her field of vision.

She rolled her head and the dark splotch followed, blotting out the left side of the room. She closed her eyes again, counted to ten. No change. Damn, that couldn't be good.

Through her working eye, she watched her mother sleep in the chair next to the bed; she at least was the same as Raven had left her. A *Cosmo* was sprawled across her mother's lap as if she'd drifted off midsentence. Though now that Raven looked more closely, the lifestyle magazine was wrapped around a disturbingly worn copy of *Surviving Divorce* by Amy Dickerman, PhD. Raven winced. So her father's pronounced absence had come to this. Or maybe it was a preemptive read, a talisman against the inevitable. As far as she knew, her parents had only separated—the burden of her illness giving rise to separate bank accounts, separate bedrooms, separate lives—in that order. Her care had become an act of full-time charity her father could not abide.

As usual, her mom was bearing the parental weight alone this morning, although the chair beside her held her older sister Avery's rosary. When had she dug that thing up? Raven hadn't seen the likes of it since their aunt had gifted it to her for her first communion. Avery had never been the praying type. Leave it to death to bring out the inner Falwell in everyone.

Did she think she could pray the cancer away? Raven snorted at the thought. *Pull the plug.* That's what she'd say if she had a say, and if she were plugged in to anything more than Mr. Drippy, her full-time fluid and drug-delivery companion. So far, she could breathe on her own and swallow, unlike the man across the hall. *Stopped the vent*, she'd heard the nurses whisper.

Lucky bastard.

"Hey, beautiful," Dr. Freemont said.

Raven rolled her head back to center, then slightly to the left so she could see him clearly out of her good eye. Dr. Freemont was a balding, portly man whose gray temples gave away his advanced age. Still, he was more fun than his stodgy contemporaries. She liked him.

"Hey, ugly," she responded, although the words sounded choked off and raspy.

His bushy silver brows sank over his bulbous nose. "What's this about? You're holding your head at an angle. Raven, can you look at me straight on?"

"No," she drawled. "Dark." Every word was like lifting a two-ton boulder from the depths of her skull and carrying it through a labyrinth of synapses to finally hoist over her lips. It was exhausting.

Dr. Freemont placed one hand gently on her head, then drew a penlight from his pocket. He swung it in front of her right eye, then her left, where the light disappeared inside the dark fog.

"Squeeze my fingers," he commanded, touching her right hand. She did as he asked, then wondered why he never placed his fingers in her left, although he'd walked to that side of the bed. Or maybe he had. She could no longer feel that hand.

As Dr. Freemont continued his assessment, she noticed a trend. Her left side wasn't working. Not just her eye, but also her shoulder, her hand, her thigh, all the way to her pinky toe. Numb. Dead. She was dying in halves.

"Why?" she demanded, but she knew.

"The tumor," he said simply. "The pressure in your brain." He kept speaking, but Raven's mind couldn't keep up with his medical explanation. She did catch the word *stroke*. It didn't matter. They wouldn't treat her for it anyway.

"Donate?" she asked.

Half cloaked in shadow, his face turned grim and he

lowered his voice. "Yes. The cancer is only in your brain. You'll be able to donate your organs. It's all arranged." His voice was funny, and she wondered if he was lying. Normally Dr. Freemont didn't talk to his patients much about organ donation, but she'd pressed him about it early on. For her, it was a light at the end of the tunnel. Every time he reassured her of her donation status, her heart leaped a little. She'd do something with this life. Leave a part of herself behind that mattered.

If he was lying, she didn't want to know the truth.

"Long?" she asked. He knew what she meant. How long until she died? They'd been at this for over five years on and off. Through railroad spikes of pain that left her begging for someone to bash her head in. Months of chemo that turned her inside out. There was nothing left to try. There would be no more chemo. No more surgeries. Raven wanted to live, but if living wasn't possible, she would settle for being free.

His pale eyes met hers, and he gripped her fingers on the right where she could feel his reassurance. "Not long now."

Not long now. She tried her best to smile. "Good."

Her mother roused, her magazine-wrapped book falling from her lap and clattering to the floor. "Oh! Doctor. Excuse me. I must have drifted off. How is she?"

When he turned to look at her, his eyes glossier than usual, his face changed. A mask slipped into place, clinical and authoritative. Raven rolled her head on her pillow to see her mother, and the dark splotch swallowed most of Dr. Freemont's head. She couldn't see anything above his shoulders when he answered.

"I would never put an expiration date on your daughter, Mrs. Tanglewood… Sarah. We both know how strong she is."

"Yes, I know. This one came out fighting." Her mother still believed Raven could beat this thing.

She was wrong.

"Raven's comfort measures are working. We'll maintain the course." He straightened as if he might leave.

Raven squeezed his hand. "Do it," she said. It was the best part of her day. She wouldn't let him leave without giving it to her.

He turned an impassive expression toward her, half light and half dark as she looked at him straight on. "I have no idea what you are talking about, Raven." The corner of his mouth twitched.

With whatever part of her face was still working, she sent him the sternest glare she could muster.

Raising one eyebrow, he backed up a few steps and glanced into the hall. "You know, I don't do this for all my patients. Only for you."

She smiled lopsidedly.

He removed his white lab coat, cleared his throat, and glanced again at the door. There was no one out there. Ceremoniously, he wrapped his coat around Mr. Drippy, holding the neck in place with one hand and gripping the sleeve with the other. He squared his shoulders.

"I get no drip from champagne…," he began to sing, deep and throaty, in the style of Frank Sinatra. He swayed with her IV pole as much as the length of the tubes leading to the port in her chest would allow. "Mere Toradol doesn't move me at all, but morphine and fentanyl too… Yes, I get a drip out of you." He cradled the screen of the IV pole and dipped it below his round belly, careful not to upset the hanging medications. His lips puckered in an air-kiss toward the screen.

Raven couldn't help it. She started to laugh. Her mother did too, which made her laugh even harder. As always, the sight of that normally stiff and paunchy man dancing with her IV pole tickled something deep inside her, something that bitch cancer hadn't ruined yet. She laughed and laughed until her throat constricted like the valve of a pinched balloon.

Her laugh turned into a cough and then a wheeze.

Dr. Freemont stopped singing.

The next moment he was leaning over her, his pale hands gently shaking her shoulders, and she realized she'd been unconscious. Not long, judging by the look on his surprised face.

"Welcome back," he murmured. He was half dark again.

"That's never happened before," her mother said nervously.

"That's just Raven's body telling us she needs rest," he said. "I'll leave you to it." He removed his lab coat from Mr. Drippy and shrugged it on before nodding his goodbye.

"Well, that sounded promising," Mom said after he was gone. "You just need more rest." She stood up and tucked Raven in, her face positively glowing with denial.

Raven adjusted her head so her good eye was pointed at the door. *Not long now*, he'd said.

That was the day cancer stole her laugh. It was the last time the doctor sang for her. The last time she was awake long enough to ask him to. There were flashes of color and light, the feel of anointing oil crossed on her forehead and wrists as prayers were whispered over her, Avery's rosary dangling from her fingertips above her chest, Dr. Freemont's humorless face as he answered her mother's questions. But most of the following days consisted of darkness.

Until, one night, *he* came for her.

2

Death stood at the end of Raven's bed, looming and dark, and she welcomed him with open arms. Open arm. Only her right was under her control. Oh, how she longed to be free of her broken body.

If any part of her had questioned the true identity of her visitor, the skepticism was short-lived. The aura of the supernatural surrounded him. Raven's first clue was his suit, or rather that he wasn't wearing scrubs. An eternity had passed since someone who wasn't a medical professional or close family had entered her hospice room. Her own father didn't come anymore. It was too sad. A lost cause.

Death's miraculous presence aside, there were stranger things about his visit. Her IV had stopped dripping. Mr. Drippy's digital face was frozen, the impossibly full belly of her next drop of morphine hovering by a silver thread at the center of the machine's plastic chamber. She shot a glance toward her mother, hoping for an explanation, but the woman was motionless and rigid, staring, catatonic, toward the darkened hospital windows. The clock had stopped. Midnight.

Raven's time had finally come.

She took stock of the man who must be Death, the new growth of her hair rustling against the scratchy pillowcase as she turned her head. It was the only sound in an otherwise silent room. Under the fluorescent lights, she studied him. This was the one who would carry her home? He wasn't what she'd expected.

Death was a babe.

Dark. Brooding. Heavy boned and unshaven. There was something handsome about him nonetheless, alluring enough for her failing body to send her a flicker of desire, something she hadn't felt in over a year. It was the eyes, black eyes that seemed to burn into her, with flecks of red and mahogany that radiated from pitch-black pupils. His substantial eyebrows were too full to be considered conventionally attractive, but they balanced a generous nose and lower jaw that had no use for frivolity. He was olive-skinned, full-lipped, and big. Really big. Professional wrestler big. Although, based on his sunken cheeks and long, tapered fingers, she got the sense he could be bigger, like he was perpetually hungry.

"Ravenna Tanglewood?" he asked, his voice lined with charcoal and grit. A Clint Eastwood voice. A burning voice. Was he taking her to hell? A whiff of campfire drifted past her nose as he neared. That was one thing cancer hadn't taken from her, her sense of smell. And he smelled like the fall, like oak leaves and pumpkin pie, like smoke and old print.

"Yes." Her voice was nonexistent, mostly lips and breath doing the work.

"You are *this* Ravenna Tanglewood." He removed a folded newspaper from his breast pocket. The pages crinkled in his grip. He thrust it toward her.

A large emerald ring on his right pointer finger glinted in the light, and she had trouble looking away from it to focus on what he was asking her. Eventually though, she zeroed in on the story he was showing her. It was an article by a reporter from the *Tulane Hullabaloo*. PSYCHIC STUDENT SAVES FAMILY. She blinked slowly, confused. Why would Death care about a piece of gossipy journalism?

Before the doctors had discovered her brain tumor, she had experienced a premonition. She'd been doing laundry when a vision of her parents' pub completely engulfed in flames brought her to her knees. Neither her father nor mother took her vision seriously, but for some reason, her sister Avery did. Avery's resulting tantrum led to the purchase of a brand-new fire extinguisher. A few nights later, an inexperienced cook set his apron down too close to the grill and the strings caught fire. Her father reached for the old extinguisher first. It didn't work. Thankfully the new one did, and consequently her father was able to save the pub and the people in it.

It didn't mean Raven was psychic. Dr. Freemont had explained that the tumor in her brain, with its octopus-like tentacles infiltrating her gray matter, was connecting different areas of her mind, making her exceptionally intuitive. She'd subconsciously noticed the expiration date on the extinguisher, and her brain had produced the vision accordingly. It was the cancer, not anything weird or unusual. The newspaper story was a bit of flamboyant reporting by a friend who hoped to use the piece to attract readers to a fund-raiser meant to help with her medical expenses, nothing more.

Death tapped his finger against the newspaper impatiently, the massive green emerald glowing like a star. "Well, is this you?"

She licked her lower lip and nodded. He slid the paper back inside his jacket. Exhausted from the effort of responding, she closed her eyes and prayed silently, *Take me. Please take me.*

GABRIEL STOOD AT THE END OF THE HOSPITAL BED, USING every ounce of willpower he had to restrain himself. When Richard had suggested the girl was a long shot, he wasn't kidding. She was more dead than alive, a porcelain doll he was afraid to startle for fear of breaking her. Still, there was something... alluring about her, the same as when he'd seen her picture. Deep within his chest, a primal urge to heal and protect demanded his attention.

He hadn't felt anything like it in his five hundred years. Not for a human anyway. Perhaps the feeling bore a close resemblance to when he found a rare and priceless item for his collection. Yes, that was it.

She appeared nothing like the picture he'd seen. The only way to describe her now was haunting. The bones of her cheeks protruded as if her skeleton was battling her skin for rights to the surface. Ravenna Tanglewood was death, propped in a bed like a body on display. Above thin lips and a gently curved nose, her blue eyes bulged from her skull, dull and rheumy. Those damned eyes were nothing short of pleading. His chest ached. If she refused his offer, it would haunt him the rest of his days.

He stepped closer to her. Was that night-blooming jasmine? The scent was faint, but he could smell it on her skin. "Is it true you were an anthropology major with a minor in history? Honors student?"

A grunt came from deep within her throat, a warm wet trail of saliva coursing down her lower cheek. Her throat contracted and relaxed, but she seemed unable to form words. He hissed. Damn human hospitals. This was torture. What type of creatures left their females to die like this?

He could wait no more. Already the curse on his ring was weakening his magic. His skin felt thick, like he might turn to stone from the inside out at any moment. He tapped his fingers, exactly three times each against his thumb. Tap-tap-tap. Tap-tap-tap. It was the only thing that helped, the only thing that reminded him he could still move. His magic wasn't completely gone. Not yet.

Still, if he was to save her, he must do so soon.

"I see," he said. "I would like to offer you a job, Ms. Tanglewood. It is hard work. You'll have to learn quickly and take the initiative."

She stared at him blankly. He wondered what she must be thinking, if she could think at all. It was possible her brain was as wasted as her body. From what he'd read, she had brain cancer. Even with magical intervention, there might not be enough left in her head for her to consent. And she must consent. He would not bind her if she didn't. To do so would be to divest himself of any remaining honor he still bore in his wasting body.

He approached her bedside and gently laid his hand on

her chest. Those too-big eyes locked onto him. Her heart pounded against his palm. Her expression pleaded for death, but her heart begged for life.

"Ravenna, do you consent? Do you agree to work for me?"

Her eyebrows dipped and her chin twitched as if she didn't quite understand what he was proposing. A tear escaped the corner of her eye. He wiped it away.

"Say yes, little one," he said. "I cannot bear to see you like this a moment more."

Her eyes widened. "Yes," she mouthed.

He smiled weakly. "Praise the Mountain."

As he held her stare, he removed his hand from her chest, the storm of magic brewing within him. His ring glowed brighter as he drew his power to the surface, the dragon within barely contained inside his human form. Opening his jaw wide, he reached deep into his mouth, his large hand wedging itself between his teeth. He heard her gasp as the sound of tearing flesh filled the room. Gabriel grunted. He was likely scaring her, but it could not be avoided. This was part of the transition. The faster she came to terms with what was happening here, the better.

A spurt of crimson blood beaded on his bottom lip as the tooth materialized, clutched between his fingers. He tugged a handkerchief from his pocket and dabbed at the blood, then held the tooth up to the light. It was thin. Pointed. With a long root still bloody from the extraction. Clearly not a human tooth.

"Never gets easier," he murmured.

Beside him, Ravenna trembled. Her arms were covered in gooseflesh. He had to soothe her, to do something to comfort her before she had a heart attack. He closed his hand and drew on the magic of the ring. When he opened it again in front of her mouth, there was no tooth, only a slim white pill.

"Swallow," he commanded.

She must do this now. They were running out of time, her life fading in front of him, his magic sputtering under the weight of the curse. He scooped an arm behind her shoulders and lifted. Her lips parted like a baby bird's, and he dropped the pill to the back of her throat. She gurgled, coughed. He raised her head higher. Her throat bobbed and the choking stopped.

Oh, how beautiful it was shining through her stomach. The red light spread through her torso and to the ends of her limbs, warming her flesh from within. And all the time, she lay helpless against his arm, staring at him with unrestrained wonder, that jasmine scent of hers growing stronger. It made him feel like a god to hold her like this, to know that he'd given her what she needed to heal, to survive.

He watched her chest rise and fall with the first deep breath she'd taken since he'd arrived.

"What did you give me?" she asked, and this time the words were strong and true, more than the breathy whispers he'd gotten before. Good.

His shoulders slumped. The magic had taken its toll. He must get home to rest.

He brought his face close to hers. "Rest. Recover. You're no use to me like this. We are bound now. I will know when you are ready." He pressed his lips to her forehead and lowered her to the bed.

Her mouth worked soundlessly, as if she couldn't find the words for all the questions she longed to ask.

The rhythmic beep of her heart monitor started again, and a drop of morphine fell within the chamber of her IV. As he left her side and the room, he prayed to the Mountain that he'd chosen wisely. Ravenna Tanglewood was his last chance.

THANK YOU FOR READING THIS EXCERPT OF THE DRAGON OF New Orleans. Visit me at https://www.genevievejack. com/books/the-treasure-of-paragon/the-dragon-of-new-orleans/ to continue the story.

ACKNOWLEDGMENTS

A Bargain with the Shadow Prince is a tale of recovery. It's a story about being at your lowest and clawing your way back to who you were before a toxic relationship stripped you bare. Battle for The Shadow Prince is a tale of growth and change. It's about being brave and risking it all for someone who is worth fighting for. Bartered by the Shadow Prince is a tale of growing closer as a couple when everything you thought you could count on is stripped away. And Bride of the Shadow King is about letting go and letting God (or goddess, or universe.)

As I write this, I am experiencing my own let it go moment. A personal storm of change has left me battling stormy seas. But just like Eloise, I know that I can weather this storm, because there is a part of me that has faced this before and far worse.

I am thankful for the shadows that lurk within me, the ones that sprouted from dark roots of experience. Dark roots that led to dark wings and dark claws. We don't often have to call upon these things, but it's a comfort to know they're there for us when we need them. For all of us, in our own time, must take back our own kingdoms.

Thank you to my editor, Lisa, at Silently Correcting Your Grammar for seeing my vision for this series and helping me bring it to fruition. This novel is so much better for your efforts. It's been an amazing experience to work with you on these last two books.

Thanks to my author circle: Sara, Brenda, Skye, and Kate, you know I'd be a mess without your steadying and enduring friendship. My deepest, most sincere thanks to all of you for your talents, ongoing support, and encouragement.

And finally, my sincere thanks to every reader who adopts a copy of any of my books to live in their home library. I appreciate you.

MEET GENEVIEVE JACK

USA Today bestselling and multi-award-winning author Genevieve Jack writes wild, witty, and wicked-hot paranormal romance and fantasy romance.

She believes there's magic in every breath we take and probably something supernatural living in her deep, dark basement. You can summon her with coffee, wine, and books, but to keep her around, simply introduce her to your dog. Her novels featuring badass heroines, fiercely loyal heroes, and breathtaking fantasy elements have sold nearly one million copies.

Learn more at GenevieveJack.com.

Do you know Jack? Keep in touch to stay in the know about new releases, sales, and giveaways.

facebook.com/AuthorGenevieveJack

instagram.com/authorgenevievejack

bookbub.com/authors/genevieve-jack

tiktok.com/@Genevievejackbooks

MORE FROM GENEVIEVE JACK!

A Bargain With the Shadow Prince Series

A Bargain With The Shadow Prince

Battle for the Shadow Prince

Bartered by the Shadow Prince

Bride of the Shadow King

The Treasure of Paragon

The Dragon of New Orleans, Book 1

Windy City Dragon, Book 2,

Manhattan Dragon, Book 3

The Dragon of Sedona, Book 4

The Dragon of Cecil Court, Book 5

Highland Dragon, Book 6

Hidden Dragon, Book 7

The Dragons of Paragon, Book 8

The Last Dragon, Book 9

The Angel of Paragon, Book 10

The Three Sisters Trilogy

The Tanglewood Witches

Tanglewood Magic

Tanglewood Legacy

His Dark Charms Duet

Lucky Me

Lucky Us

Knight Games

The Ghost and The Graveyard, Book 1

Kick the Candle, Book 2

Queen of the Hill, Book 3

Mother May I, Book 4

Logan (companion novel)

The Wolves of Fireborn Pack Trilogy

Fated Bonds

Feral Instincts

Forever Mated